SCREEN OF DECEIT

A DCI Henry Christie Mystery

Nick Oldham

Severn House Large Print
London & New York

This first large print edition published 2010
in Great Britain and the USA by
SEVERN HOUSE PUBLISHERS LTD of
9-15 High Street, Sutton, Surrey, SM1 1DF.
First world regular print edition published 2008 by
Severn House Publishers Ltd., London and New York.

British Library Cataloguing in Publication Data

Oldham, Nick, 1956-
  Screen of deceit. -- (A DCI Henry Christie mystery)
  1. Christie, Henry (Fictitious character)--Fiction.
  2. Police--England--Fiction. 3. Juvenile delinquents--
  Psychology--Fiction. 4. Detective and mystery stories.
  5. Large type books.
  I. Title II. Series
  823.9'14-dc22

  ISBN-13: 978-0-7278-7884-7

Severn House Publishers support The Forest Stewardship Council
[FSC], the leading international forest certification organisation. All
our titles that are printed on Greenpeace-approved FSC-certified paper
carry the FSC logo.

Mixed Sources

Product group from well-managed
forests and other controlled sources
www.fsc.org Cert no. SA-COC-1565
© 1996 Forest Stewardship Council

Printed and bound in Great Britain by the
MPG Books Group, Bodmin, Cornwall.

This one is for Bob Tanner

Prologue

It started to rain hard just after midnight, big spats of water exploding like tiny bombs on the windscreen. Henry Christie shivered and hunkered down even further in the front passenger seat of the decrepit but non-descript Vauxhall Astra, reached out to the dash and twisted up the heating a notch in an effort to keep warm – his nose was red with cold – and to clear the fogged-up screen. But the heater fan, rattling in protest, wasn't working as effectively as it should have been – no surprise there – and Henry had to sit up again and run the back of his hand over the screen to get a half-decent view down the poorly-lit street.

He sighed and slumped back, cupping his hands around his mouth and blowing warm breath into his palms to circulate it around his nose, which was now dripping unsightly beads of snot.

'Just how good is this intelligence?' he asked, discreetly checking his watch for the umpteenth time. He turned to the man in the driver's seat, a newly promoted detective inspector called Rik Dean. The two cops had known each other for a number of years and Henry had been instrumental in getting Rik from uniform into plain clothes in the first place. He'd spotted and nurtured the younger man's thief-taking potential early on. Rik's subsequent rise from detective constable to DI had been entirely his own doing.

'It's good,' Rik said confidently. 'He'll be here, don't worry.'

'I'm not worried. It's just that at moments like this I realize the benefits of being a shiny-arsed headquarters Waller, nine to five, weekends off, warm office, long lunches ... luscious secretaries,' he concluded wistfully.

'You make it sound very appealing, especially the secretary bit, but you did volunteer for this, remember?'

'Aye ... truth is, the job I do at HQ is as boring as bat shit and the fact is I'd give anything to be doing this sort of stuff day-in, day-out ... waiting for bad guys to turn up ... what could be better?' He adjusted his position and shivered. 'Except the car, maybe.'

'Best we could do at short notice,' Rik apologized, 'but at least it's not out of kilter with the surroundings.' He indicated the rain-sodden back street, consisting of a few dilapidated terraced houses, some lived in, others boarded up, and the high gated wall surrounding a warehouse at the far end of the street with the area of derelict land opposite which looked like a World War Two bombsite.

A companionable silence descended on the two men as they maintained their observations, waiting for their prey to arrive so they could pounce, claws drawn.

Earlier that day – 9.30 a.m. – Henry had been sitting in a meeting at Blackpool Police Station, listening with a growing sense of boredom to the regular monthly get-together of the divisional management team, hoping his expression did not betray his inner feelings. He was there as a visitor, the head of Headquarters Special Projects Team, and was required to give a short presentation to the DMT on a new stop-and-search initiative that was shortly to roll out force-wide. He had visited all the other divisions in Lancashire Constabulary – and been greeted with stunned apathy at another hare-brained HQ scheme – and this one, Blackpool, was his last gig of the tour.

His mind wandered as he sat through the usual plethora of agenda items, wishing he could have been put on first, as in other divisions, but not here. In reality he should have been glad of the distraction afforded by days out around the county, but he wasn't. His head was still full to bursting with the mush and emotional turmoil from the last time he'd managed to worm his way out of HQ and get involved in 'real' police work. He'd found himself mixed up with a murder which had led him into a real nest of vipers – not all criminal ones, either – which had ended badly. Henry was only just getting through his inner pain barrier, and scooting around the county giving meaningless presentations should have taken his mind off things ... but it didn't.

He wondered if he would ever shake off the way he was feeling – but of one thing he was completely certain: attending meetings overpopulated by career-minded brown-nosers who spent most of their time up their chief superintendents' backsides was not the cure.

Talking of which, the chief superintendent of Blackpool division drew a riveting discussion on budget allocations to a close and moved on to the next item on the agenda.

Henry forced himself to concentrate. He wasn't good at meetings at the best of times.

'And now we come to Operation Nimrod,' the chief super said, looking around the table and zeroing in on DI Rik Dean – unfortunately for him, a fully paid-up member of the DMT.

Welcome to management, Henry thought sourly, and kiss real coppering goodbye.

He pricked his ears towards Rik and what he had to say. At least Nimrod had some connection to the business of front-line policing.

Nimrod was an ongoing, countywide operation, aimed solely at disrupting the drug business and targeted at dealers and their set-ups. 'A raid a day' had been the grand motto and there had been some notable successes, even though everyone knew the honest truth: no matter how much the police did, how many dealers were arrested and brought to trial, the drugs trade was so widespread and sophisticated that, even as one dealer was banged up, another was stepping up to the mark. Not that this prevented the cops from doing their job – and Nimrod showed the public that the cops were hard at work – it just meant that the deep-rooted social issues related to drugs were never really being tackled. That was a job that the politicians ducked and weaved around.

Rik inhaled nervously. This was his first DMT as a fully-fledged member, and his stress showed as he shuffled his papers, cleared his throat and began...

'...and some more good news, Tommy "the Crud" Hawthorn appeared at Preston Crown yesterday and after pleading guilty to importation and supply was sent down for eight years' – an audible Mexican wave of 'Well dones' and 'Good stuffs' murmured around the table. Rik acknowledged the plaudits without too much of an ego-show. He'd been the one who'd nabbed and nailed Tommy 'the Crud' in a previous Nimrod raid a few months before. Henry gave him a wink – 'which brings me to tonight's Nimrod operation, subtitled "Wiggum"...'

Henry saw a few creased eyebrows but no

one had the courage to ask 'Why Wiggum?' Henry, though far removed from any form of youth culture himself, did know that Chief Wiggum was the police chief in the Simpsons cartoon, which he happened to love.

'Obviously I can't share any of the intel or operational details at this forum,' Rik went on. All intelligence gathered prior to a Nimrod strike was closely guarded and only disseminated when necessary. It was vital to keep the whole operation watertight – until the moment of the fateful knock on the door. 'But the briefing's at ten tonight in the parade room and a lot of detectives and uniforms'll be showing up for this one, because it's a biggie,' he concluded with a grin.

'And you have all the resources you need?' the chief super asked.

'I think so,' Rik nodded. He vaguely explained a few more details before winding up and asking if anyone had any questions. There were none – which then brought the meeting round to Henry.

He took a deep breath and prepared to bore his colleagues into oblivion.

The meeting dissolved, the attendees drifted back to their real life jobs. Henry quickly gathered his notes and slotted in behind Rik Dean as he left the room.

'So who are you going to nail tonight?' Henry asked him mischievously.

Rik raised his eyebrows. 'Can't tell you

that, Henry,' he said, mock-affronted.

'Yes you can.'

'You might be a bent cop for all I know.'

'As a nine-bob note ... go on, come on, tell me, mate.' Henry cajoled.

They walked down the narrow corridor on the fourth floor of the station, then twisted to the stairs, Rik ahead of Henry, taking the steps two at a time as he descended.

'Come on,' Henry whined pathetically.

Rik stopped on one of the dog-leg landings between floors. Henry almost crashed into him.

'You may well be a DCI, but you know how secret Nimrod is.' Rik looked furtively around, up and down. There was no sign of anyone else in the stairwell. He leaned toward Henry and whispered a name in his ear which made Henry go weak at the knees.

Henry drew back. 'You jest!'

Tight-lipped, Rik shook his head.

'Hey, look,' Henry said hurriedly, 'Kate's away for the night,' he said, referring to his ex-wife, with whom he lived, 'and the girls,' he added, talking about his two daughters. They were in London to catch *We Will Rock You*. Henry had been invited, but had made a poor excuse not to go.

Rik grinned knowingly.

'Can I come along for the ride?' Henry pleaded. 'Can I?'

It was just the sort of tonic he needed.

★ ★ ★

Which is how he came to be sitting in a battered pool car with a dickey heater, shivering, and watching nothing in particular in a back street just off Blackpool's town centre, wishing he hadn't volunteered himself so hastily. Like most of his rash decisions, it had seemed a good idea at the time, but now, two hours after the briefing, with nothing moving but sodden cats and a rat, he was repenting at leisure. But only up to a point, because deep down there was always that chance of action. He just needed to be patient – but for how long? At the back of his mind he was thinking that whatever happened, whatever time this job went on to, he had to be back behind his desk at nine next morning.

'So how you doing, H?' Rik asked, breaking their silence. 'I know you've been through the ringer.'

'Out the other side now,' he lied brightly.

'Must've been tough,' Rik commiserated.

Henry nodded. Yeah, it had been tough. Seeing the bodies of two of his colleagues who'd been butchered by terrorists and having the same almost happen to him and then – very big 'then' – shouldering all the guilt, however misplaced, that maybe he had been responsible for their deaths.

'I can see you'd rather not go down that route,' Rik said. He smiled wanly at Henry.

'Wiggum Alpha Four to Wiggum Alpha One,' their personal radios blared in stereo. They were tuned into an encrypted frequency dedicated solely to this operation and all the other officers involved had been designated call signs beginning with Wiggum. WA4 was the call sign of the plain traffic car parked up on a bridge spanning the M55, one of the two routes most likely to be used when travelling into Blackpool. WA4 was equipped with a state of the art ANPR – Automatic Number Plate Recognition – which locked on to the registered number of every vehicle heading towards Blackpool and checked it against numerous computerized databases, including various intelligence ones and the Police National Computer. The resultant search was almost instantaneous.

Rik exchanged a quick glance with Henry. 'Alpha Four, go ahead.'

'Bingo!' said the officer in a less than professional manner. 'Target vehicle, the black Lexus' – he gave the registered number – 'has just passed under my point on the M55, heading towards the golden city.'

'Roger, thanks for that,' Rik said, a quiver of excitement in his voice. He locked eyes with Henry. 'The consignment's on the way in,' he said gleefully. Into his PR he said, 'All other patrols acknowledge.'

Which they did, one by one.

'No one is to move from their positions,' Rik instructed them, 'until I say.'

He gripped the steering wheel. Henry saw his tension.

'The guy is supposed to be mega-surveillance conscious,' Rik said. 'If he even smells a cop, he'll be off ... shit!' Rik saw a movement down the street and slithered low in his seat, as did Henry, who had spotted the same thing: a car, no lights, turning slowly into the street by the area of derelict land, creeping inch-by-inch towards the warehouse gates.

'Who the hell's this, then?' Henry hissed.

'Dunno,' Rik breathed.

'Wiggum Alpha Five to Wiggum One,' their radios called up. WA5 was a pair of plain-clothed PCs huddled in the back of an old Transit van on an adjoining street. 'A Ford Focus has just turned into your street.'

'Yeah, got eyeball,' Rik confirmed. 'Nothing else, though ... maybe two occupants, but it's a good one-fifty yards from us ... did you get the reg number?'

'No.'

'Bollocks!' Rik said, but not into the PR, smacking his hand on the edge of the steering wheel.

'Uninvited guests,' said Henry.

'Lookin' that way.'

'Always expect the unexpected,' Henry said unhelpfully.

Rik glared sideways at him. 'Maybe this has nothing to do with us,' he said hopefully.

'You mean a car creeping suspiciously around with no lights, on the street where you expect a drugs drop to take place, and at the same time of day, i.e., the witching hour?

16

Pull the other one, Rik old pal.'

The offending car pulled in by the warehouse gates. Behind these gates was a partly derelict warehouse, Henry knew from the briefing, where a consignment of drugs was supposed to be being stashed, and at the moment they were stashed, the cops were going to leap into action and ensure that all the baddies were banged up. It was as straightforward as that – a dozen cops dotted around, hidden from view, ready to be given the 'Go, go, go!' by Rik ... but another car and another two players on the scene had caught them on the hop a little.

'They could be scouting, checking the place for any signs of us,' Henry thought out loud.

'They could be waiting to nab the drugs for themselves.'

'Or they could be out screwing.'

'Or they could be here for any number of reasons,' Rik said, wrapping up the speculation. 'Question is, what do we do with them?'

'Sit tight, keep everyone informed, see what transpires,' Henry said, now starting to thoroughly enjoy the slowly unfolding events. The intelligence was that the biggest drug dealer in town was bringing in a consignment to hide in the old warehouse and, quite simply, the police were going to nab him. No one else was expected to be turning up to the party. But Henry did not believe in such coincidences. The guys in this car were definite gatecrashers.

The Ford remained motionless. Even through the pouring rain and the obstruction of a car parked in front of their Astra, Henry could see exhaust fumes rising from the tailpipe of the newly arrived car. He peered through the night, squinting, to establish there were just two figures in the car.

'Switch off,' he said quickly to Rik. 'If I can see their exhaust fumes, they can see ours.'

'Good point.' He flicked off the ignition.

The rain continued to bat down. The Astra began to steam up almost immediately.

'Wiggum Alpha Six to Alpha One.'

'Alpha One,' Rik acknowledged. Alpha Six was a cop sitting at the motorway exit at Marton Circle, just on the outskirts of Blackpool.

'The Lexus has come off at junction four and is heading into Blackpool on the A583.'

'Roger,' Rik said unsurely, then, 'Shit!' as the doors of the Focus opened and both occupants climbed out. He relayed this development to all the other participants in the operation and told them all to stay put. 'Not good, not good,' he said to Henry.

The two guys split up, one crossing the street, then they started walking slowly down the street towards the Astra.

'If they are mixed up with this and they spot us, cover's blown and maybe the opera-

18

tion,' Rik said bleakly. Henry's thoughts entirely.

'And there's no doubt about it, they're gonna spot us.'

The men were getting closer.

Henry and Rik were rigid in their seats, nowhere to go, nowhere to hide.

'Whaddaya reckon, pal?' Rik said through the corner of his mouth.

'I think our goose is cooked and we've about ten seconds to make a decision.'

'One way or the other, they need to be neutralized, because if they are spotters or even rivals, this op will go tits up if we don't get them off the street like now. You up for it?'

'Shiny-arsed I may be—' Henry began, but didn't finish.

Rik was speaking hurriedly into his PR: 'For info of patrols, Alpha One is challenging occupants of the Ford Focus ... Alpha Six, get yourself on to the street now ... intention is to get these two out of play now, no messing...' He was uttering these words as he opened his door, Henry following suit just a fraction of a second behind him. They would have to work quickly to deal with the two men, get them off the plot and get everything back to normal.

The two detectives were out of the car speedily, Henry approaching the man making his way down the left side of the street, Rik moving diagonally across to the other,

19

each cop reaching for his warrant card; Henry also curled his fingers around his extendable baton which hung from the belt of his jeans.

He glanced over at Rik, seeing his hand extended with his warrant card in it. Henry turned his attention back to the man he was going for, seeing him more clearly now as they closed on each other, although the guy's face was still a mix of shadow and light.

'Police,' Henry said, 'need to have a word, please.'

Across the road, Henry was aware of a similar confrontation taking place.

The man Henry had challenged stopped in his tracks, but did not speak.

At the far end of the street, a vehicle swung in, headlights blazing: Alpha Six.

Henry breathed an inner sigh of relief. Now they had these two jokers, whoever they were, whatever they were doing, out-numbered and boxed in and could take them off the plot quickly and efficiently.

Just as long as it all went swimmingly...

Suddenly there was a 'crack' from the other side of the street. Henry knew im-mediately what he had heard – a gunshot.

He ducked instinctively.

Rik groaned and went down, clutching his thigh.

These two were not going to be easy.

The man in front of Henry reacted. He lunged at him, taking him by surprise. He

20

was a big guy, as was Henry, but he barged Henry aside and pushed him roughly against the wall of a house. Henry crashed painfully against the brickwork, but bounced straight back and launched himself at the man who had begun to run. Henry's warrant card skittered away (never to be found) as both his hands grabbed the man, who twisted into him and powered a big fist up into Henry's guts.

Even in the darkness, Henry saw it coming, although there was little he could do to prevent it connecting other than to tense his stomach muscles and try to pull back.

It was still a good punch. Henry's breath shot out of him. He curled double, holding himself.

The police car raced down the street.

Henry – ashamed he'd taken such an early punch – staggered backwards a step, righted himself, then leapt at the man as he turned and attempted to run away again.

This time Henry succeeded in wrapping his arms around the man's waist. He gripped him tight, head tucked in for protection, and heaved him round, trying to slam him against the wall. The suspect pummelled Henry's head with his fists, shouting obscenities at him as he fought.

But Henry clung on like a limpet, even though one particularly powerful thump crashed into the side of his head, sending a flash of lightning through his brain.

21

And then help arrived as one of the cops from Alpha Six piled in and felled the guy with a blow across his back with his baton, narrowly missing Henry's head. Henry reared away as the officer sprayed him with a faceful of CS gas just to be on the safe side, ensuring the man was then skilfully taken down and handcuffed within seconds.

'Pin the bastard down – and call for an ambulance,' Henry ordered the bobby, who jammed a size eleven Doc Marten boot into the middle of the man's back, not allowing him the chance to clear the CS away. Henry extracted himself, thankful he hadn't been clattered with the baton or given an accidental shot of CS, and ran across the wet road to Rik Dean who lay there groaning, holding his right thigh.

'Ah, shit, shit,' he grimaced in agony.

The other cop from Alpha Six was kneeling next to Rik, saying soothing words and holding something that looked like a hankie to Rik's leg wound.

Rik looked up at Henry. 'Bastard shot me ... Christ, this hurts...'

Henry bounced down on to his haunches. 'It's OK, pal, ambulance is en route ... where is he?' he asked. Having been involved in his own little fracas, Henry had not seen what had happened on this side of the street.

'In there,' Rik gasped as more pain shot through him, whipping him back and causing him to smack his head on the pavement with a horrible, hollow sounding thud. 'Shit.' He pointed to the warehouse gates and Henry saw a Judas gate set within the larger gate. Rik's pain eased momentarily and he looked up pathetically. 'Am I going to die?'

'Not bloody likely.'

'Shit – I always get into trouble with you.' He was referring to a previous incident when, with Henry, he'd been stabbed by a psychotic child molester they'd been questioning. Henry had saved his life that time.

'You'll be OK, honest. He's only shot you.'

'Your bedside manner is crap ... ahhgh!' More pain speared through him.

In the distance Henry heard the ambulance siren closing in. They were a pretty efficient bunch in this neck of the woods. Now he knew he needed to take a step back, take stock of the situation. He stood up, groaning as his stomach muscles tensed from the blow they'd received. He needed to get his thoughts into gear quickly and re-prioritise what was going on as, by default, the running of this operation had now dropped into his lap.

What had started as an attempt to catch a major drug dealer had deteriorated into farce. Nothing new there, Henry thought cynically. Story of my life. Question was, what, if anything, could be salvaged? The priority was to get Rik urgent medical treatment, then to catch the guy who'd shot him and, way down the list, try to achieve the original objective of the operation.

Henry's mind buzzed.

He'd just come along for the ride, nothing else. A bit of a jolly whilst Kate was gallivanting in the Big Smoke with the kids; something to do on what would have been a long, boring evening. A bit of gung-ho policing. Fun. Chasing baddies. Not having any responsibility – that had all been on Rik's shoulders, but not now.

He squatted back down. 'How's it going?'

Rik's face was creased in agony, but he still managed to give Henry a withering look. 'As well as can be with a slug in my leg.' Rik shivered and Henry recognized the onset of shock. He had been going to tell Rik was what going to happen now, but he decided Rik probably wasn't all that interested.

He stood up and spoke into his radio.

The dog patrol arrived seconds after the ambulance had departed with Rik in the back of it. The whole wet street was now alive with cops and their cars, with Henry, now sporting a hi-viz yellow jacket, directing everything.

Lancon Albert looked greedily up at Henry, his eyes shining like diamonds in the dark, his big teeth very apparent, his long, sloppy tongue drooping out, hot breath making steam.

Henry was glad that his handler, a squat, tough-looking copper called Craig, was holding tight on to the German Shepherd's leash because Albert obviously wanted to get working, all the movement and flashing lights obviously exciting him. He wanted to sink his teeth into something.

'He ducked into the Judas gate,' Henry was telling Craig and Albert. 'He didn't come back out and no one followed him. As far as I know there's no other exit ... it's an old warehouse, partially falling down...'

'Yeah, I know it,' Craig said. 'I searched for a missing kid in it about a month ago.'

'This is no missing kid ... it's a guy with a gun who just shot a cop.'

Craig nodded and gave Henry a look which said, 'Tell me something I don't know.'

'I'll kit Albert up, then send him in to play. It's what he does best, isn't it, pal?' He ruffled the dog's head and Henry thought he heard the canine reply, 'Yeah, yeah.' The pair headed back to the dog van.

Henry read his mental check list again: the warehouse was surrounded, tick; four armed cops were on the plot, tick; the dog was about to be let loose, tick; Rik should be at the hospital by now, tick; senior officers had been informed, tick; the Lexus was being taken care of, tick. All bases covered.

Craig returned with Albert, who looked like a *Star Wars* extra, now wearing doggie body armour and a small camera on his head, known as a FIDO cam – an acronym

25

for Firearms Incidents Dangerous Operation – which could transmit pictures and also allowed the handler to speak to the dog as it was running free as it searched.

Craig handed Henry a mini-monitor that was already getting pictures from the dog's point of view.

Craig patted his thigh and said, 'C'mon, Bert, let's go play,' to his eager partner. Man and dog stepped through the gate into the warehouse yard.

Henry heard Craig's shouted warning which was repeated three times before the further warning that the dog was being let off the leash. Henry went to sit back in the Astra out of the rain, but the truth was he could not have been any wetter. The rain had been relentless.

He settled back to watch Albert's progress through the dark, dangerous corridors and rooms of the old warehouse.

It was a bouncy, jarring ride on the dog's head, reminding Henry of the camera work on some US TV cop shows, but the image transmitted by the tiny camera was clear, despite the lack of light.

Albert worked his way diligently through the building.

Then suddenly he became still.

Henry found himself tensing up. Had the dog found someone?

The dog moved slowly. Was he now stalking someone?

Henry was transfixed by it. His knuckles were white as he gripped the monitor.

Then there was a sudden rush.

Two bright flashes.

Henry heard two bangs from inside the building. Gunshots.

His insides churned as he watched the blurred images on the screen.

Albert had found the gunman – but had he been shot?

The images kept moving – and then Henry watched in amazement as the screen showed the figure of a man getting larger and larger as Albert rushed at him, then leapt.

Henry saw the man's face, abject terror on it, then his forearm came up in a protective gesture as Albert powered into him and did what police dogs love doing: sinking their fangs into bad guys.

'Remind me never to go out on a job with you again.'

Henry looked down at the woozy, drug-ged-up Rik Dean on the hospital trolley. A tangle of tubes and wires had been inserted into him and he was in pre-op before going under the knife to have the bullet removed. Rik managed a weak smile.

'As if,' Henry responded. 'Anyway, just thought I'd let you know – we got the guy who shot you up. He'll probably be in the operating theatre after you after the mauling the police dog gave him. It just wouldn't let

27

go, apparently.' Henry smirked. 'His mate's in custody.'

'What about the Lexus?'

'I got it pulled and searched.' Henry shook his head. 'Nothing.'

Rik tutted, rolled his eyes.

'Guy driving it was clean, said he'd just bought it.' Henry shrugged. 'It's obvious he was a decoy. I think the drugs'll have come in by another route. *C'est la vie.*'

'So he out-thought us.'

'Seems that way.'

'And another police operation fails to net the biggest drug dealer this side of the Irwell.'

'Aye, the Crackman lives to fight another day, whoever the hell he is … one day, eh?'

'Yeah, whatever.' Rik had lost interest.

A nurse came into the room and told Henry it was time to leave. He touched Rik's arm and went just as the nurse inserted a hypodermic needle into the back of his friend's hand and he started counting down from ninety-nine.

One

Mark Carter knew he was going to get a battering.

'I don't do drugs,' he said. 'You know that.'

He was standing astride his Diamond Back Igniter BMX bike, staring guardedly at the three lads in front of him. They were arced around in a semicircle to prevent him from pedalling away, all noisily chewing gum, looking menacing, their heads tilted to one side as they glared at him.

Mark knew all three by name and reputation. As his eyes darted from one to the other, he kicked himself for choosing this route home. Normally he would have circled the estate, but because he was running late, he'd decided to cut through instead.

Big mistake.

Now he was going to pay for the big mistake.

Big style.

These were the most feared lads on Shoreside, even though none of them was older than him, that is to say fourteen. Their leader and biggest troublemaker was Jonny Sparks, Sparksy or JS to his mates. It was he who was standing directly in front of Mark, the front wheel of the BMX gripped securely between his legs, his bony, spider monkey-like fingers curled tightly around the handlebars. Jonny was as tall as Mark, but thinner, wiry, pale, his face pockmarked from a childhood disease. Mark would say he was as evil-looking as a weasel.

'Maybe you should start. They're good for you,' Sparks said with a sneer.

'Drugs screw you up. I don't need 'em,' Mark replied.

'Unlike your sis, eh?' Sparks taunted.

Mark's mouth clammed shut. His guts were jittering, his insides trembling. He was frightened, no doubt about that; too frightened to respond to Sparks. He just wanted to get away unscathed and as far as he was concerned, Sparks could bad mouth his family to hell and back if it meant not getting hammered.

However, Mark was canny enough to know that whatever he said, or didn't say, was unlikely to help this situation. They were out for blood. Mark could sense it.

They beat up people just for the fun of it, sometimes to rob them, sometimes for a laugh. They were into happy-slapping, too, recording their exploits on their mobile phone cameras to watch back later and post on the Internet. And they were known to use knives and hammers as well as fists and feet. The fists and feet didn't bother Mark too much. It was the possibility of weapons that terrified him.

He tried his best not to look intimidated, staring impassively at Jonny. He blinked, said, 'I don't want any drugs, thanks,' and did not rise to the nasty remark about Bethany, his older sister.

Mark wondered what was going to happen now. He knew that others had been beaten up for refusing to buy drugs off this crew. In a one-to-one confrontation, and unarmed, Mark was pretty sure he could equal any of the three, even though he didn't consider himself a fighter. But these lads never operated singly. They always ganged up, hunted in a savage pack, which was why they called themselves 'The Hyenas'.

A heartbeat of silence passed between Mark and Jonny Sparks.

Sparks leaned in closer. 'Your sister's a slag, y'know,' he hissed, with a dirty expression on his face.

Mark bit his lip hard, trying to stay cool, not get wound up. His mind raced as he tried to figure out how to extricate himself from this mess, but try as he might to hold back, he could feel that the tremble inside him was morphing from fear into anger, especially when Sparks taunted, 'She'll shag anyone just for a score.'

Sparks eyed Mark with a triumphant smirk, knowing he was succeeding in touching a raw nerve and winding him up. A

31

twisted smile played on his thin lips, as he added, 'Shagged her meself,' really turning the screw.

Jonny Sparks had been after Mark for a long time, never missed a chance to goad him and it was well known he wanted Mark to have a dig at him, just to give him an excuse. Mark had no idea why this was because, for sure, he'd never knowingly done anything to annoy Sparks so much. He just stayed out of his way, avoided him at all costs, and maybe that was reason enough for Sparks. That's how it was on the Shoreside council estate in Blackpool, Lancashire. People often hated others for no definable reason. They just did, and that was good enough. Just like Jonny hated Mark. It was probably all about some sort of perverted 'respect' thing – fights often started because one lad had 'dissed' another by showing disrespect, often innocently. That was part of the jungle that was Shoreside.

Mark couldn't ever recall knowingly dissing Sparks. Maybe his avoidance of Sparks amounted to disrespect? Maybe that's what wound the little toad up – because he could not get to Mark, could not get his claws into him. And Jonny liked having his claws in as many people as possible.

Mark swallowed. His nostrils flared. He glanced quickly around for some help, but he knew there would be none. This scenario was nothing out of the ordinary around here

– a scrap brewing between lads outside the boarded-up Spar shop. It happened all the time and you could guarantee no one would intervene or get involved in any way. Nobody would call the cops either, except maybe when it was all over and Mark was sprawled in the gutter with his head kicked in and blood gushing out of his nose and the danger was over. Nobody saw anything, nobody got involved. Everybody was scared, usually.

Mark Carter was on his own.

'Can I go now?' he asked.

The Hyenas cackled with laughter, more like a coven of witches than a gang of hoodlums. It was like Oliver Twist asking for more.

Not a hope in hell.

Sparks released the bike's handlebars, sort of eyed Mark as if weighing him up and, amazingly, said, 'Yeah, sure you can go, Mark, mate.' But he didn't move. The front wheel of Mark's BMX stayed firmly trapped between Sparks's legs. He was lying, surprise, surprise; obviously there was a condition to Mark's release. Mark didn't even try to cycle away. Jonny Sparks did not just let people off the hook. He looked at the BMX, leaning from side to side, admiring it. 'Nice bike.' He winked, creasing his whole face as he did so.

Mark remained silent. His heart was slamming in his chest.

'You can go, but the bike stays. Like a

pressie, from you to me.' He arched his eyebrows, licked his lips and eyed his gang members, Eric King, known as The Kong, and Sam Dale, known, without explanation, as Rat-head. They were Jonny Sparks clones in the way they dressed, spoke and treated folk; nasty devils, but with no independent thought processes of their own. They relied on Sparks to lead the way and jumped at his command.

'Nice one,' The Kong said enthusiastically. He had a lazy left eye and sometimes it was hard to know which one was looking at you. It didn't stop him being a hard swine, though. He took a drag of the rolled–up ciggie he always seemed to have dangling from his bottom lip, hacked up and gozzed revoltingly on the ground. Then he sniffed up disgustingly.

'Yeah, we can get a few quid for it down at Tonno's,' Rat-head piped up. He was a broad-shouldered lad, good-looking, with a shock of blond hair, but he had even less up-top than The Kong, which was saying something. Sam Dale was Jonny's powerhouse. The guy he could wind up and set off to do the heavy battering. He had big fists with lots of scrapes on the knuckles, and he used them well. When he talked about Tonno's, he was referring to a second-hand shop in town through which most of the estate's stolen goods ended up being sold on.

'What d'you think?' Jonny asked Mark.

'It's my bike and you're not having it,' he said, feeling a tightness across his chest. Things, he thought, are about to get out of hand.

'Whoa! Tough words from a soft kid,' Sparks spat. 'Tell you what, then – you pay *me* for your bike and I'll let you keep it. Ten quid now, ten at the end of the week. That's fair, innit?'

'Like I said – it's my bike.' Mark was fiercely proud of the Diamond Back. He'd worked hard on a double paper round in the mornings before school, one after school and a Sunday round for nine months to get the dosh together. In fact, he thought it was probably the only bike on the whole estate that wasn't stolen, or didn't have any knocked-off bits on it. 'You're not having it, Jonny,' he squeaked.

The 'look' came down on Jonny Sparks's face. The look that didn't need words, that itself said, 'Game's over, business is just about to begin.'

Except this was no game – not for Mark, anyway – and the business was violence.

Mark braced himself. As frightened as he was, there was no way he was going to let go of the bike – they'd have to prise it out of his fingers; nor was he going down without a fight.

Sparks flicked his head at his two mates. They stepped forward menacingly, but halted suddenly as Jonny's mobile phone rang.

He held up a hand to stop the attack, looked warningly at Mark and said, 'Don't move, or else. I need to get this.' He shuffled the phone out of his trackie-bottoms pocket, the polyphonic ring tone being Green Day's 'Boulevard of Broken Dreams', which Mark recognized instantly. Green Day was his favourite band and that was his favourite track. It made him feel sick that scumbag Sparks liked it too.

'Me,' Sparks said into the flashy phone, his eyes still intently on Mark. 'Yeah ... yeah ... understood...' He adjusted his position slightly as he talked, his feet moving a couple more inches apart so that the wheel of Mark's bike was no longer trapped between his legs. He probably didn't even realize he'd done it – but Mark did. 'Yeah, so it'll be there? I'll sort it ... yeah...'

To Mark it sounded as though the conversation was coming to an end.

This was his chance.

He took in the scene: Sparks standing dead ahead of him; Eric and Sam a couple of feet either side of Sparks's shoulders. Mark could tell they were interested in the phone call, trying to earwig. He realized this would probably be the only opportunity he'd get. His fingers tightened on the handlebar grips. He tensed up.

'How much?' Sparks asked down the phone, listened to the answer, his eyes still fixed on Mark. However, when he got what was obviously a good reply from his question, he could not resist looking around at his chums with a big snigger on his face and a thumbs-up with his left hand.

Now!

Mark yanked the front wheel of the bike upwards. He knew the bike well, intimately, could reel off every fact about it, including its weight, and because he spent so much time playing moto-x in the fields behind his house, knew exactly how much effort was needed to yank the wheel upwards to best effect.

Which he did.

He caught Sparks off guard and rammed the wheel up into his unprotected groin.

Sparks emitted an unworldly howl of pain, dropped his mobile and staggered backwards as both hands went instinctively downwards to cradle his nuts. The surprise attack also caught the other two off guard, giving Mark the fraction of a second he needed.

Without a pause, Mark did a quick reverse, dropped his left leg and skidded the bike round spectacularly, making grit shower the three lads like a hailstorm. With as much power as he could muster – that's to say, every ounce of it – he drove his right foot hard down on to the pedal, rose high on the bike and shot away from the scene, leaving the two goons clucking fussily around their wounded ringleader like mother hens.

Mark pedalled like hell, head down, bum right up in the air, and aimed for the narrow alleyway that ran behind the old Spar shop. Just before he reached the gap, his head flicked round to get one last look at the three troublemakers.

If it hadn't been so scary, it would have been hilarious.

The Kong and Rat-head had been brushed roughly aside by Sparks as he stomped around, doubled over, cupping his most precious assets. Mark's wheel had hit him slap-bang on target and the agony was clear to see on Sparks's scrunched-up face – but he did manage to look up at the same moment Mark glanced back over his shoulder and, though the two lads were fifty metres apart by then, their eyes locked.

'You're dead!' Sparks screamed furiously. 'You're gonna get...' But Mark skidded expertly into the narrow ginnel and heard no more of what was a long bout of ranting, raving, effing and blinding, and threats by Jonny Sparks.

Mark pushed himself hard, head down, face up into the wind, the air pounding his ear-drums, his lungs hurting with the combination of relief and escape.

He stopped for nothing, emerging at the far end of the alley on to the road, not even pausing to check for traffic. He just shot across – fortunately there was nothing coming – avoided a couple of little kiddies on their bikes, though he did manage to drench them as his BMX cut through a dirty puddle. He went on at this relentless pace until he reached home on the far side of the estate, an end quasi-semi council house that had recently been partly renovated by the council.

He rode up the garden through the non-existent front gate and up to the front of the house, where he applied the brakes for the first time and screeched to a swervy halt. He sat astride his machine, panting, desperately out of breath. It took a couple of minutes for him to come back down to earth from his exertion, but even then he was sweating like a demon.

The bike was kept in the hallway, together with loads of other stuff. There was an old coalbunker at the side of the house, big enough to walk in, and though there was a lock on it, it had been broken into so many times that nothing was kept in it at all. Now it was just a den for Mark and his mate Bradley. The inside of the house was the only safe-ish place for the BMX and he kept it there despite the occasional outburst from his mum and sister when they tripped over it. But it was too valuable to lose, as had just been demonstrated.

He bounced it up the front step, in through the front door and rested it against the radiator in the hall. The house seemed quiet, but that didn't necessarily mean there was no one home. He didn't bother shouting 'I'm home' or anything like that, because nobody really cared if he was, or wasn't.

Instead, he went into the kitchen, found some bread without mould on it and made a jam butty. With a glass of orange squash and a bag of pickled onion Monster Munch, he ran up to his room, locked himself in, sat on his creaky wire-framed bed and swigged down the drink in one.

He was parched after his little adventure.

Just then, as he placed his cup down on the old TV stand he used as a bedside cabinet, it dawned on him what he'd done.

He'd basically kicked the hardest lad on the estate in the knackers. Well, not kicked, but 'wheeled' – yes, 'wheeled' the hardest, baddest, meanest, cruellest lad on the estate in the goolies and in so doing he'd converted Jonny Sparks from someone who had been just 'after him' in a fairly leisurely way into a deadly enemy with a grudge.

Nothing was more certain. Jonny Sparks had been humiliated and he would want revenge. Lots of it. With icing. And cherries.

Mark's hot sweat turned into a cold one as he realized the enormity of what he'd done.

Two

Mark liked his room, his refuge from the real world. It was lockable from the inside and he could go into it, close the door behind him, slide the big bolt across so no one else could get in, and retreat to his own inner space.

Everything in it was his. Whilst he knew that some of the things might have been a bit 'iffy', he'd paid good money in good faith for most items and found the others.

His bed had always been there. Everything else in the room he'd got for himself. He'd painted the walls a sort of grass-green from a tin of paint he'd found dumped by the roadside, using a brush he'd also found. It was a good colour, like the Man U pitch. The old TV stand that doubled as his bedside cabinet had been chucked out by a neighbour, literally dumped on the street outside, and Mark had helped himself to it. Someone else had dumped a three-piece suite (people on the estate didn't usually bother with council collections if it meant it might cost them something) and Mark had snaffled one of the armchairs. With Bradley's help he'd managed to squeeze it up the stairs into his room. It had taken ages and both lads had struggled to see how the chair could even get into the room, but they'd done it with much huffing, puffing and muscle.

The desk was just a decorator's pasting table he'd bought from a cheapo DIY shop in town, then strengthened with a few extra lengths of wood to make it more substantial. He still needed an office chair, which was on his 'to get' list.

He had a PlayStation games console and loads of games for it that he'd got through trading at school, but he wasn't really happy with it. The graphics were rubbish and dated and the games too easy. He wanted an Xbox 360, but they were hellish expensive and the cost of the games was scary. Nevertheless this piece of kit was also on his 'to get' list. He was saving for it now. His TV was an old portable with an inbuilt DVD player, given to him by his brother Jack when he left home years before. It was OK but needed upgrading too.

So that was Mark Carter's room.

He had few toys, but loads of books. He loved reading because that was truly an escape to a different world. Books set his mind going, unlike computer games, which just numbed it. He was always at the library and always scouring the second-hand book stalls on the market for bargains.

His favourite book, even though it was written in an old-fashioned way, was *Treasure Island*. He'd read it a zillion times.

Mark'd been home about an hour and his guts were rumbling. The jam butty and crisps had not been enough to satisfy a growing lad and he was wondering what to do for his tea.

There was not much chance of his mum making it. She was either out gallivanting or at work, Mark didn't know which. Meaning he'd have to fend for himself. His elder sister, Bethany, who was seventeen, was in, but she was slobbed out in front of the telly in the living room and Mark couldn't even remember when she'd last cooked anything for anyone other than herself.

His mind's eye was working through what he'd seen in the cupboards earlier. Lots of beans, spag hoops and stuff like that; a couple of eggs, Pot Noodles ... now that was an idea – Pot Noodle – something he loved, though he did blame it for making him a bit spotty in the chin area.

As he thought what best to do, there was a knock on the front door.

Mark tensed immediately, listening hard. He paused his computer game. He was pretty sure Jonny Sparks wouldn't come near the house. Like the hyena he was, Sparks hunted in the open spaces of the estate, where he tracked and brought down his prey with his pack. But you never knew.

More knocking.

'I'm bloody coming,' he heard his sister

yell, then heard her stomp out of the lounge to the front door. There was a loud crash, then a, 'Bloody soddin' bike!' as she caught her shin on the pedal. Mark smiled. She always seemed to be able to trip over it, even though she knew it was there in the hallway. The front door was opened, there was a short conversation followed by the door slamming and the sound of footsteps running upstairs.

Mark relaxed, resumed the game, shouted, 'It's open.' He had recognized the footsteps.

Bradley Hamilton, Mark's best mate, poked his head round the door.

'Hey!' he called.

Mark beckoned him in, pretended to be concentrating on his game and jerked a thumb in the direction of the bed. Brad sat down quietly, watching Mark on the old armchair, playing the game, ducking and diving with the character on-screen as he negotiated the tortuous route.

Bradley was in Mark's class at school. They had known each other since they were little kids and got along really well. Both lads lived on the perimeter of Shoreside and had managed to keep their noses clean, even though it would have been easier to get involved with the bad crowd on the estate. Not that either of them was a saint. Far from it. But both saw what they called 'the dark side', after *Star Wars*, was ultimately not worth the hassle. It had been a hard choice with much temptation. Everyone stole. Everyone cheated. Everyone fought and everyone hung around in gangs harassing everyone else – or at least it seemed that way. But Mark and Bradley had realized that if they got dragged into that, their lives would be screwed up for ever.

The hardest thing was that the temptation was always there, always dangling like a carrot. *Always.*

Thing was, though, Mark had a good role model – his brother Jack. He had a dad somewhere, obviously, but he'd done a bunk a long time ago, leaving Mum, Jack, Bethany and him to fend for themselves and Jack, being older than them by quite a few years, had done well for himself. He had an apartment overlooking the marina at Preston docks; a Porsche Cayenne, one of those four-wheel-drive ones with darkened side windows; he had a cool bird for a girlfriend; had a great job selling computer software and had loads of dosh. He was Mark's hero. Showed that it could be done, that getting out of the gutter was possible for anyone if they wanted it enough.

'Finished!' Mark announced with a flourish as he triumphed on-screen.

He gazed round at his tolerant friend who, like Mark, had a short haircut – a grade four and a two – with train tracks zigzagged across the side of his head rather like a swastika, though unintentionally so. There was something in Bradley's expression that made Mark say, 'What?'

Bradley shook his head in disbelief. 'You've really done it now.'

'Done what?'

'I think you know. It's all round the estate. Jonny Sparks says next time he sees you, you're dead.'

'Oh, that,' Mark said glumly. He exhaled. 'Has he said anything more?'

'Does he need to? I think it's all pretty well summed up in that phrase, don't you? "I'm gonna kill Mark Carter."'

'Mm, possibly,' Mark conceded.

'I mean, what the hell made you ram your bike into his goolies? Have you got a death wish, or summat?' Bradley's astonishment was obvious. 'You made him look a fool and now he's out to get you.' Bradley's lips were curled into a kind of unbelieving sneer. 'And he will, y'know. Get ready for your head to resemble a crushed tomato.'

'You think I don't know all this? It's been on my mind ever since, strangely enough.'

'You're going to have to watch your back, pal. What on earth made you act like such a plonker?'

'Two things – right?' Mark stood up and counted on his fingers. 'First off he called Beth a slag.' He paused, waiting for some reaction from his mate. All he got was a blank look that could have meant agreement or disagreement with the statement. Mark

46

didn't push it, mainly because he knew that Beth's reputation around Shoreside wasn't exactly squeaky clean ... all the same, it didn't mean someone could say it in public, to his face. 'And second, he wanted *me* to give *him* my bike, or twenty quid.'

'Ahh,' Bradley said, beginning to understand. That was a different matter.

'And there was no way I was going to give him either.' Mark rubbed his eyes wearily. 'Shit!' he said.

Bradley was nodding, scratching his head, thinking. 'Can't you find twenty dabs? Might get you off the hook ... maybe.'

Mark shrugged helplessly. 'Even if I could, which I could, and I gave it to him, he'd still bother me. He's got a downer on me and that's that. I'm just gonna have to keep me head down for a while.'

'A lifetime, don't you mean?' Bradley corrected him.

'Nah, Jonny Sparks has the memory of a goldfish. He'll have forgotten in a week or two.'

Bradley's face reflected that he did not believe that. He sighed. 'So what're you going to do for a fortnight? Stay in here, holed up like that guy across the street did?' He was referring to a crim who'd done a less than daring escape from Kirkham Open Prison – by simply walking away from the place across the fields – and then spent his entire time on the run, it was rumoured, underneath a bed in his mum's house, where the cops eventually caught him. 'Life goes on, mate. You got to go to school. You've got paper rounds. You've never skived off school and you've never missed a paper round. He'll get you, sure as eggs is beans.'

'Maybe if I just steer clear of the estate, that's where Jonny mainly hangs around ... anyway,' Mark changed the subject breezily, 'I need some food. You had your tea yet?'

'Not yet. Mum hasn't landed home.'

'Fancy going down the front, see what we can cadge?'

Bradley gave an uncertain shrug. 'I do, but...' He huffed, screwing his face up, obviously torn.

'Come on,' Mark encouraged him, a little unfairly really. Bradley had what Mark called a 'proper family', a mum and a dad who worked normal hours, came home at normal times and did things that a proper family did – at least what Mark thought a *proper* family did. Not like his ragbag excuse for a family: a mum who worked weird hours and was always staying out or, worse, bringing home a succession of boyfriends; and a sister who was too busy with her own life to be bothered about him. Mark often speculated what it would be like to be Bradley. Sometimes he was envious, sometimes not. At least, he would think, I can come and go as I please, do what I want when I want. I haven't got somebody watching over my shoulder all the time.

Then sometimes he wished he had...

'I'll have to leave a note for Mum,' Bradley decided, 'and I'll have to be back for eight. I think that'll be OK.'

'Fair dos.'

They raced through the streets on their bikes, down alleyways and other short cuts, riding like feral boys, screeching round corners, leaving braking almost too late, nearly knocking people over and tearing across busy roads without stopping. From Shoreside down on to the front at Blackpool took less than ten minutes.

They surfaced on to the promenade just north of the main entrance to the Pleasure Beach and turned right with the grey Irish Sea across to their left as they pedalled up the prom. Sticking to the wide pavement, they meandered more slowly now towards Central Pier and the Golden Mile, that stretch of the prom which was all amusement arcades, fast food outlets, pubs, clubs and tacky shops – and, of course, Blackpool Tower.

Mark had grown up in the resort and knew it intimately, and also a lot of the people, which was handy when on the scrounge for a food handout.

It was that time of year between Easter and summer when, during midweek, the town was pretty quiet, so riding up the pavement was possible without crashing into people. They reached a pub called the Manchester at a point where the tram tracks crossed the wide road and cut inland from the sea front. Once across this wide junction, there were more pedestrians knocking about, so Mark and Bradley dismounted, pushed their bikes.

On the way down from the estate they'd been shouting to each other, wondering where would be best to try and get a free burger each. They settled on Tony's Burger Bar. It was basically nothing more than a serving hatch to catch passing foot traffic and sold a delicious range of greasy burgers and carbonated drinks. It was owned by a guy called Ray, not Tony – Tony had been the previous owner and Ray couldn't be bothered to change the name – and Ray occasionally let Mark and Bradley do odd jobs for him in exchange for payment by food. The jobs were usually horrible cleaning jobs associated with chip fat, grease and cockroaches, and drains blocked with congealed fat. Despite the small size of the business, Ray always shut down after the illuminations in November and decamped to Tenerife for the winter where he ran a similar business in Playa de las Americas.

As well as giving them food, Ray allowed the lads to leave their bikes around the back of the shop, where they would be safe.

Even though business was light that evening, Ray grudgingly gave them a burger, fried onions, chips and a cheap cola each based on the promise they'd return at the weekend and clean up the accumulated mess behind the shop as payment.

With the bikes securely stowed away, they set off on foot up the Golden Mile towards the tower, hoodies tugged over their heads, munching their feasts.

'They're actually really horrid, these,' Bradley whined, but kept eating as though it was his last meal before execution. 'Taste like cardboard.'

'Fried onions're nice, though.' Mark stopped in his tracks and slurped a particularly long piece of juicy onion into his mouth. He sighed with pleasure as he bit into it. 'Perfect.' The more burnt, the better.

They crossed the road at the junction opposite Central Pier, their hunger slightly assuaged, and reached the more crowded pavement near to the tower, just two lads cruising amongst many others. They drifted aimlessly through a few amusement arcades, banging their fists hopefully on fruit machines and pressing the buttons in case they got lucky and money fell into their hands, and having a go at some of the arcade shooting games without actually putting any money into them.

Not much was happening. None of their other mates were around and soon they became bored with this feckless activity ... and they were hungry again, their growing bodies demanding some proper sustenance.

But such was the lifestyle of a kid in Blackpool. It was pretty boring and pointless, mostly. Especially if you didn't have money.

'I think I'll head off home. My guts're churning,' Bradley complained. He was a bigger lad than Mark, more of him to fill, and was forever eating. He said it was because of a growth spurt, but to Mark it seemed that his mate was always going upwards.

'We could see if Ray'll sub us another burger,' Mark suggested hopefully. He didn't particularly want to go back home, even though he was bored, because there would probably only be him in the house. Bethany would have gone out by now and his mum ... well, his mum ... Mark just didn't expect her to be there.

More hours spent alone in front of the telly didn't really appeal to him.

'Nah, I want summat proper in me belly.' Bradley rubbed his tum. 'Me mum'll be home by now.'

Mark pulled a face and almost said, 'Lucky sod.' Instead he shrugged and said, 'Whatever.'

'I could ask her if she'll let you have tea with us.'

'Eh? That'd be great,' Mark blurted enthusiastically.

They walked back toward Tony's Burger Bar, but none too quickly. Neither lad could resist checking out the arcades, mooching from machine to machine, seeing if anyone had missed collecting their winnings, but they were singularly unlucky that day.

Crossing back over the Chapel Street junction, they passed the MacDonald's where Bill Clinton had once had a burger as part of some witless publicity stunt.

It was getting colder as the night drew in, a wind slicing through the air like a knife from the sea. Both huddled down into their hoodies and quickened their pace as they left the arcades behind.

At the Lonsdale Arms they waited for a tram to trundle past, then legged it before the lights changed, passing the pub as a gaggle of people crowded into the door. Mark wasn't really taking much notice of them, but as they crushed through the revolving doors, he heard a girl's laugh he thought he recognized. He stopped and yanked Bradley back, almost pulling him over.

'What?' Bradley demanded.

'Come on.' Mark dragged him.

'What?' Bradley bleated, struggling.

'I wanna go in here and have a look.'

'What for? It's a pub!' Bradley was nonplussed. 'You're only fourteen.'

'I know. I just want a look, OK?'

Mark set off to the side door on Lytham Road. Usually they had bouncers here and Mark was wary. Even though he believed he looked older than fourteen, doormen were pretty good at estimating the age of kids. Probably more to do with body language than appearance: youngsters who shouldn't be in pubs, who weren't used to being in pubs, were awkward in their movements because they were always expecting the fateful hand on the shoulder. Those who sneaked into pubs regularly looked and acted more naturally. Mark didn't go into pubs – and as he walked up to the door, putting on his cocky walk (always a dead giveaway), he felt as if a big inflated finger was pointing down at him from the sky, singling him out and a booming, God-like voice saying, 'Underage! Underage!' As luck had it, probably because it was still early, there was no one on the door. He entered with Bradley behind.

For the time of day, the place was heaving with bodies. Thumping dance music blared out of huge, ceiling-hung speakers, stuff that Mark did not like. He was more into straight-up rock, not drum and bass crap. People crushed together, shouting to be heard. Lots of smoke rose, despite the non-smoking policy, with some strange niff within the normal smoke, something sweet smelling.

Moving through the pub he expected to be identified as being too young, then dragged to the door to be ejected by some ape of a bouncer, but no one looked at him twice. They were all engrossed in their own worlds.

Bradley stayed up close behind him, very uncomfortable in this environment.

'What're we doing here?' he demanded in Mark's ear.

'Lookin', that's all.'

Bradley gave the back of Mark's head a confused grimace.

They went once around the pub. Mark thought he might've been mistaken. Maybe he had misheard.

As they circled back to the door they'd come in at, Mark stopped abruptly and Bradley walked into him.

He wasn't wrong after all. The laugh he thought he'd heard coming from the bunch of people entering the pub *was* Bethany's. Mark had come in hoping to surprise her and her mates, but now, as he spotted her, he edged backwards, using his arms to get Bradley to walk backwards too, a kind of fear ripping through him.

There she was, Bethany Carter. As large as life, in the centre of a throng of youths, part of a gang, all seated in a dark corner of the pub. She had a drink in one hand, a fat-looking cigarette dangling from her fingers. Mark knew it was a spliff – cannabis.

He melted further back, his eyes fixed on the group, Bethany in particular.

At one point she turned and looked directly at him and he didn't know what to do. Duck? Dive? Wave? He just stood as if frozen.

It didn't matter, though. She might've been looking straight at him, but she didn't see him. Her eyes were hazy, watery and bleary. Her head seemed to be wobbling as though it might drop off at any moment, like it could not balance. She was looking but not seeing a thing, not Mark, not anything. Then her head swivelled back, a slightly contorted smile on her lips, and she burst into a sort of inane laughter, a strange, disjointed cackle, as if she wasn't all there. A sandwich short of a picnic.

But as unsettling as all that was – Mark knew she was into drugs, though he'd never seen her under their influence – it was something else that really scared the living pants off him.

He watched her lean sideways and start snogging the guy sitting next to her. A real, full-on snog, tongues, slaver, everything. She was almost eating him alive. To Mark it looked horrible, doing something like that in public, in a pub full of punters.

But that was still not the worst of it.

The worst of it was that the guy she was kissing was Jonny Sparks.

Three

It was 2.20 a.m.

Mark was in bed, his Man U duvet pulled up tight over his head. Even so, he was cold, shivering. He could not sleep, couldn't even doze off. He was wide awake and there was an empty, carved out feeling in the pit of his stomach. He just found it impossible to rid his mind of the vision of Bethany's lips attached to Jonny Sparks's face like a limpet. A repulsive sight, it made him feel weak and ill. He'd tried a few pages of *Treasure Island*, but even that didn't help.

He tugged the duvet down, blinked and stared at the cracked ceiling.

Mark, generally speaking, was proud of himself. Most people would have thought that Mark Carter wouldn't have had a chance growing up on the estate with no dad, a mother who worked hard and played even harder, surrounded by drugs and criminality. Actually, he often wondered why he hadn't been lured to that sort of life, but from early on, he'd somehow known that nicking other people's stuff was wrong. He just knew instinctively. Add to that he'd had stuff pinched from him, nearly had his bike robbed, and he knew what it was like to lose something valuable. He could never have inflicted that feeling on somebody else. Just wasn't right. It was probably down to a bit of Jack's influence, too. He'd always preached right and wrong – sometimes Mark had been bored rigid by his elder brother's sermons – but the words had stuck and therefore Mark avoided the worst of the estate and did his best.

Obviously the same hadn't rubbed off on Beth. What the hell was she doing with Jonny Sparks?

OK, she was Mark's older sister and had always moved in different circles to him, but he'd always thought she was doing all right. Not that he could ever recall having a heart-to-heart with her. Didn't mean he didn't love her. He did. Lots. They just didn't live in each other's pockets.

But Jonny bloody Sparks!

Mark thought she had more sense than to fall in with a bad sod like him. He'd been excluded from school time after time and was known to be a drug dealer, the rumour being that he worked for the Crackman.

Mark didn't know whether that was true or not. Certainly Jonny would have everyone believe he was on the Crackman's payroll, even tried to make some gullible fools think he was the Crackman himself. Mark didn't believe that for one nanosecond – Sparks

didn't have the intellect to run a business –
but he certainly believed Sparks was a runner, dealer and maybe occasionally a taxman
for the Crackman; that is, someone who
went around collecting debts and kicking
people's heads in if they didn't pay up.

The Crackman was a bit of a legend on the
estate and in Blackpool. He was supposed to
be the main man who controlled all drug
dealing on Shoreside and in large chunks
of the rest of town. He specialised in crack
cocaine – hence his nickname – but also
dealt in huge quantities in every other illegal
drug imaginable. He was supposed to have a
complex web of dealers and a chain of command that meant he was untouchable.

That's if he actually existed. Because no
one knew who he was. No one had ever seen
him, other than in the shadows. No one had
ever spoken to him. Could there really be
one person with such immense power? Maybe he was just an urban legend ... but, whatever the truth about the Crackman, big time
drug dealers did exist in town and they made
life a misery for hundreds of people, and
Jonny Sparks was definitely a dealer, even if
he wasn't big league.

Which, among others, was one of the reasons why Mark avoided him and why he
could not believe Beth had been stupid
enough to get involved with him.

Admittedly Beth had been really distant
recently, more so than usual, but to be

honest Mark hadn't been too concerned. But as he thought about it, he realized she had been acting a bit strangely, as though she was in a different world completely. She didn't spend much time in the house any more, but because she'd got a job on the tills at Tesco, Mark assumed she was out working. Maybe he was wrong. Perhaps she'd been knocking around with Jonny and had been dragged into his lifestyle.

Damn, I wish I talked to her more, Mark thought regretfully. He knew she had smoked a bit of dope in her time, but hanging around with Sparks would almost inevitably lead to much harder stuff. That worried Mark, made him quiver inside.

He had to do something about it. Not that he was into screwing up any relationship she might have with a boy, but Jonny Sparks was the exception to that rule and he decided there and then he would do whatever he could to make her dump him. He'd no idea what. That would come with time, but there was no way he was going to allow his big sister to mess up her life by hanging around with a shit-head like Sparks.

As his mind whirled Mark started to drift off towards sleep.

The sound of a key in the front door brought him back fully awake.

He shot upright, threw back the cover and sprang lightly out of bed. Keeping the light off, he crept to the window, peeled the curtain back an inch and peeked out through the crack.

There was a car outside the house with a couple of people inside. Mark stood on tiptoe and peered down to the front door, which he could just see if he squished the side of his face right up to the glass.

Bethany was down on the front steps.

So was Jonny Sparks.

They were embracing, kissing, body-to-body, tight, up close. Jonny's hands ran all over Beth.

Mark's face screwed up in revulsion.

Thing was, Bethany was giving as good as she was getting. Her hands were everywhere, too. She threw her head back and Jonny kissed her neck, slavering all over her chest. She blatantly rubbed her groin against Jonny's.

Mark's fists clenched in sickened rage.

Then they stopped and, forehead resting on forehead, they murmured intimately in low tones. Beth giggled, Jonny uttered a dirty laugh.

Mark's teeth grated and he growled deeply like a wolf, something primitive moving inside him. He wished he'd done a proper job on Jonny now. Not just one smack in the balls. He should've crushed them.

The driver of the car tooted the horn and shouted for Jonny to hurry up.

The lovely couple gave each other one last

61

grope. Jonny then turned and sauntered down the garden path. He went a few steps, stopped, turned back and looked up at Mark's bedroom window. Mark reacted instantly by drawing his face back, but not before he saw Jonny's middle finger jerking up at him.

Mark flattened himself against the bedroom wall, teeth still grinding, fists balled up, every muscle inside him scrunched up, his nostrils flaring with rage.

He heard the front door open. With a snarl on his face, he pushed himself away from the wall and ran out of the bedroom. He was going to confront Bethany and have it out with her.

Mark was in her face the moment she stepped through the door.

'What're you doin' with that piece of crap?' he yelled at her.

She looked at him strangely, forehead furrowed, her expression perplexed. Her eyes were watery and seemed distant, the pupils dilated unnaturally. She was looking at him but it was as though he wasn't actually there, she wasn't actually seeing him.

She screwed up her nose, gave a sort of shrug and shouldered past without saying a word, brushing him out of her way as though she was passing someone she didn't know in a crowd.

Astounded, he grabbed her, spun her

round. 'I said, what're you doing knocking round with Jonny Sparks, you idiot? He's trouble.'

She wriggled free from his grip. 'Leave me alone,' she protested. 'What the hell's it got to do with you?'

'He's a shit,' Mark said fiercely. 'He's no good and you're my sister.'

'What?' she spat. Her face told him exactly what she thought about that sentiment. 'Just get lost, Mark. Leave me be. I'm having a good time, OK?' She swayed where she stood, as if drunk. Only thing was, Mark couldn't smell booze on her, so he knew she hadn't been drinking. Mark wasn't thick. He could add up the sums – and the simple maths came to only one answer: drugs. 'Just piss off, you pathetic dick-head,' she snorted.

Mark took a step away from her. 'You be bloody careful,' he warned her with a dangerous whisper. 'And he's only fourteen. You're seventeen.'

'I've got along fine without a dad this long; I don't need one now,' she sneered. 'It's none of your business. Stay out of it.'

He regarded her critically for the first time in a long time, standing under the bare light in the hallway. What he saw scared him. There were changes he'd not noticed before that moment.

Beth used to be on the chubby side. Not fat, but some of Mark's mates had passed lewd comments about the size of her boobs. As Mark quickly scanned her, he now saw a thin, pasty ghost of the girl who had once been a picture of health. She looked like a skeleton. Her cheekbones stuck out against her skin and her face had deep valleys in it, with gloomy shadows on it. Her eyes were sunk in, surrounded by unhealthy bags. Her mouth had become thin, almost lip-less and her neck was like a scrawny turkey. She looked dreadful. Mark knew intuitively that her condition was not because of smoking a few spliffs or going on a diet. Cannabis alone did not do this to a person. She was into hard drugs.

Why hadn't he seen the change?

He swallowed. 'Please.' It was all he could think of to say. The word was barely audible.

It had no effect on Bethany. She shook her head. 'Do me a favour – piss off and leave me alone. I'm old enough to know what I'm doing.'

'Yeah, right.' His tone was sarcastic.

She ran upstairs and banged into her room, leaving Mark standing in the hall, staring after her. He sat down on the second step, elbows on knees, head in hands. He began to cry softly, somehow believing all this was his doing, his fault. If only he'd seen the signs.

The tears lasted maybe five minutes before he crept quietly upstairs. On the landing, he paused outside Beth's door, listening but hearing nothing. A few steps further and he was outside his mum's room. He tapped gently on the door and pushed it open, poking his head inside.

Her big double bed – unmade – was empty. He knew it would be. She was probably out at her latest boyfriend's. Mark would be lucky to see her even in the morning. She'd most likely be out all night. He slid into her room and perched on the edge of her bed, running his hands over the sheets, thinking about her. He had vague recollections of sneaking into bed with her when he was a lot younger. He had felt warm and protected and she had held him close against her in those days. That was just after his dad had done a runner. Those days hadn't lasted long. Soon, there was no chance of getting into bed with her unless you wanted to curl up with the latest 'uncle'.

But now, sitting there, Mark wasn't too upset about the dim, distant past.

It was the here and now that terrified him.

Four

Next day, school was a bit of a haze.

It began solemnly, with assembly, when the whole school was asked to stand for a minute of silence to show respect for a sixth-former – a girl called Jane Grice who had died from a drug overdose a fortnight earlier; today was the day of her funeral. The head teacher said a few words about her, warned everyone of the dangers of drugs and then led the school in an incantation of the Lord's Prayer after the minute's silence – during which there was a lot of farting, pushing and giggling going on. Some respect.

Mark went along with it, the little tirade about the dangers of drugs hitting a chord within him. He didn't know the girl who had died, though, and wasn't really affected by her demise. But he could see others who were. Some of her friends were openly weeping. He had a vague sort of memory of seeing her knocking around with Jonny Sparks before he got excluded.

After assembly, the kids all trooped to their classes as if nothing had happened.

Mark actually enjoyed school, couldn't understand anyone who didn't. He had some good mates here, had a laugh and sometimes even knuckled down and did some work and usually enjoyed the subjects. He was half-good at maths and sciences, not so brilliant at metalwork, adored Spanish, was ace at English – literature and language – and history ... and, of course, sport. His perfect day would have been a morning reading and an afternoon playing footie.

He knew he would have liked school even if he didn't have any ambitions, but even at the age of fourteen he was planning ahead and saw school as the best way to cut free from Blackpool. He didn't want to end up in a dead-end job. He could easily have got work around the resort when he left school, even without any qualifications, but he had a different life planned.

First off, he was going to stay on for 'A' levels, then he was going to go to university. Part of what he earned from his paper rounds was already going towards those costs. Yes, university, in a town or city far, far away.

Then a job in London, or New York, or Madrid.

At that moment he wasn't sure what sort of job. That would come, he thought.

For now, he was dreaming with his eyes open.

Except, in Mrs Fletcher's history class, he

was actually *day*dreaming with his eyes open, staring out at the football pitch. And he wasn't thinking about London and the future. Nor was he thinking about the Victorians and the past, which he should've been doing. He was thinking about Bethany. And Jonny Sparks. And how to split them up.

A nasty crack on the head made him jump back to the reality of the classroom. Mrs Fletcher's 'dink' with a pencil on the skull – her favourite means of getting someone's attention. His head spun around and he looked stupidly up at her, rubbing his head and saying, 'Ow.'

'Away with the fairies, Mark Carter?'

The rest of the class giggled.

'Sorry, Mrs Fletcher.'

She regarded him warmly. She quite liked him. 'So,' she asked, 'what did the Victorians ever do for us?'

'Brought sanitation?' he responded hopefully.

She blinked. 'Yes, you're right. They got rid of poo.'

Inwardly, Mark was relieved, thinking he'd got off lightly. He shuffled cockily on his chair. But Mrs Fletcher wasn't to be put off by a lucky answer – even a good one. 'And what else?'

He groaned and shifted in his uncomfortable chair, his mind now a blank.

'Jet engines?' he guessed – an answer that

68

received another pencil crack on the bonce.

Word travelled fast. Before he knew it, Mark Carter was a bit of a celebrity, albeit an infamous one.

He picked up the vibes during lunchtime as he walked with Bradley from the form classroom towards the dining room. Some year eight girls saw him and started giggling and whispering behind their hands; next a couple of year nine lads moved quickly out of his way, giving him more respect than he'd ever had before.

In the dinner queue, some guys behind him, who were in the year above him, scrutinized him strangely.

In the end, Mark gave up, turned and said, 'What?'

They backed off a couple of steps.

'What?' Mark demanded more fervently.

'Sorry,' one of them said. He had real fear in his eyes. Mark didn't even know the lad's name, just knew he was a head taller than Mark was and pretty hard with it.

'What you sorry for?' Mark shook his head and turned away.

Bradley laid a hand on Mark's arm.

'What's going on?' Mark asked.

The dinner queue moved on a few feet. Mark and Bradley made up the distance, but not before a couple of year tens had seen the opportunity and cut rudely in.

'Oi!' Mark snarled.

They spun with ferocity, ready to put him firmly in his place. Then they saw who he was, who they'd just transgressed. They mumbled some sort of pathetic apology and scurried away like mice.

Mark looked askance at Bradley, who had an amazed grin on his face. Mark gestured with his hands as though he was trying to grab something that wasn't there. 'Help me here.'

'Word is you battered Jonny Sparks, mate.'

Mark blinked.

'Word is, he dissed you and you leathered him.'

'Word is wrong,' Mark said quietly.

'I know that ... rumours grow. The real story gets twisted. Y'know – the fact that what you actually did was hit him and run for your life. Somehow that seems to have got lost in the mists of story-telling.'

Mark was thoughtful as he collected his tray and moved across the serving hatch, picking up his Jamie Oliver-inspired dinner of healthy stuff. Mark desperately needed a burger and chips, not rabbit food. He chose lasagne and boiled potatoes and sticky toffee pudding for dessert, which was the un-healthiest thing on the menu.

He ate in silence. The buzz, chatter and laughter of the other kids in the room was just background. He didn't even hear it. Bradley sat opposite him, knowing it best not to disturb his pal's thinking.

Mark was brought back with a bump when a year ten lad walked past him, again, someone he hardly knew, and gave him a slap on the shoulder.

'Way to go, mate,' the lad said. 'Respect to you. The twat deserves all he gets.'

'Cheers,' Mark responded dully.

'New-found fame,' Bradley smirked when the lad had gone. 'How you going to handle it?'

'Mm,' Mark mumbled doubtfully. Thing was, though, as he thought about it, the respect was pretty cool and he was beginning to enjoy the notoriety a little, even if the story of what really happened had been twisted. Trouble was, it could all go wrong once everyone got to know the real truth, or when another lad found the courage to challenge him and discovered that Mark wasn't really much of a fighter. So, as much as it was a good feeling to have guys cowering under his gaze, Mark wasn't foolish enough to believe in his own press. He knew he had to put an end to this – and fast. Particularly before Jonny Sparks found out and got extra mad at him for embellishing the truth, even though he wasn't the one who had. It had just happened.

But ... just for a few more minutes, maybe even for a few hours, Mark decided to bask in the glory.

He pretty much kept his head down for the

71

rest of the day: maths and science, his two poorest subjects. A few people gave him sidelong glances which were a mixture of awe and respect and not a little fear.

Thinking about it, Mark could perhaps see where they were coming from.

Jonny Sparks had been – still was – one of those kids beyond anyone's control. His background made Mark look as though he'd been brought up in a wealthy, caring family with all the privileges imaginable. Jonny's parents were smack-heads, real heavy-duty drug addicts who were in and out of the police station on a weekly basis for stealing stuff to feed their habits. The only bit of luck Jonny'd had was not to be born a heroin addict. He'd been brought into this world before his mother, who was seventeen when he was born, had staggered down that path.

Jonny had grown up into a hard, streetwise kid with no social skills whatever. He terrorized other kids and disrupted lessons (when he was actually in school); when he beat up the PE teacher, ambushing the guy in the changing rooms, attacking him with a dumbbell and putting him in hospital, he'd finally been excluded for good. Most of his life had been spent in and out of children's homes, being chased by the courts and social services.

But – in Mark's estimation – none of this excused Jonny's violent behaviour.

It had been a good day for the school when

he was kicked out, but rumours still abounded, as rumours did, that Jonny might come back because that was the way the ridiculous system worked. If you were out of control, it seemed, they bent over backwards for you.

So, yeah, Mark could see why he was a bit of a hero. Few people liked Jonny, most were scared of him, and anyone who got the better of him was to be applauded. Unless they became like him, which Mark had no intention of doing.

He was relieved when the bell rang: 3:30 p.m.

Mark hurriedly packed his books into his shoulder bag and did a runner.

Even though it seemed a cliché to Mark, the bike sheds tucked away at the back of the school were where lots of iffy things happened. Pre-arranged fights, for instance, smoking, snogging and one of Mark's mates even claimed he'd once had a hand job here from the girl known as the school bike, appropriately enough. A used condom had even once been found and the school idiot, a dim, bespectacled boy called Fosdyke, had blown it up when encouraged by the crowd who had gathered to gawp. He had then managed to get it on to his head like a swimming cap. Mark had witnessed this and the thought still made him shiver with disgust. A used condom? It would have been bad enough using one straight out of the packet.

Mark's BMX was in the shed, secured by two thick chains with sturdy padlocks.

He was hunched over unlocking it when he became aware of someone standing behind him. Dread moved inside him, like a reptile. He rose slowly and turned, his fears being realized, that fear emptying his mouth of all moisture. He knew his tenure as king of the castle had just come to an end.

The Kong and Rat-Head, Jonny Sparks's lackeys, aka Eric King and Sam Dale, aka the Hyenas, were towering there with menace.

Mark stood up on weak, creaky knees, the bike chains in his hand.

They looked tough and ferocious.

'Jonny wants to see you,' Sam said. For the first time Mark noticed that Eric had an occasional twitch, which made the left hand side of his face jump about, his eye wink and his lip curl like Elvis. Mark supposed it was the first time he'd ever been this close to Eric. It wasn't a regular twitch. It was sporadic, but quite noticeable once you knew it was there.

'I don't want to see Jonny,' Mark retorted.

Sam gave a 'Don't care what you want' gesture. 'Get your bike and push it and don't try anything funny.' He twitched, but with the twitch he stepped suddenly forward, quicker than Mark could react, and drove his fist hard into Mark's guts. The move, the blow, took him entirely by surprise. The breath shot out of him like from a steam pipe. He doubled over, clutching his stomach, knees bending, head drooped low.

Sam stepped back and flat-footed the side of Mark's head, sending him crashing against his bike, knocking it over, then falling on his side in agony. Sam stood over him. 'That was just for fun, mate,' he snarled. 'Now get up, get yer bike, stand between us and walk out of school nice 'n' easy as though you love us.'

Teeth clenched, Mark rolled on to his knees and, using the frame of the bike shed, heaved himself painfully to his feet, reluctantly standing up and pulling his bike up with him. He wrapped the steel chains around the neck of the saddle and put his hands on the handlebars.

'Ready,' he said.

Eric and Sam smiled wickedly at him. Sam grabbed an arm and they began to walk out, one either side of him.

Tears of pain welled in Mark's eyes.

'I got a Stanley in my pocket,' Eric hissed into Mark's ear. 'A three-blader. You try anything and I'll slash your face with it, just the once. You won't even feel it for a few seconds, but the doctor won't be able to sew it up. Understand?'

Mark nodded, blinking back the tears. He knew about triple-bladed Stanley knives and the damage they could do.

Most kids had gone home, but there were

a few left dotted around the school. There were no members of staff around who could've helped him.

Mark's girlfriend, Katie Bretherton, was waiting at the school gates. She always did and they usually walked to the newsagent's together, where Mark did his paper rounds. Katie was a year older than him and, to be honest, not really his girlfriend in the truest sense. She was a girl and they were friends. They had a laugh together and that was about it. They'd had a kiss once, but nothing more. Mark lived in hope.

Katie and Mark's eyes locked as he approached her flanked by his escorts. Her expression betrayed that she was appalled by what she saw – on the face of it, Mark and two bad lads in cahoots. Her face, wordlessly, asked him what the hell was going on.

He replied with a little shake of the head, diverting his eyes from hers.

'All right, fittie?' Sam leered at her.

'Sod off,' she responded. She was exceptionally pretty, but the look she was pulling screwed up her little nose like a scrimped-up piece of paper, as if there was a stink on her top lip. She looked worriedly at Mark.

'It's OK,' he said, trying to reassure her, though his own face told a different story. 'Can you tell Aziz I might not make it?'

The trio walked past her, Sam continuing to leer. She held his gaze, trying to appear unafraid.

They paused at the front gates where Sam and Eric exchanged a look across Mark.

'Down by the Swannee,' Sam said.

'Oh yeah,' said Eric.

The Swannee was a piece of boggy, derelict land on the outskirts of Shoreside where kids often met and played. How it had got its name, no one knew, but it was a great place to hang out because it was not overlooked by any houses and it wasn't far away from the motorway. It was a pretty desolate place where someone could easily get beaten up and have their bike stolen from them without any witnesses.

Mark quickly weighed up the chances of legging it, ditching his precious BMX and just running ... but his guards seemed to read his mind. They stepped in closer and Sam said, 'No chance.'

Mark's shoulders sagged. He started to shake as a wave of terror washed over him. His head spun and he looked back imploringly at Kate, who shrugged her shoulders and raised her hands helplessly.

Face facts, Mark Carter, you are definitely going to get a battering this time.

His saviour came in a black Porsche Cayenne, one of those big four-wheel drive monsters with smoked glass windows, huge tyres and a big attitude – fifty grand's worth of attitude.

Mark, Sam and Eric had walked about a

hundred metres – slowly – at the pace of a condemned man being led to the gallows. Things were not helped by the evocative description Sam was gleefully relaying to Mark about the extent of the beating he was about to get from Jonny.

'He's gonna kick yer 'ed in,' he said with relish.

Eric added his own salt to that particular description. 'Even yer own mum won't be able to recognize ya.'

Mark began to feel that Eric and Sam were interchangeable, two peas out of the same pod, their thought processes almost identical. They could've been brothers, but Mark knew they weren't related ... but, then again, maybe they were and they just didn't know it. Stranger things than that had happened on Shoreside. Same dad, different mums.

Mark's face had set like concrete. He did not hear the car at first, just became aware of its presence behind, hovering like a ghost. Mind, the engine was quiet, purring away, almost inaudible.

His captors didn't notice it either, not until the horn blasted out and made all three of them leap out of their skins. They all spun around.

Mark's eyes widened.

The Porsche drew up alongside and stopped. A man climbed out.

He was wearing designer shades, covering eyes which Mark knew were as keen as an eagle's. The man's hair was close-cropped, but styled all the same, trimmed with scissors by a hairstylist, rather than just with a mini lawnmower. There was a square chin and a tanned face. He wore a pure white D&G T-shirt underneath a superbly cut leather jacket, complementing his expensive jeans and loafers, his feet sock-less.

'What's going on?' the man asked. His voice was soft.

'What's it to you?' Eric sneered defiantly, though with a bit of hesitance.

'I asked what's going on.'

Eric stepped aggressively forward. 'An' I said, what's it to you?'

Wrong move.

It was just a blur of speed. So fast. A kind of double-punch to the face and Eric went down as though a ten-ton weight had smashed into him. He hit the ground hard.

Sam moved at the man then – launched himself with a scream at this mystery attacker.

Wrong move number two.

The man pivoted and drove his fist into Sam's stomach, making Mark go 'Oooh!' and wince, even. Then he twisted Sam around and shoved him head first against the school railings. As Sam's head made contact with the iron, the man let him go and he flopped uselessly to the ground.

The Porsche driver cast a critical eye over his handiwork and rubbed his hands. He then looked at Mark with a wry smile and slowly removed his sunglasses.

'Can you not keep out of trouble?'

'Thanks, you saved my skin.'

'I know.' The man's attention turned to the two defeated miscreants on the ground. Eric was sat up on his backside, knees up, hands covering a crunched, bloody nose. Sam was on his knees, both hands covering the top of his head. The man gave Eric a tap with his toe just to get his attention. 'Get lost, unless you want more – cos I'd be happy to dish it out.'

They clambered unsteadily to their feet, but before they hobbled off, the man said in a low voice that was really a growl, 'You leave Mark Carter alone, OK? If I ever hear you've even been near him, I'll be back and you'll be dangling by your feet from a motorway bridge – now piss off.'

They ran, or shuffled, away, like the beaten dogs they were.

Jack Carter turned to his younger brother and gave him a look of deep affection. 'They won't bother you again – promise.'

'Thanks, mate.'

It was one of those rare moments in Mark's life. It didn't happen often, but it still felt very, very good to have a big brother who could look after you now and again.

Five

Jack was wearing that sardonic smile he had perfected so well. It sort of hovered on his lips. That, coupled with one raised eyebrow – something else he'd perfected – and his easy good looks had the effect of making Mark squirm under his gaze – but not uncomfortably so – and go, 'Whaaat?' before chomping into his chicken burger and savouring a real treat, unlike Ray's pieces of cardboard that doubled as burgers. It was something Mark could rarely afford – a three-piece meal. Bliss, and bless Colonel Sanders.

They were in the Kentucky Fried Chicken near to Preston New Road. Jack shook his head with twisted amusement. 'You don't half get yourself into some scrapes,' he chuckled.

'Yeah, yeah I do,' Mark admitted through his munching, revelling in Jack's attention, even though the truth was he actually did his best not to get into scrapes.

'And big bro has to come along and bail you out.'

'Yep.' Mark shoved a bunch of salty chips

81

into his mouth.

'What was that all about then?'

'Oh, nowt,' Mark said, trying to play it down. 'Just trod on some tough guy's toes. Nowt really. Big mistake.' To be honest, Mark didn't want Jack to get involved. Jack's life had no connection with what went on at this low level on the streets of Blackpool. Jack was a high-flyer, a businessman who always had bits of computers and paperwork strewn around the inside of his car.

'I see. You don't really wanna tell me, do you?'

'Nah – just glad you came along when you did, that's all.'

'OK, fair dos ... but I'll tell you something, those guys won't bother you again.'

Mark placed a half-eaten chicken drumstick down and squinted thoughtfully at his brother. 'Jack, you won't be here to do anything. I mean, once you've gone, you've gone, if you know what I mean. I mean, thanks for leatherin' them, but they'll get me sometime. It's just how they are. The way of the world. And you won't be here, because your life's not here.' Mark interlocked his fingers on the table in front of him.

'No!' It was barked harshly, making Mark jump a little. Jack placed a big hand over Mark's hands and squeezed reassuringly. He leaned forward, looking closely into Mark's eyes. A strange, hard, determined expression came over Jack's face, a bit scary, even.

Mark's eyes narrowed. Jack said, 'I mean it – they won't bother you again.'

'You can say that, Jack, but—'

'Yeah, I can.' Jack sat back, pulling away from Mark. There was another look on his face now which made Mark feel slightly edgy.

'How?'

'Trust me ... I might not be here in person, but I'll be here in spirit.'

'Mm, OK, then,' Mark said, not wanting to fall out with him, but knowing that as soon as Jack hopped into his fancy motor, he, Mark, would be alone again and would have to rely on his own wits and cunning to avoid Jonny Sparks and the Hyenas.

'Don't believe me, do you?' Jack said.

'Jack...' Mark shrugged, opening his arms, wiggling his fingers as he tried to put his doubt into words that wouldn't offend Jack.

'You'll be all right, mate. I'll be watching over you.'

'If you say so,' Mark conceded, not wanting to fall out.

Jack's mobile phone rang. It was on the table between them. He picked it up and inspected the caller display. 'Need to get this – sorry.' He pushed himself to his feet, putting the phone to his ear and walking out of the restaurant in to the car park out front.

Mark watched him leave as he folded more chips into his mouth and washed them down with Fanta Orange.

God, he thought, it was fantastic to see Jack. He always did this: didn't see him for weeks on end and then, when you least expected it – bam! – turned up out of the blue. Mark loved it when he came, even if it was only for a fleeting visit. And he hated it when he left, drove off into the sunset, back to his business, his girlfriend and his own life. Mark really looked up to Jack, seeing what his elder brother had achieved, having dragged himself up and away from a shitty council estate and made something of his life. Good job, great car, some fantastic women, too. What Mark wanted was just to be happy and have a family of his own some day – a steady, dull family. Even at the tender age of fourteen he knew that was what he ultimately wanted and that's what he was working towards. Get the education, get the degree, get the job, have a ball, see the world and leave this sink-hole and people like Jonny Sparks behind.

Mark's thoughts skittered to Bethany and his face darkened.

Mark needed to speak to Jack about her. Maybe he could do something. But he knew that Jack didn't hold much sway over Beth. No one did. She was hot-headed and in-dependent, didn't listen, knew best, didn't like being told. Mark just hoped she wasn't a lost cause.

He would speak to Jack.

Jack was in deep, animated conversation

on the phone, gesticulating, emphasizing points with his hands, stomping around in circles, looking at the ground. Probably pulling off some business deal or other, Mark thought. Jack seemed pretty annoyed at something, but Mark could not hear any words, nor even guess at what was being said.

Mark's eyes roved round at the other customers. There were only a few people in the place. A young couple, all gooey-eyed, lovey-dovey, feeding chips to each other making Mark want to retch; one bloke sitting with a coffee, reading a broadsheet newspaper; two lads in their late teens were huddled in one corner by a window. Mark paused on them and they immediately locked on to his gaze, glowering back at him nastily. Mark quickly averted his eyes. He knew that even glancing at someone could end up with a head-butt and the two lads looked mean. He gave them a quick label: dealers. They reeked of drugs ... or maybe he was being unfair to them.

He looked outside again. Jack was now leaning on his Cayenne, facing toward the restaurant, still in discussion. He spotted Mark and held up two fingers, meaning two minutes. Mark nodded. He was in no rush. He sat back, relaxed, hands behind his head, watched a blue Subaru Impreza pull into the car park. It was that fantastic shade of blue, with gold-rimmed wheels – a real speed machine. Quite a lot of dosh for four wheels, though not as expensive as Jack's Porsche, which was a real beast of a motor.

The Subaru rolled on to the tarmac and stopped as though the driver was deciding where to park. Not a difficult decision, Mark wouldn't have thought. There were loads of free spaces. Or maybe it was a hard decision. Too many free spaces. Too much choice.

Mark watched idly.

There were two lads in the car. Their features were indistinct, faces hidden in shadow, but Mark could tell they were young and actually, as he looked harder, they were both wearing baseball caps with the peaks pulled down. Mark sat up as his eyebrows knitted together and a deep but unsubstantiated suspicion rattled through him. Something about it just didn't seem quite right.

Was it a stolen car? Were they car thieves, maybe? Maybe they had targeted Jack's motor. Mark had heard stories about people nicking good quality cars and exporting them, even carjacking them, literally robbing the owners.

Just as quickly as he had made up his mind about the 'dealers' sitting in the corner, he now decided the Subaru was either stolen or the lads on board were looking for their next car to nick. Two lads, peaks pulled down over their faces, fast car: it all added up.

Mark's brain jumped and bounded. Was the car connected to the two dealers in the restaurant? Had they come to do a deal? Was something about to go down here?

Or was he letting his vivid imagination run riot?

The Subaru was still stationary. Jack, leaning on his car, was located between it and the entrance to the restaurant, concentrating on his phone call.

Mark shook his head to clear it and sat back again.

But only for a second.

The passenger window of the Subaru slid down.

Suddenly the car screamed forward with a howl of its powerful, well-tuned engine, and Mark jerked upright in his seat. The car veered left so it was travelling parallel to the restaurant, placing Jack and his vehicle between it and the front door.

Mark's guts lurched and he sensed real, serious danger now, not just imagined. His eyes glued to the car and in particular the passenger who was now leaning out of the window – with a heavy-looking pistol in his hands, tilted over, held parallel to the ground. Mark knew nothing about guns, but he knew one when he saw one. This one needed two hands to hold and point it. He'd seen such things in plenty of American cop dramas. It was huge, almost the size of a machine gun.

There was a dull but horrible 'Crack-ack-ack!' – the gun being fired. Jack twisted round, screamed something unintelligible and dived to the hard ground, taking cover by the side of the Porsche.

Mark, stupidly, rose to his feet, like he'd been hypnotised.

Everything was a blur.

The Subaru accelerated past the restaurant, with Jack still caught between it and the intended targets – Mark assumed in his racing, tumbling mind that the two lads who he'd put down as drug dealers were the intended victims. So he had been right after all.

One of the large plate-glass windows at the front of the restaurant shattered spectacularly as bullets smashed through it.

Now Mark reacted as he should have done initially – by throwing himself down between the chair and table legs and his own chair clattered away as he upturned it.

There was a high-pitched, female scream.

Mark hit the deck hard, catching a glancing blow on his forehead as he caught the edge of a table.

A man shouted.

More shots were fired – a dull, sickening sound, unlike anything he'd ever heard before and totally unlike the sound effects of gunshots on the telly.

An engine revved. The Subaru?

Had Jack been hit accidentally?

Mark lay on the floor, his hands over his head, terrified. He had no idea how long he was there amongst the chair legs. Probably only seconds and then he was being hauled to his feet by strong hands and there was Jack's cool face in his. He was OK.

'Let's get out of here,' big brother said calmly.

'What happened?' Mark babbled.

'DBS,' said Jack, yanking his younger brother across the restaurant and then out through the front door.

Mark just went with the flow. His head was in a vortex and he allowed Jack to man-handle him away from the scene. Still, he managed to utter, 'What's a DBS?'

Drive-by shooting!

Mark Carter sat there stunned, dumb-struck, in the front passenger seat of Jack's Cayenne, Jack at the wheel, driving away from the KFC cool as an icebox. Mark's brow was deeply furrowed, his eyebrows almost touching with his perplexity as he tried desperately to work it all out. A drive-by shooting. Hell! Something he'd only ever heard of. Something that only ever happen-ed in London or Birmingham, or Notting-ham – or the Bronx. Not here in Blackpool.

He turned and studied Jack's profile. He couldn't even remember being bundled into the 4x4. It was all a sort of muzzed-up haze as Jack had dragged, prodded and forced him out of the restaurant and into his motor. Mark was now in shock. He was starting to shake a little. He held out his right hand in front of him, palm down, and watched it tremble uncontrollably. A look of horror morphed his face.

'You OK?' Jack asked, not taking his eyes off the road. 'I hope that's not your gun hand.'

Mark quickly dropped his hand back into his lap and blurted, 'Yeah, yeah ... Shit, Jack, a drive-by shooting?'

'I know. I can hardly believe it myself.'

'You seem dead laid back about it, though.'

Jack shrugged.

'What was it all about?'

He shrugged again. 'Dunno.'

'Who were they shooting at?'

'How would I know? Somebody in the Kentucky, I guess.'

Mark's mind was beginning to clear a little. He cast his thoughts back to the few moments before the Subaru had rolled in to the car park and everything had gone to rat shit. The seconds when he was looking around, taking in the other people there. The bloke reading the newspaper, the lovey-dovey couple and, yeah, the two lads. It all slotted neatly into place for him then.

'It had to be those two lads,' he gasped. 'Real seedy looking guys, druggies if ever I saw any.'

He tried to picture what had happened to them in the chaos of a hail of bullets, but couldn't. It was all a blurred, frightening mess, and he couldn't recall seeing them when Jack was dragging him away. They were probably flat on the floor. Had they been hit? Had anyone been hit?

'Yeah, must've been them. Looked just like dealers.'

'You know what a drug-dealer looks like, then?' Jack asked.

'Spot one a mile off,' Mark said confidently.

Jack chortled.

'What?'

'Talk about stereotyping – what, shell suits, baseball caps and Reeboks?'

'What do you mean?'

'The guys who usually look like drug-dealers or pimps, usually aren't, but they'd like people to think they were. It's the ones who don't look like 'em are the ones who usually are. Still, you're probably right. They were probably the targets.'

'Think anyone did get shot?'

'Couldn't say,' Jack responded, not sounding too concerned.

'What about the police?' Mark asked.

'What about 'em?'

'Shouldn't we go to them?'

'I don't think so,' Jack said stiffly.

'But we're witnesses!'

Jack's eyes closed and then reopened in a moment of disdain. Now he looked slowly round at Mark. 'What planet are you on?'

'Eh?'

'Things like that, you don't get involved

with. Once you get hooked up with a job like that, it's like a noose around your neck.' His voice was brittle.

'But suppose someone's got shot—' Mark began.

'Not our problemo.'

'But, those guys, they could get away with what they've done!' Mark persisted.

'Then let 'em get away with it. What could we tell the cops, anyway? Two guys in a blue Subaru? No good description? They'll get that from the other people. Or – supposin' we did finger those guys – have you ever thought what could happen to us? They'd be after us. Witness intimidation at the very least. Death threats, houses burned down. All that sort of thing could happen. We'd end up on the witness protection programme. They'd hunt us down, those kinds of people. We were in the wrong place at the wrong time, our paths crossed, so let's leave it at that, eh?'

'Jack – that's a bit far-fetched isn't it?'

'Trust me – forget what you saw. Being Mr Sensible and putting your head over the wall will only get it shot off. Guys like that mean business and if you mix it with 'em, they don't take kindly to it. Not worth it, believe me.'

Mark scowled and folded his arms haughtily.

Jack pulled the Cayenne into the side of the road, sat there for a few moments, then

turned in the leather seat and looked square-
ly at Mark. 'Hey.' He touched Mark's right
elbow affectionately. 'You're a good lad and
you'll make good when you're older. You
know the difference between right and
wrong and most of the kids round here
haven't a clue' – he pointed a finger at Mark
– 'but you've got to realize the world's a grey
place and you need to know when to step in
or step back. Today was nasty, big boy stuff.
Serious.' His pointing finger reinforced his
next words. 'You do not want to get involved
in this, not if you want to stay unhurt, yeah?'
He peered closely at Mark. 'The important
thing is that you *wanted* to do the right
thing.' Jack leaned over and embraced Mark
with a big bear hug.

'Right, right, I get what you say, but what if
we've already been identified by someone
else? Say someone took your car number
and the cops come knockin'?'

'You worry too much. Let's cross that
bridge when we come to it, eh?'

'OK,' Mark conceded. 'I'm being an arse.'

'Yep, you surely are.' Jack smiled, looked
slightly relieved. 'So keep it zipped' – he
imitated pulling a zipper across his lips –
'keep mum and it'll all pass over.'

'OK, will do.'

'Good lad.' He patted Mark's knee.

Jack drove the Cayenne back into the
traffic, whilst next to him Mark stayed tight-
lipped. Yet, as much as he would like to have

been comforted by Jack's words, he couldn't help but think he hadn't heard the last of it.

Drive-by shootings don't just curl up and die.

Jack dropped him and his bike – which was in the back of the Porsche – close to the estate, then, after giving Mark a tenner out of his wallet, he pulled away.

Mark realized two things.

First, he hadn't had a chance to talk about Bethany.

And second, there was a bullet hole in the rear wing of the Porsche.

Sleep would not come. Impossible. The images of the day wheeled in circles around Mark's inter-cranial TV screen and prevented him from even nodding off.

1 a.m. came and went.

At 2.15 a.m. he heard a noise outside.

He jumped up and peeked through a crack in the curtains, knowing, but dreading, what he would see: Bethany arriving home accompanied by Jonny Sparks.

Again – Mark felt sure it was for his benefit – Jonny made a big show of snogging Beth and when he slid his hand up her top, Mark twisted away from the window and threw himself back on to his bed, face down in one pillow, another pulled over the back of his head.

He cursed himself for not gripping Jack

about Bethany. But that chance had passed for the time being.

Mark's thoughts spun to his mother. She was out somewhere, probably at 'Uncle-bloody-Jim's', or whoever else she was seeing at the moment, staying overnight. It was really her job to get Bethany sorted, but there was no chance of that. She was as out of control as her daughter and didn't seem to care. She just made sure there was food in the house – sometimes – clean clothes and bedding, turned up occasionally and that was it. As far as she was concerned the kids were just a nuisance.

Then he wondered about his dad ... but his feelings became all confused and emotional, so he tried to put everything out of his mind except the new computer game he'd just got, one of the Harry Potter ones. He imagined each stage of the game as he walked through the levels, a lone boy against the world around him.

He began to tremble, though, as he confronted the darkest wizard of them all.

Six

Next thing it was 5 a.m. and his alarm clock was clattering in his ear. Mark leapt awake, plunged out of a strange, deep dream into the reality of the morning. He was sweating, breathing heavily as though he'd been running hard. Something had been chasing him in the dream, but as he rubbed his eyes he found he couldn't recall any detail. He groaned and swung his legs out of bed, sitting there, dying for a pee, his hard-on tenting his boxer shorts, his bladder aching.

Light chinked through the gap in the curtain, the one he'd looked through to watch Bethany and her boyfriend trying to swallow each other in a gunge of saliva. He jumped up and got moving. Within five minutes he'd splashed water on his face, had that wonderful relieving pee, got dressed. Before heading downstairs he checked the other bedroom doors on the landing. His mum's was open. He tiptoed to it and put his head round. The room was empty, bed unmade, clothes strewn everywhere, the stench of stale cigarettes hanging there. Mark's face screwed up distastefully as he withdrew and

96

glanced at Beth's door, which was closed. He didn't recall hearing her come in – obviously he'd dropped asleep quickly with his head sandwiched between his pillows – but he didn't look in.

He trotted downstairs, thought about shoving a piece of toast down his throat, but decided he didn't have time. He manoeuvred his bike down the hallway and out through the front door, making as much noise as possible in the hope of waking and annoying Bethany. He slammed the door – satisfyingly – behind him and pedalled off into the dawn.

It was the start of a beautiful day. Early June, lots of light, lots of birds singing. A fantastic time of day, and as he rode slowly around the edge of the estate, no one else around, it felt good to be alive.

The newsagent's he delivered for was in a row of shops just off the south side of the estate. It was in a fortunate position, not being actually on Shoreside, because all the shops on the estate itself had all been vandalised, put out of business and the owners forced to move out. There wasn't a single legitimate business on the estate and everyone had to leave to buy anything. The newsagent's was just far enough away to have escaped the attentions of the more destructive criminal elements and if it had been on the estate there was no way in which it would have lasted more than a few days anyway. An Asian family ran it and they would have been hounded out from day one. As it was, they still suffered daily racial abuse even off the estate, but they tolerated it because the shop made good money.

Mark liked Mr Aziz. He always treated Mark fairly and paid slightly more than he should in order to keep his paperboys and girls. They were like a little army, descending on the shop and delivering to a wide area. Mark had two rounds in the morning, six days a week, one in the afternoon, also six days a week, and a huge, heavy one on Sunday mornings which nearly broke his back and took about four fours to complete. He worked hard, was paid reasonably for his efforts, and quite enjoyed it – especially in summer.

The hi-viz delivery bags were already loaded when Mark arrived, yawning, at 5.25 a.m. Mr Aziz was up at 3.30 a.m. each day, opened at 5 a.m., closed at 10.30 p.m., seven days a week. He made a small fortune, Mark guessed, yet despite the hours and the harassment, he was always cheerful and perky. Mr Aziz handed Mark the first bag of the day and a cup of tea in a lidded Styrofoam cup. Mark apologized profusely for missing yesterday afternoon's rounds. Mr Aziz said OK, said at least he'd sent someone to let him know, told him not to do it again, smiled and shooed him out on to the road, then did the same with the next boy. It was like a little production line.

Mark wobbled on his bike, getting his balance, ensuring the shoulder bag was perfectly arranged for weight distribution, took a sip of the tea, which was thoughtfully provided each day for the little team, and hit the road.

The route was embedded in his brain. He could have done it with his eyes closed – riding using one hand, drinking tea with the other – but that morning his eyes were wide open as he enjoyed the start of a great sunny day and breathed in the already warm air into his chest whilst whizzing from house to house.

Just before eight he'd finished the second round of the day.

Things were busier now. The world had woken up. People were rushing around, traffic had clogged the roads and it was all a bit less pleasant.

He landed back at the shop with an empty canvas bag and threw it down on top of the pile of other empty bags. One of the Aziz specialities, sold in the shop as part of a takeaway breakfast menu, was a double fried egg roll. As he charged only cost price to the paper-round kids, Mark, who was usually famished by the time his rounds were over, occasionally took advantage of the offer and succumbed to it that morning. He gave Aziz the 'feed me' look and Mrs Aziz set about creating a mega-butty for him.

'Give him three eggs today,' Aziz told his wife. 'He deserves it. He's a good worker, this one.' He ruffled Mark's short hair – having no effect on the style whatsoever. 'In fact, you can have this one on the house.'

'Thanks,' Mark responded enthusiastically to the generosity. Three eggs was good. Free even better.

Unlike most of the other kids who delivered, Mark did not want his money at the end of each round. He preferred it to accumulate over the week because he knew that if he did take it each day, he would only end up spending it like the others. As it was he got Mr Aziz to pay him each Saturday morning, then Mark would fly round to the building society and salt ninety per cent of it away in his savings account. Then he would blow the remaining ten per cent.

Whilst waiting for the sandwich, Mark hovered by the magazine rack, leafing through a few comics he couldn't afford. He thought they were a waste of cash anyway.

'Eeeh, dear, dear,' he heard Aziz mutter behind him. Mark turned. Aziz was behind the counter. Unusually, there were no customers in the shop. Mostly there was a never-ending stream of them. Aziz was taking a precious moment to have a sip of tea and a snatch-read of a daily rag.

'What is it?' Mark asked curiously.

'This town, this town,' Aziz sighed, shaking

his head sadly, reading an item inside the paper. He laid the paper down on top of the stack of other newspapers and swivelled it round. 'What is it coming to?' Mr Aziz laid a finger on what he'd been reading. 'So dangerous now. You can't even eat safely anymore.'

Even before he read it, Mark knew what Aziz was referring to. His throat suddenly constricted, dry like he'd just eaten a mouthful of dust, and his heart began beating unhealthily quickly.

It was an item on the inside pages of one of the tabloids. The headline read, *'Waitress Critical After Shooting'*. Next to the headline was the KFC logo – the kindly looking Colonel Sanders with the goatee beard.

Mark bent over and read the first few lines of the story. *'A young waitress is critically ill in hospital following a drive-by shooting in Blackpool yesterday...'*

'Very bad, uh?'

Mark looked slowly up, feeling colour creeping up his neck. It was as though Mr Aziz knew, was taunting him, even though Mark realized he couldn't know anything.

'What's it say?' Mark asked with a choke.

'Oh, not much ... a waitress got shot in the chest...' Mr Aziz swivelled the newspaper back, closed it and replaced it on the appropriate pile. 'Police want any witnesses to come forward ... but who would?' Aziz shook his head again. He did a lot of that. 'The

101

world is such a dangerous place, eh, Mark?'

'Yeah.' He just wanted to turn and run.

Everybody knew! He was the witness the police wanted to find. *Him and Jack.*

'You OK, my boy?' Mr Aziz asked. 'You look white as a sheet.'

'I'm good.' He wasn't. He felt ill.

Mrs Aziz appeared from the rear of the shop bearing Mark's free three-egg sarnie in a paper bag. Already at least one of the eggs had burst and the yolk was seeping through the paper, turning Mark's stomach. Mark took one look at it, wanted to retch. He turned and did a runner from the shop, leaving the couple open-mouthed.

'Wonder what's eating him?' Mr Aziz speculated.

Outside, Mark leapt on to the BMX and pedalled furiously away.

He had to stop, get his breath, calm down. He veered into the side of the road and sat astride his bike, trying to slow everything down so he could think. If only he had a mobile phone. But Mark had always thought there were more important things in life than mobile phones – and he wanted to use his hard-earned cash for more exciting things – but just at that moment he could have done with one. He could get on it, call up Jack, and tell him they were now witnesses to an attempted murder, maybe even a murder if the waitress died. But what would Jack say?

He'd only shrug it off, say chill out, don't worry, not our problem, don't get involved.

But here he was, fretting away like a steam train on drugs. There was a word for it. He searched his mind ... that was it: hyperventilation.

The story had gone national. The big papers had got hold of it. It might even have been on the telly. Probably had been, definitely would be. And the cops were after witnesses to come forward.

And a girl had been shot.

Mark remembered her. There had been two members of staff at the front counter, a lad and a girl. She'd been quite pretty.

What was it like to get shot? he wondered. He'd seen all the American TV shows with bullets flying through the air in slow motion, then slamming into the flesh of a human being, entering a body and doing incredible damage. Slick TV. Didn't go any way to describing how it must feel to have a lump of hot lead piercing your body, causing horrendous internal damage.

His nostrils flared as he tried to imagine.

Smack!

He winced, feeling the pain, then feeling sick.

Suddenly he lurched, almost fell off his bike. He scrambled to the edge of the footpath where it met a stone wall and spewed up nothingness from his guts.

But he knew what Jack had said was true.

What his brother had meant was that the DBS would only be a noose around their necks if they came forward as witnesses ... what he should have said was that, whether they came forward or not, there was still a noose, an inescapable noose, which was tightening around Mark's neck because, whatever, he and Jack were involved and the cops would find them. How the hell do you hide a Porsche Cayenne in an almost empty KFC car park? And the fact it drove away after a shooting? That it had smoked glass and a personal plate ... and also a bullet hole in it?

But worst of all was the noose of conscience. Someone had got shot, could die, and if he and Jack contacted the police, their evidence might just catch a killer.

Why was nothing simple?

Mark threw up again. Horrible, green-grey bile, making him wish he'd eaten the egg sandwich. At least there would have been something to bring up. As it was it felt like he was wringing out his intestines.

He crawled back to his bike, then with his head down, he pedalled for home, deciding he would give school a miss today.

Arriving home minutes later, he manoeuvred his bike into the hallway and burst into the living room, switching on the TV in the corner of the room, channel hopping to see if he could find any mention of the shooting.

It was all fashion tips, political crap and cartoons. He went on to the local Teletext news page – 160 – and found the index. Sure enough, page 161's headline read: '*Police investigate Blackpool shooting*.' Mark sat down heavily in front of the screen and waited for it to scroll to page 161.

As it revealed, he read it slowly.

The details were sketchy, but enough for him to feel rising panic.

He slumped back against the settee and read it a few times more.

He knew there was nothing he could do. Just follow Jack's advice. Keep quiet and keep your head down and hope it goes away. One thing was for sure – he wouldn't be going back to that KFC in a hurry.

The problem was, something inside Mark told him he should do the right thing and go to the cops.

But he wanted to keep on Jack's right side too and he could see the logic of his big brother's argument. Eventually he came round to accept the situation.

He and Jack had been in the wrong place at the wrong time. Just one of those things. Bad Karma, he'd heard people say, whatever that meant. One of life's little hiccups. Fate. All that sort of crap...

...Just so long as the girl didn't die.

He pointed the remote at the TV and it went blank.

The house was quiet.

All he could hear was his own breathing, which had calmed down now.

Suddenly his hunger returned with a vengeance. He needed something to eat. Beans on toast sounded good. Maybe he would go to school after all. Maybe nothing would happen now. Maybe the cops wouldn't come knocking – and why should they? Maybe, maybe, maybe. He stood up stiffly, trying to shake it off.

Food, he decided, then school.

Face it head on.

Mark left the living room and turned in to the hallway. The kitchen door was at the far end of the hall, closed. With his mouth screwed up thoughtfully, his mind still a raging mess, he walked the few steps in the direction of the kitchen, pausing at the door, his hand resting on the handle. He turned it slowly and pushed the door open and stepped into the kitchen.

It was as though 100,000 volts of electricity had hit him, arcing with searing agony through his whole being.

Mark stood open mouthed, hysteria rising rapidly through him as he sagged down to his knees next to the body lying across the middle of the kitchen floor.

'Beth?' he gasped. 'Beth?' This time more desperately. *'Beth?'* He touched her face, and her skin was cold.

He knew she was dead.

Seven

She must have been lying there for some while, spread-eagled face up on the tatty vinyl floor, dressed only in her bra and knickers. The blood in her body had settled to the lowest parts of her, making her top half a kind of marbled bluey-white and her bottom half – buttock, thighs and back – red with blood.

Her eyes were still half open, her head skewed in the direction of the kitchen door. Her pupils were a milky colour, her mouth twisted open with dribble, vomit and blood having trickled out, mingling in a horrible concoction on the floor, underneath her head, neck and shoulders.

The palms of her hands were open and lying across her right hand was a hypodermic needle, a small, tiny one really, half filled with blood. There was a tourniquet around the bicep of her left arm – a belt trimmed down to size to do the job – and red pin-prick-sized marks in the soft flesh of her inner elbow, showing where she had been injecting herself.

Mark looked desperately at her chest.

Was it his imagination? Did it just rise and fall? Was she breathing? Mark stared, hoping it would be true. *Please be alive*, he intoned silently to himself.

He kept staring.

But she did not move. She had not moved.

Mark knelt over her, knowing she was dead, but not wanting to accept that truth.

His sister. Dead.

'Beth?' he said hopefully, his voice cracking. He bent his head low so he could look into her eyes. 'Beth.' They were blank, milky, no longer seeing anything.

It took a great deal of courage to do what he did next.

He touched her. Remembering the lesson on first aid at school – how to check for a pulse – he placed his first two fingers on her neck, trying to discover the artery there, hoping there would be a beat.

Touching her reminded him of touching a fresh chicken from Asda.

Quickly he pulled his fingers away with a shiver.

Nothing.

It was building up inside him again.

He began to rock back and forth on his knees.

The pressure grew. Bursting point approached.

His face distorted as the agony and pain of the gruesome discovery hit him harder than anything had ever hit him before. His whole being convulsed, then his hands tore at his own face and he scratched himself madly as though afflicted by some horrendous disease. A kind of non-human roar burst out of his lungs.

'*No-o-o-o-o!*'

He sank back on to his heels, howling at the ceiling, then toppled over on to the floor beside Bethany, so his face was only inches away from hers.

His sister. Bethany Carter. Aged seventeen. Dead.

He huddled on his bed, knees drawn up to his chin, his duvet wrapped around his shoulders – but not stopping him from shaking. His head rested on his forearms and his eyes were tight closed as he unsuccessfully tried to stop his tears from falling. Deep, raking sobs tore his whole being, making him feel as if he too was going to die. Just at that moment, death felt as though it would have been a good option. His grief was all consuming, all pervasive, like nothing else he had ever experienced. He moved his arms and, keeping his forehead on his knees, covered his ears with his hands and started banging his head against his knees in a rhythmic beat.

Bang, bang, bang...

'Mark Carter?'

Mark continued to pound his head.

'Mark Carter?' a voice asked again from

109

somewhere a million miles away.

Still he did not respond. The voice did not really penetrate his world, meant nothing to him.

Then somebody touched his shoulder, sending a jolt through him like a crack of static. He stopped the banging and raised his ravaged, anguished face.

A man stood there. Mark could only guess at his age, maybe forty, maybe fifty. He had a stern, lived-in face, hard, yet with a compassionate edge to it. His hair was closely cropped, a grade two on the clipper scale. It wasn't a close enough cut for it to be threatening, but near enough to give him a bit of a fear factor. He was wearing a suit, looked smart. He was about six-two, broad shouldered and had a middle area that could've done with a few sit-ups. He looked cool, in control.

He was a cop.

'May I come in?'

'You're already in.'

The man shrugged.

'Who are you?'

'My name is Henry Christie ... I'm a detective chief inspector, what they call a senior investigating officer. I work at Blackpool nick and I'll be in charge of this ... incident.'

'Oh, right.' Mark had switched off. The words were just an incoherent babble, meaning nothing to him. He dropped his head on to his knees again.

'Mark ... I need to ask you some questions.' Christie sat down uninvited on the foot of Mark's bed. 'I know this'll be a tough time for you, I know you must feel terrible—'

Mark cut in, instantly enraged. 'You don't know sod-all,' he blasted the cop. 'Not a thing. No idea how I'm feeling. That's my sister down there, dead in the kitchen.'

Christie blinked, allowed Mark his rant, not in the least sidetracked by this outburst. 'I need to establish facts,' he said calmly with an undercurrent of assertiveness. 'That need won't go away, however you might be feeling ... and yeah, it will be hard for you, but it has to be done.'

Mark glared at him, eyeballing him ferociously. Christie held the look impassively, with a slight sadness behind his eyes. Mark tried to outstare him, but eventually he dropped his eyes and replaced his forehead back on to his knees again. He convulsed with sobs.

Christie sighed and laid a comforting hand on Mark's arm, letting him cry until the torrent subsided. In due course Mark raised his head again. His eyes were red raw, nose running, snot and tears mixing down his face. Christie removed his hand.

'I hate crying.'

'Everybody needs to cry at some time. Nothing wrong with it.'

'Feels so pathetic.'

111

'But you have good reason.'

Mark's eyes looked into Christie's once more, this time without the anger, trying to weigh up the cop. 'I need to wash my face.'

Christie nodded. 'Do it.'

Mark shrugged the duvet off his shoulders and slid off the bed, leaving the detective in his room while he went to the bathroom. He ran the water cold, as cold as he could get it, and filled the washbasin. Then he dunked his face in it, keeping his eyes open, holding himself there until he thought his lungs would bust, then lifted his face out of the water, gasping for air, sending water splashing everywhere.

He reached for a towel and dried himself off, then regarded his reflection in the mirror. He looked ravaged and older. He felt like he'd aged ten years since finding Beth's body. The image of her corpse came back into his mind and his chin started to wobble as he attempted to hold back further tears.

The detective, DCI Christie, was looking along the titles of the books on the shelf in Mark's bedroom. There were lots of them, all carefully chosen by Mark, mixing classics – such as his favourite, *Treasure Island* – with more up to date stuff like Harry Potter and some thrillers. He was particularly fond of James Bond, preferring the books to the films. There was even a book of poetry.

Christie looked around at Mark when he

came back into the bedroom. He'd taken about ten minutes, but the detective hadn't pushed him by knocking on the bathroom door or anything like that.

'You still here?' Mark snapped.

'Oh yes.'

'They're not stolen, you know. Nothing in this room is nicked.'

'I never thought it was, Mark.'

'I mean, don't tar me with the same brush as the rest of the shit-heads on the estate. I don't steal. I don't do drugs.'

'Hey,' Christie said quietly, 'that's enough, less of the defensive, Mark. I only come to conclusions about people when I get to know them, OK? I'm here to investigate your sister's death, not to worry about whether you nicked a library book, or not.'

The two faced each other across the room.

'All right,' Mark relented sullenly. He sighed deeply, then sat on the edge of the bed. 'What do you wanna know?'

'Where's your mum, first?'

Mark shrugged. 'Dunno ... she comes and goes ... could be anywhere ... don't see that much of her, really.' Mark's jaw line tightened as he tried to hold back his tears for a whole different reason. 'She's probably at work. I've phoned my big brother, Jack, though; he's on his way. He lives in Preston.'

'And how old are you?'

'Fourteen.'

'I need to interview you in the presence of

an adult.'

'Why? I didn't kill her.'

'Did somebody kill her?' Christie asked quickly. 'Or was it just a terrible mistake?'

Mark shrugged again. It was becoming a horrible habit, but somehow he could not find the words to respond properly. He rubbed his eyes.

'Just tell me about this morning, eh?' Christie said softly. 'From getting up to actually finding her and calling the ambulance.'

Reluctantly Mark began to retell his morning's activities up to the point where he stepped into the kitchen. He didn't mention reading the paper about the drive-by shooting and the angst that had caused him.

'If only I'd looked into the kitchen before setting out,' he moaned sadly.

'I know it's no consolation,' Christie said, standing by the bedroom window, half-eyeing what was going on outside, 'but I don't think you could have done anything to save her, Mark. The doctor said she probably died about three this morning. She was dead when you left for your paper round.'

The front door slammed. From the front hallway there was the sound of an argument. Banging, raised voices.

Mark became alert.

'This could be your brother,' Christie said.

Mark shot off the bed, out of the room and down the stairs.

'What the hell d'you think you're playing at?' Jack snarled, enraged and red-faced. He was shouting at the detective who'd been speaking to Mark. 'You are way, way out of line questioning a kid without an appropriate adult present. I'm going to see my solicitor about this. I'll have your job for this!'

'Jack!' Mark protested.

'Keep outta this, kid,' Jack snapped. 'They think they can walk all over you, this lot. Cops! Huh! I've crapped 'em.'

They were in the hallway of Mark's house. The kitchen door was closed. A uniformed PC stood this side of it, guarding what Christie had described as a possible crime scene. Christie and Jack were head-to-head, but the detective was more in control than Jack, who had lost it totally to Mark's eyes.

'I was talking informally and none of it is on record,' Christie retorted, 'and if you don't settle down, Jack, you'll find yourself locked up for Breach of the Peace – and I will do it.'

'You wha—?'

Christie held up a warning finger. 'I'm investigating a possible – and I do say possible – murder here. Every sudden death starts with the presumption it's a murder until we know different, and I'll talk to anyone – that means *anyone*, Jack – who is a possible witness, kid or otherwise, including Mark, whether you're there or not.'

'Don't push me around, cop,' Jack uttered.

Mark looked quizzically at his brother. 'Jack, he was only doing his job. Don't you want to know what happened to Bethany?' Mark suddenly felt very mature. 'It starts with me, dunnit? I found her, so course they're gonna want to talk to me first.'

Jack glared, his nostrils flaring. 'Never,' he snorted, '*never* trust a cop.' He turned fearsomely to Christie again, eyeballing him. 'They'll screw you and fit you up and before you know it, you'll have said something completely innocent that they verbal up, and you'll be facing a murder charge.'

Mark grimaced as he tried to add up what the hell had got into Jack.

Christie said, 'Jack, belt up, eh?' He checked his watch and looked toward the kitchen door, which opened as if on cue. A white-suited crime scene investigator poked his head through the crack. The uniformed constable stepped aside.

'We're about done here, Henry.'

Christie nodded. He turned to the two brothers. 'That means the scenes of crime and scientific people have finished,' he explained. 'Now we have to move Beth's body to the mortuary. Then I'll inform the local coroner who will order a post-mortem and I'm pretty sure he'll want a full inquest because of the circumstances.'

The words seemed to have a soothing, salutary effect on Jack. He leaned against the wall and raised his face to the ceiling. Mark could tell he was about to cry. He grabbed Jack around the waist and buried his head in his older brother's chest. Jack's arms encircled him and both of them gave convulsive sobs, desperately clinging to each other.

Christie stepped back, allowing them their moment of grief.

'Let's get up to your room,' Jack said through his cascade of tears. 'I don't want to watch her body being dragged out.' He shot Christie a look of hateful contempt and ushered Mark upstairs.

Eight

The undertakers arrived twenty minutes later, a local firm in a black Ford Transit Van specially adapted for the carriage of the dead. Not a hearse, but simply a means of transporting dead bodies. Two stone-faced black-suited men climbed out. Mark watched them from his bedroom window, repulsed but fascinated. He expected to see a coffin, but instead all they had was a big, grey zip-up bag, reminding him of a guitar bag, and a folding trolley, rather like waitresses use to carry dirty pots and pans, though twice as long.

Christie met them at the missing front gate, spoke to them, obviously giving instructions.

They nodded. Their faces said they did this sort of thing day in, day out. They walked past the detective and Mark heard them enter the house.

He remained at the window, his eyes on Christie.

Jack's Porsche Cayenne was parked a little way down the road. Mark saw Christie clock it, saw him react, then turn his head toward the bedroom window.

Despite feeling he should duck down out of sight, Mark stayed where he was and exchanged a look with the detective.

Mark gulped. A cold shiver ran through him. Did he know? Did the detective know that a Porsche Cayenne had driven away from the scene of a shooting with two males on board? One mid-twenties, the other early teens? That they could possibly be witnesses to an attempted murder? Mark prayed that Christie wouldn't take a close look at the car and see the bullet hole.

Christie looked at the Porsche again, gave Mark another quick glance, then walked back up the path to the house.

In that instant, Mark experienced two conflicting things. First, relief that Christie hadn't inspected the car; then the certainty that the DCI had done some sums in his head and was just working on the answer.

The bedroom door opened, Jack entered. He'd been washing his face, which looked drained. There was going to be a lot of face-washing today, Mark thought sadly. A lot of tears would need to be cleaned up, cleared away.

He decided not to share his thoughts about what he'd just seen outside with Christie and the Cayenne, but just said flatly, 'The undertakers are here.'

Mark expected that Bethany would be zippered into the body bag, heaved on to the fold-out gurney and wheeled out of the kitchen, down the hall, out of the front door, down the few steps, along the path and slid into the back of the Transit. He caught his breath when, unexpectedly, the two undertakers emerged from the front door with the body bag slung easily between the two of them, carrying it with the light body inside, to the van. She was so light they didn't even have to put her on to a trolley. It was so ... Mark searched for the word ... *undignified*. She didn't even get wheeled out, just heaved out between two blokes who were chatting to each other, who didn't know her, like they were moving sacks of veg in ASDA.

That was all his sister had become.

A commodity to be moved.

The harrowing thought he had then was that there was no dignity in death. You might meet your death with honour – or not, as in Beth's case – but beyond that you just became something to be shifted about, to be poked at or investigated, then buried or burned to ashes.

Footsteps on the stairs made him turn.

DCI Christie again.

Jack stood up. He'd been sprawled on the bed, a pillow pressed down over his face in an effort to smother his sobs.

'We've finished in the kitchen now,' Christie said, poking his head around the bedroom door. 'I can recommend someone to come and do a clean-up if you want.'

'Stuff that,' Jack said, wiping his eyes, 'we'll do it.'

'Whatever,' Christie said. 'I need to follow the undertaker down to the mortuary for evidential reasons, so I'm going now.'

'What happens now?' blurted Mark.

'As I said – coroner, post-mortem, inquest, maybe a full police investigation.'

'What happens at the post-mortem?' Mark asked.

'An expert finds out how Bethany died.'

'In other words, you cut her up?' Jack snarled.

Christie eyed Jack as though he were an imbecile. 'That will happen as there's no other way of doing a PM ... now, I need to go. I want you,' he turned to Mark, 'and you,' he looked at Jack, 'to be at Blackpool Police Station at 1 p.m. today. I need to interview Mark and take a statement, OK?'

'Why there? Why not here?' Jack demanded.

'Fewer distractions. Trust me, it'll be easier for us all.' Christie turned to leave, hesitated, spun back. 'I am sorry for your loss,' he said sincerely. He glanced at both brothers, then left with a curt nod.

As the door closed, Jack said, 'Like hell you are.'

It became a madhouse, especially when his mother turned up – eventually – and began weeping and wailing and throwing herself around the house, as well as chucking ornaments and anything else she could lay her hands on that would fly and smash. People started coming and going, folk Mark hardly knew or had never seen in his life. A succession of his mother's friends knocking on the door, coming in and entering the 'who could cry the loudest' contest to show they were more upset than anyone else.

Mark despised it.

He watched them come and go, a sneer implanted firmly on his face, his cold eyes taking it all in.

Everyone got a big hug from his mum.

He didn't.

Whether by accident or design, he could not tell. But one thing was for sure: his mum didn't grab and squeeze him and as much as it would have repelled him, it was something he craved.

He needed her to give him a hug. To feel her arms encircle him and hold him tight so he could sob with her. Just her. Her and Jack. No one else. Not these 'best friends' who were crawling out of the woodwork like worms. He just wanted it to be him, Mum and Jack. The family that didn't exist.

Instead it was like Piccadilly Circus.

And he hated it.

He gave up hoping and retreated to his room again, his haven of peace, his comfort zone; the world he had made his own. He

122

didn't want to see anyone, especially after having had to recount his experience with Christie down at the nick. That had taken nearly three hours and he was mentally exhausted.

Up in his room he sat in his armchair, sunk deep in its knackered cushions and stared at nothing. That was all he did: stare and brood, deep anger and resentment boiling up inside him, building like a volcano. Much of it directed at his wayward mother. He had once seen an episode of the 1980s' American TV series *Dallas*, about a mega-rich oil family in Texas. The episode had been on Bradley's TV on one of the satellite channels and he'd watched it by accident, but there had been one bit in it that had always stuck in his mind. A guy having a real dig at his ex-wife, calling her 'a drunk, a whore and an unfit mother'.

A description fitting his own mother to a 'T'.

There was another knock on the front door.

Mark looked at the clock. It was 8 p.m. now. Mark ignored the knock, so deep was he in his black thoughts.

In the living room there was still lots of crying and caterwauling going on. More knocking: probably another bunch of his mother's long-lost friends come to commiserate and enter the crying competition.

He heard footsteps in the hall and the door

123

open, then Jack's voice booming up the stairs. 'Mark, it's for you.'

Mark shook his head. He inhaled deeply and, reluctantly, pushed himself out of the armchair, no desire whatever to go down. But he forced himself on legs wobbling like jelly. The front door had been closed on whoever it was and Jack had obviously returned to the fray in the front room, leaving the caller standing outside. Very welcoming – not, Mark thought, and opened the door to find Katie Bretherton on the front step.

They stared at each other for a few moments, before Katie's bottom lip quivered, her face crumpled and she said, 'Mark, I'm so sorry.'

'News gets around fast,' he responded sullenly, taking her aback.

She composed herself. 'I just thought I'd see how you were.'

'Thanks,' he said, less than graciously.

'OK, fine. It's obviously a bad time.' She turned to go, fuming that he was being so cold and distant with her.

But Mark reached out and grabbed her shoulder, turning her back to face him.

'Sorry,' he said meekly, with a pathetic shrug. 'Bad day all round.'

'Do you wanna talk?'

'Uh – no. I don't know what I want,' he admitted.

'Do you wanna hang out with me, or something? No pressure, like.'

He half turned and gestured down the hallway to the living room. 'I think I'm kinda expected to stay, but actually, I wouldn't mind someone to hang out with ... d'you fancy coming in, upstairs?'

She had never been in his house before and because of today's tragedy, he fully expected her to refuse. She didn't.

And obviously, she had never been in his bedroom. It was a strange feeling having a girl in the room, even if it was Katie.

'Nice room,' she said appreciatively, eyeing everything.

'All my own work,' he said proudly.

'Could do with new wallpaper and some nice curtains, though.' She glanced at Mark with a slight grin. 'Girl thing. Not keen on the green.'

'Fancy a go on the PlayStation?'

'What games you got?'

Mark reeled them off and Katie chose a racing car game they both could play. Ten minutes later, they had both squeezed on to the armchair and were well into the game. They were side-by-side, legs crossed over each other, the closest Mark had ever been to her for any length of time.

It felt very good when he got used to it. He could feel all her bumps and curves and bones and the longer he sat there, the better it became.

'Beat you again,' Katie said.

'Yep.' His throat was dry and his neck and face were red with the heat. He balanced the controller on the chair arm, Katie did likewise with hers. Their faces were only inches apart, so close it was almost impossible to focus. Especially when your heart was thumping like something going crazy and there was an amazing sensation deep and low inside.

'You're easy,' she smirked.

'Yep,' he croaked.

In the distance the sounds of anguish still emanated from the ground floor. People came and went. The noises seemed a long way away, as the beat of Mark's heart made his ears pound.

Katie budged up a bit and twisted slightly so that they were no longer side to side, but wedged in the armchair in a 'V' shape, facing each other properly without having to crick their heads. Mark's left arm was trapped underneath him.

He could smell her breath. He could smell her skin. He could see her complexion close up and it was smooth and flawless. His breathing was short and stuttery.

She blinked and angled her face downwards slightly so she looked up seductively at him through half-closed eyes, her pupils wide.

Mark shifted slightly, very uncomfortable, yet wonderful, because of what was happening to him as his jeans became tight and constricting.

Katie's lips parted slightly. 'I'd like you to kiss me.'

They had kissed once before, nothing more than a rushed playground snog in front of other kids, a messy clash of teeth, nothing really.

This was altogether on another plane.

'How *do* you kiss?' he asked daftly.

'Slowly and softly,' she murmured, as though highly experienced. Her right arm was wedged down between them, but with her left hand she touched Mark's face, drawing a sharp intake of breath from him.

'You an expert?' he asked.

She shook her head and moved her head nearer.

Their lips came softly together at first, then started to mash as the kiss grew with ferocity and young passion.

Both groaned, their hormones working overtime.

Mark grabbed her with his free hand and pulled her tight to him, lost in the moment, the death of his sister – for the time being – a zillion miles away.

Katie had quite short-cropped hair, but Mark managed to muss it up well. She was as red-faced as he was, short of breath, and after ten minutes of intense kissing, just about ready for a breather.

She pushed herself away from Mark, rotating her jaw, and stood up.

Mark sprawled on the armchair, his eyes – slightly mad – following her every move.

She brushed herself down, straightening her clothing and patting her hair flat.

Mark felt like he was on the verge of bursting. He swallowed and caught his breath, more exhausted than after a hard session on the BMX.

'Wow,' Katie said with a smile. 'So you do know how to kiss.'

'So it seems,' he preened.

She held out her hands and twinkled her fingers. He placed his hands in hers and she eased him to his feet and dragged him towards the bed, turned him around and backed him against it and, with a hand at his chest, pushed him on to the edge and stood in front of him between his legs.

'Can you lock the door?' she asked.

'Yeah, why?'

'Use your imagination.' She gave him a smile and went to the bedroom door, which had an inner bolt on it. She flicked it across with a click. Next she crossed to the window and drew the curtains before returning to Mark, who sat there mesmerised, his mouth sagging open.

Katie sat down slowly next to him and before he knew what had happened they were lying side by side on the bed, kissing like mad again, but Mark was totally unsure as to how things should progress. He had never been this far with a girl before.

Somewhere in the background he heard a knock at the front door, which he dismissed from his mind – more of Mum's bloody mates, he guessed – as Katie took the initiative, as ever, grabbed his hand and placed it on her tee-shirt over her left breast, causing Mark to shudder with pleasure.

Still in the background – voices in the hallway.

Mark's hand on Katie's boob did not move.

'Squeeze it,' she insisted breathlessly. 'Gently.'

He did. And, oh God, it was wonderful.

A door slammed.

Something incredible was building up inside him.

Downstairs – more talk, voices, urgency.

'Touch me here,' Katie gasped. She lay back and moved Mark's shaking hand from her breast and guided it down towards her tummy.

'Mark! Mark!' a voice from the real world yelled.

A look of horror broke on his face. 'Oh, hell no!' he uttered desperately.

'Mark – get yourself down here now,' Jack's voice boomed.

The deflation for both teenagers was instantaneous.

'I don't believe this,' Mark grunted unhappily, pushing himself off the bed and standing up, his legs wobbly with a lack of blood which had surged to other, more demanding parts of his body.

Katie lay there panting, dishevelled, frustration visible in her face.

'Mark!' Jack shouted again.

'I'm coming,' he replied. He looked despairingly at Katie, who gave him an expression that summed up both their feelings. 'Sorry,' he said meekly.

'It's OK. Bad day anyway.'

Mark turned away from her and adjusted himself in his jeans before opening the door and stepping on to the landing. At the top of the stairs he could see down into the hall where Jack stood.

'That cop's come back, Christie, so get your arse down here. He has something for us all to hear.'

Nine

Detective Chief Inspector Christie spoke sombrely and very seriously. Mark saw and felt that the man had a certain authority, something about him that made everyone in the living room listen to him, hang on to his every word, despite their grief.

Mark's mum was in one of the armchairs. Jack leaned back into the settee, steepling his fingers underneath his chin, watching the detective with a degree of cold calculation, as though trying to weigh him up. Mark's eyes kept flicking back to Jack, wondering what was going on in his head.

There was also a woman in the room who Mark's mum referred to as her cousin Ellie, but Mark wasn't sure whether or not she was a relative or just a boozing buddy. She was just slumped on the floor, sitting back against the wall with a bottle in her hand – supporting his mum in her hour of need.

Mark watched Christie, the detective dealing with Bethany's death, the one who had interviewed him earlier that afternoon at Blackpool nick in the presence of Jack, the adult, and taken a statement. It had been a

131

pretty painless, if exhausting, experience, as much as it could be in the circumstances, but Christie had been deep and probing at the same time. There was definitely something about this Christie guy. On the face of it he seemed to accept everything that was said to him, but underneath there was an undercurrent that suggested he didn't believe a bloody word anyone said. He was someone, not to be frightened of, but to be very wary of ... which was maybe why Jack was scrutinising him so closely.

Cigarette smoke hung thick and still in the air. Mark's mum and her alleged cousin were chain smoking, clogging the atmosphere. There was a bottle of gin on the little table next to his mum's chair and an empty bottle of whisky laid out on the carpet. She'd been hitting the bottle and was watching Christie through watery, blood-shot eyes. Her head kept sort of bobbing around, too, as though she'd lost control of her neck muscles.

Mark glanced at her contemptuously, then looked back at Christie.

He was saying, 'And the post-mortem was carried out late this afternoon...' He stood in front of the fireplace, having decided not to sit as he delivered the news. With all the smoke in the room, his head was just above the clouds, like the tip of some mountain or other. 'As a result of the examination, the pathologist has determined that Bethany died of a massive drug overdose, but' – he paused – 'further tests are going to have to be carried out to identify the drugs and see if what she had in her body was contaminated or cut in any way, or not. I intend to fast-track these tests.'

Mark had a quick flashback to yesterday's school assembly and the dour message delivered by the headmaster about another drug death, that of Jane Grice.

'Are there some bad drugs going about?' Jack asked.

Christie looked at him. 'It's a possibility, one we need to check out – something we always do in cases like this. Thing is, two people have now died from drugs overdoses in a short space of time. It's public knowledge that Jane Grice overdosed by taking a very unusual concoction of drugs, including heroin. A fatal cocktail, I think the local press called it. She'd taken the drugs in such a way that made it look like she could've been force fed them, which of course makes that murder.' Christie paused to let the words sink in. 'Therefore forensic analysis of the substances in Bethany's body will possibly link to Jane's death. If that is the case, and there is a connection...'

'Whaah ya mean?' Mark's mum slurred, interrupting Christie and then flopping back into the chair drunkenly.

'I mean, Mandy, it's possible Bethany may have been forced to take a concoction of drugs and that then means I'm conducting a murder investigation until I find out different.'

'The Crackman!' Mark uttered under his breath.

Both Jack and Christie turned quickly to him. 'What, Mark?' the detective asked sharply.

'Nothing,' he said, his face set hard and determined.

'So what happens next?' Jack asked Christie.

Mark saw himself as tough and streetwise, but he had to admit he didn't know much about drugs, didn't want to either; he just knew they were bad news, which is why he had to ask Jack to explain what Christie was talking about when he mentioned 'cutting' drugs, even though he knew his brother didn't know much about drugs either.

'What it is, is this,' his elder brother patiently put into plain words. 'Drugs usually start off in a foreign country a long way from here. Heroin, for example; quite a lot of it comes from Afghanistan. Gets carried on the backs of donkeys, over the border into Pakistan. It starts off as opium from the poppy, then gets converted to heroin, then it finds its way across Europe and gets into this country through a huge network of dealers and some folk who don't even know what they're carrying. Then it gets cut down and bulked out, usually with something like milk powder, and gets sold on the streets. Somebody makes a profit at every stage of the journey.' Jack wiped his tired face, rubbing his eyes with the balls of his hands. Mark could see it was all getting to him. 'Thing is, though, sometimes it gets bulked out with something not so nice, such as scouring powder, for example. Something that if it gets into your bloodstream will kill you, even if the heroin doesn't.'

'So that's what happened to Beth?'

The two brothers were sitting on the front garden wall of the house. It was getting late, after nine now, and Mark had been up for over sixteen hours. He was wasted and drained, but knew he couldn't have slept even if he'd wanted.

Jack shrugged. 'Maybe, maybe not. Probably she just put too much into herself, y'know, misjudged it. It's what junkies do occasionally,' he said blandly. 'Anyway, the police tests'll tell us.'

Silence fell between them.

'I'm gonna find out who gave her the drugs,' Mark declared suddenly, 'and then I'm gonna get them.'

Jack slowly turned his face to him and eyed him sardonically, shaking his head sadly. 'No, you're not.'

'Oh yeah I am, and I know where I'm going to start.'

'Mark – don't be silly. If there's anyone to find, the police will do it. So let them. It's their job, not yours. I know that's what you feel you should do. I feel it too, but it's not going to happen.'

Mark pushed himself off the wall and began pacing around, building up inside, clenching and unclenching his fists. 'No, it's what I have to do, Jack. For Beth. I let her down in life, let her get hooked on drugs and didn't even notice. You don't have to be involved and I understand that. This is something for me, something for the streets here in Blackpool. I know you've no connection here anymore, so it's OK.' The idea was blossoming inside him, like it was the most important thing he had ever decided in his life. Something he had to do for his dead sister: investigate her death relentlessly and track down the person who sold or gave her the drugs.

Jack regarded him with a mix of sympathy and contempt. 'I'd hazard a guess that this thing is way out of your league, bud. Take it from me, don't go poking your nose into a very dangerous world where you'll find yourself getting injured, or worse.'

Mark spat on the ground. With bravado, he said, 'I'm not frightened – and anyway, I know who I'm going to see.'

'Who?'

'Jonny Sparks.'

'Why him?'

'Cos he's been hangin' around Beth and I know he deals drugs and I'll bet he gave 'em to her.'

Jack sighed and clicked his tongue. 'Why didn't you tell the cops this?'

Mark shrugged. 'Dunno. Something at the back of my mind stopped me. Maybe I knew it was my job to get him, but I don't know why I didn't say.' He squinted at Jack. 'Do you know what I mean?'

'Not really,' Jack said wearily. 'Look, Mark, tell the cops, eh? That DCI left his card. Give him a bell. Tell him what you know. Let him do the dirty work.'

'He won't do anything. Cops're rubbish.'

'He seemed pretty sound to me, even though I'm not that impressed by his methods.'

Mark shook his head. 'No, it's down to me. Whatever happens, I'm having words with Sparks and then, depending on what he tells me – or not – I'm going for the Crackman. He's the one behind it all.'

Jack looked at him as though he'd gone off his head. 'All right then, who the hell is the Crackman?'

'Nobody knows,' Mark said mysteriously, 'except that he's a big drug dealer and brings misery and I'll bet he supplied the drugs to Bethany. Yeah, one way or the other, even if Sparks doesn't know anything, I'll bet the Crackman is the one who supplied the supplier who supplied Bethany.'

'Mark – listen to yourself. You're talking rubbish. You're a fourteen-year-old lad who

137

feels bad. Just tell the cops what you know, then back off and leave it to them. Don't do anything stupid.' Jack stood up and faced his younger brother and placed his hands on his shoulders, looked into his eyes. 'And don't go around making wild accusations you can't back up with evidence, either. You know I'm talking sense, don't you?'

Mark avoided Jack's eyes and looked at the ground, then shrugged his hands off his shoulders.

He had made his decision.

It became all-consuming, the only thing he could think of. He had to find out who had supplied the drugs to Bethany. As he lay on his bed in the middle of the night, unable to sleep, his brain raced like an F1 Ferrari. Not that he was making any great attempt to get his head down. He didn't want to sleep because he believed he would have a nightmare and he knew exactly what that nightmare would be: Bethany on the mortuary slab being cut open and examined by some white-coated doctor who made sick jokes while he sliced her apart and ripped out her heart.

That he could not face, even in a dream.

He stood up, crossed to the window through which he had seen Bethany coming home, Jonny Sparks snogging her, touching her up. Mark's top lip curled at the thought of Sparks's hands on his sister's body ... the sister who had gone off the rails, but who had not deserved to die such an awful death.

He didn't even remember falling asleep. Next thing he knew he stirred and his clock told him it was ten in the morning and he had missed both his paper round and the start of school. But he didn't care about either. He couldn't be bothered. The thought of them made him feel sick and he knew he didn't have to explain anything to either of them, the newsagent or his teachers.

He dressed quickly and, without even washing himself or brushing his teeth, or putting on clean clothes, or underwear, he left the house – which was empty now. His mother had disappeared, to where he had not a clue, and nor did he care either. She hadn't even hugged him once yesterday, so caught up was she in her own histrionics. As far as he was concerned, she could get lost. He had no time for her, would survive without her.

Dragging his bike out of the hallway, down the front steps, he mounted up and pedalled furiously in the direction of the sea front. He arrived sweating and tired, suddenly extremely hungry, realizing he hadn't eaten for over twenty-four hours. His arms and legs were dithery and weak and he needed some sustenance. He cruised hopefully to Tony's Burger Bar, but it was too early to be open, so he rode around the back and secreted his bike behind some big wheelie bins, covered it with flattened cardboard boxes and set off on foot into town.

His wandering was aimless, his head still swirling with thoughts of Bethany and revenge for her death. He was hoping to bump into Jonny Sparks and beat a confession out of him, but didn't know where to start. Jonny lived somewhere in North Shore and hung around the arcades when he wasn't pushing drugs up on Shoreside. It would be more luck than anything if Mark found him.

But one thing Mark believed he had was luck ... and hunger. Deep and empty, his guts roared for something to fill them.

Mark strolled into Boots the Chemist. They sold sandwiches and drinks. Just like any other shopper, he picked up a basket and meandered to the sandwich display cabinet. BLT – bacon, lettuce and tomato – sounded excellent. A three pack. On nice, thick brown bread. It went into the basket, as did a bottle of Fanta.

He queued up at a till behind a few people.

He did not know why he was doing this. He couldn't afford the food because he had no money on him.

He was going to steal it.

His mouth went dry. Heart started pounding. Breathing went dithery. He got nearer the till.

Mark had never stolen anything in his life

before, not that he knew of, anyway. But he didn't care, because nothing mattered anymore.

His eyes constantly looked around.

He spotted a grey-uniformed security guard, arms folded, chatting to someone further back in the store.

The queue moved on a couple of steps.

He weighed up his escape – basically out through the front door, which was an automatic sliding one about four metres further on than the till. Timing was going to be everything. Courage, too. And fitness.

Hunger and the lack of dosh made the theft OK in his eyes. Boots made millions. They wouldn't miss a couple or three quid for a BLT and a Fanta. All his firmly held beliefs about stealing something from someone else suddenly didn't seem to matter any more.

One person was ahead of him now, a woman buying perfume.

Mark's eyes narrowed. He was still sweating. That, added to the lack of a wash, and he knew he hummed badly. He could even smell himself. Fear was also a factor. This was his first offence. Should he dump the stuff and just walk out the store now? It was an option. The woman in front paid for her perfume. Now, if he could just time it right...

He stepped up to the till.

What did it matter if he stole?

He smiled at the young Asian lady on the

checkout.

She smiled back, but then her nostrils flared slightly. Could she smell his intent? A brief shadow of suspicion clouded her face.

'Mornin',' Mark said.

'Hello, love.'

He glanced at the woman who had bought the perfume. She was the key to his escape. She was looking at a display of Boots catalogues, stacked just inside the door.

Mark emptied his basket and tossed it into the stack by the checkout. He saw the uniformed guard, his face turned in Mark's direction, but still chatting.

The cashier ran his two items across the barcode scanner. They beeped and Mark saw the price displayed.

BLT: £2.35

Fanta: 99p

Total £3.34

My very first theft, costed up right in front of my eyes, he thought wildly. Big money!

The cashier slid the goods into a flimsy carrier bag. That made things easier.

'Three thirty-four, please.'

Mark took the carrier bag. Act natural, he thought ... his right hand slipped into his pocket as though he was searching for the change. Through the corner of his eyes he clocked the perfume-buying woman, who was approaching the doors, which hissed open for her.

Spot on.

Mark gave the cashier an arrogant grin, then legged it.

Without warning he ran and as the doors opened fully, he danced around the woman who had unwittingly become a player in his crime, and raced off down the street, tearing away from the scene, the wind howling in his face, no idea if anyone had even shouted a thing. He did not look back, just dived into the crowds of shoppers, kept low, kept running. Stolen property in his grip and a surging feeling of euphoria pulsating through him as the adrenalin in his system was released, giving him extra power, more speed.

He dodged through the streets like an urchin in a Charles Dickens' novel. Cutting down by Woolworth's on to the prom and, without pausing, he dashed across both lanes of traffic, instinctively avoiding being clobbered by cars, and ran to the railings at the sea wall where he stopped, panting heavily. He turned to face the town – expecting to see an army of burly security guards on his trail, closing in for the arrest. There was no one.

He had committed his first crime and he had escaped.

Holding up two fingers at the town, he yelled, 'Stuff the lot of you.'

Ten

And that, Henry Christie thought, puts a whole different perspective on the matter – just that one name, the Crackman.

He was driving back to Blackpool Police Station after having spoken to the mixed bag that was the Carter family, having told them what the result of the post-mortem on Bethany had been, at least as much as he knew.

And Mark had uttered those magic words under his breath, 'The Crackman,' catching Henry sharply.

He hadn't pursued the remark, but that didn't mean he wasn't going to and as he drove back from Shoreside to the nick he reassessed just how he had got to this point and mulled over how things would progress from hereon.

Henry Christie truly believed he had been born to do the job of senior investigating officer – in other words investigating sudden, unexpected, violent or unusual deaths. Death kept him going. He thrived on it and – if there were a word that described his feelings better he would have used it – *relished* the prospect of tackling the biggest challenge a detective could face: hunting down and bringing to justice someone who had taken another's life.

The ultimate job for a detective: catching killers.

Unfortunately his job, his vocation, his raison d'être, had been cruelly taken away from him by higher-ups in the organization that he'd had the temerity to upset.

The fact he'd slept with the wife of his boss, a detective chief superintendent, and the resulting furore may very well have hastened Henry's departure from the Force Major Incident Team (FMIT) and into the backwaters of an office-bound desk job at headquarters about as far away from the front line as could be. Even though Henry had committed the dirty deed many years earlier, even before the lady in question had become the guy's wife, this did not seem to count for much in his defence ... which meant Henry had been busted from FMIT kicking and screaming, threatening legal action and grievance and employment tribunals until he was blue in the face, but to no avail. When he realized he was fighting a losing battle – once the organization has got it in for you, you might as well wave the white flag – he decided to keep a low profile and take whatever scraps were offered and make the best of a bad job.

He did manage to get promoted to chief

inspector on the promise he would keep his mouth shut, but he did refuse to relinquish the title of detective, even if he was technically no longer one. He knew this was pretty sad, *but hey*, he thought, *I like being called a detective*.

And, being the stubborn ass that he was, and not wanting to sit on an ever-expanding backside in a badly-lit office, he did his best to stay in touch with the sharp end of policing as best he could. He therefore ensured that his name was on as many call-out duty rotas as possible and provided cover for the divisionally based DCIs when necessary, making him quite a popular fellow with one or two people. He also volunteered for just about anything else if it meant getting out of his fishbowl office; Rik Dean's ill-fated Operation Nimrod was an example of this.

He knew he was like a dog around the supper table, waiting for throwaways, but he was prepared to take what came his way, good or bad, deal with it as best he could and therefore walk around with a bit of self-esteem, knowing he hadn't been entirely defeated by the powers that be.

Henry had been at home when he received the call about Bethany Carter's death by drugs overdose.

He had awarded himself a late start that morning but only because he had slept through his alarm, as had Kate, and when he eventually surfaced he found he had the biggest cranium-bashing hangover he'd experienced in a long, long while.

He and Kate had had a particularly heavy night down at the Tram and Tower, their local pub. There had been a two-piece band on, all backing tracks and digital music machines, but they'd played a good selection of '60s and '70s music which Henry appreciated, being stuck in the musical time warp that he was. After their second set of the night, Henry – who'd already had too much to drink – introduced himself, bought them a round of drinks, then the rest was history.

Following a 2 a.m. lock-in by Ken, the tame publican, Henry and Kate had staggered the mile home and after a Jack Daniel's night cap and a box of microwave chips each, they fell into bed in a drunken stupor which failed to be infiltrated by the alarm.

Hence the late start.

He dragged himself into a sitting position on the edge of the bed just after nine, groaning when he saw the time, but then shrugging. Nobody would miss him for an hour or two today. There was nothing urgent on his desk, no pieces of paper that needed to be rushed anywhere, no meetings, and no pressing emails, so he decided to roll in whenever he got there.

Kate yanked the duvet over her head with a warning snort and Henry, depressed that his job seemed nothing more than an administrator's position, staggered to the shower, scratching the parts that men are prone to scratch in the mornings.

It was as he was drying himself and half-returning to the sober world that his mobile phone rang.

'You're not in your office!' a voice accused him.

'No, mate, I'm not.' Henry recognized Rik Dean's voice immediately. It was nearly three months since he'd been shot and Henry knew he was already back at work, office-bound for the time being.

'So where the hell are you? On a tryst? The chief constable wants to know.'

'Tell the chief constable to go and frig himself.'

Rik laughed. 'No, seriously, where are you?'

'Butt naked, still in bed, half-pissed, fighting crapulence – and that's a hangover, not the shits, by the way.'

'I knew that! So, still in Blackpool?'

'Yep.'

'Even better ... fancy covering a job for us?'

Henry squinted, felt a little nauseous. 'What sort of job?'

'Drug OD. We're strapped out here, nobody to cover ... unless your office job is too tying, that is?'

'Name, address.' Henry picked up a pen next to the pad he kept bedside for such eventualities.

'Who was that?' Kate enquired, her voice muffled from underneath the bedclothes.

'Just work. They want me to cover a suspected drug overdose down on Shoreside. Some girl ... hell, don't feel like it,' he admitted.

However, twenty-five minutes later, spruced up, sharp looking, breath smelling fresh and the headache held more or less at bay by a double dose of Nurofen, Henry was walking up the path leading to Mark Carter's front door. He slotted back into his SIO role like pulling on a pair of comfy driving gloves.

He kept it simple, telling them he was an SIO from Blackpool Police Station. No point in complicating matters for people already under stress. He managed the scene, talked to the family, then arranged for the body to be taken to the local mortuary, hoping he had hidden just how badly his hangover was affecting him. He had come close to snapping when the elder brother, know-it-all Jack, had a dig at him for questioning the kid, Mark, especially after he'd been so sympathetic to the lad.

Henry had been proud of himself that he hadn't actually locked Jack up, because he had severely pissed Henry off, but he'd held back and ridden Jack's tirade and been mildly amused when Mark had actually leapt to his, Henry's, defence.

Whilst waiting for the body removers,

149

Henry had noticed Jack's Porsche Cayenne parked a little way up the road. Something nagged at the detective about the car, but he couldn't exactly say why. He'd simply filed it on the back burner and got on with the task of following the body down to the mortuary.

In over twenty-seven years of policing, Henry Christie had seen many bad things and although he had become thick-skinned to most, the death of a youngster, natural or otherwise, always gave him pause for thought.

When he looked down at the pitifully thin and wasted, waxy cadaver of Bethany Carter, he shook his head sadly and thought it was such a terrible waste. So unfair to die at such a young age. Then he thanked his lucky stars that his own daughters, both older than Bethany, had managed to avoid the drug scene in the town that was Blackpool. This was due to good mothering rather than his wayward fathering, he knew that, and was ever grateful to Kate for the way in which she had steered the girls along the straight and narrow.

He shivered at the prospect of what might have been, then got on with the job. He pulled on a pair of latex gloves.

With the assistance of the pasty-faced and rather creepy mortuary attendant, Henry stripped Bethany, bagged and tagged her clothing, then inspected the body. He took hold of one arm and eased it outwards, exposing her inner elbow.

His mouth became a tight line and his nostrils dilated as he nodded sagely to himself. He placed her arm back and looked at the soft, fleshy parts at the backs of her knees, nodding to himself again at the sight of the scabbed-over needle marks he found there.

A junkie.

He drew a white sheet over her head and nodded to Dr Death, the mortuary assistant: She could go into the chiller now.

There was no pathologist available until the afternoon, so Henry headed back to the police station to begin to pull together the bones of a report and to tell the coroner what he was up to.

Just another dope-head, self-inflicted death, he guessed.

Still, a million times better than sitting on his bum at headquarters, pen pushing.

Henry poked his head around the door of Rik's office.

'Mind if I hot-desk here for today?'

Rik looked up and smiled warmly. 'Just so long as I don't get shot or knifed.'

'Hey, live dangerously.'

'I do when you're about,' Rik mumbled.

Henry parked himself on a plastic chair on the 'public' side of Rik's desk. 'How's the leg?'

'Had a bullet in it – what do you think?' He gave Henry a withering 'Duh!' look.

'Get over it, that's what I think.' Henry raised his eyebrows. 'Any progress on the job?' He was referring to Operation Wiggum.

Rik shrugged. Negative. 'Nah ... the Crackman's still out there, mysterious as a shadow. We don't have a clue who he is, where he is, or anything ... just odd snippets of information, on which that operation was based, to be honest.'

'So it wouldn't have stood the five by five by five test?' Henry asked, referring to the way intelligence was graded.

Rik gave him a guilty look. 'I kinda exaggerated it ... but it wasn't far off. The two guys we jumped on were definitely involved in something there – obviously' – he rolled his eyes – 'but they've said nothing, so all we've got 'em for is what they did – shoot me and assault you. They're having it and they'll go down for it, but they won't be saying anything more. Bastards. And the gen about the Lexus was spot on, but we got the wool pulled over our eyes with that.'

'Previous owners?'

'Checked out ... not a hundred per cent, but they're saying nothing either.'

'And your source, whoever gave you the information?' Henry asked.

'Still keeping his ear to the ground.' They looked at each other. 'So that's that, I reckon ... anyway, thanks for covering that death, by the way. Run of the mill?'

'Probably, but I'll do the full works on it.' He rubbed his face. 'PM's later this afternoon ... just taken a statement from the younger brother...' Henry was carrying the start of a sudden death file and he fished out the statement he'd taken earlier from Mark Carter, leafed through it. 'This lad, the dead girl's brother, didn't even know she was on dope ... not a close family ... mum's a slapper, older brother's a big shot businessman who's right up his own arse.' Henry regarded Rik. 'I don't think I've got everything from the young one, though. Get the impression he's holding back.' He pouted, shook his head. 'However, we'll need to kick-start investigations into her supplier, as you do. You'll probably have to delegate that to one of your DCs. Her boyfriend will be worth a look at. His name's in the file. I know him of old.'

Rik nodded. 'No probs.'

'Once I've overseen the PM, I'll probably hand it all to you because Headquarters cannot possibly function without me for more than a day.'

'I can see that.'

'And anyway – what's so all-fired important that I had to cover a job for you lot?'

'We're all-out on that drive-by shooting the other day ... getting nowhere fast.'

'Oh, I recall that one.' Henry's eyebrows furrowed as he tried to dredge something up, but got nowhere. 'Anyway, I need to speak to the coroner, cross a few Ts and then get back to the mortuary – after I've had something to eat, that is.'

Henry's mobile phone rang as he was about to slide into his car. He had just attended Bethany's post-mortem and not enjoyed it at all.

'Hi Rik,' he said, recognizing the number on the caller display.

'Hi ... the drugs death? Carter?' Rik said without any formalities.

'Just leaving the PM. Looks like a concoction of drugs.'

'Suspicious circumstances?'

'Yeah, a concoction of drugs.'

'You know what I mean – any evidence she'd been forced to take them?'

'Don't think so ... hard to tell. Why? What's eating you?'

'Come down to the nick if you've got time. I'll have coffee brewing.'

'Did you say, "Please, boss" then, or not?'

'Boss.'

The coffee was good, strong. Rik had a reputation for filtering the best fresh coffee in the building. Henry sipped it black, no sugar. He looked over the rim of the 'Rik's a Great Leader' mug that had been provided for him.

'I glanced through this.' He held up Mark

154

Carter's witness statement, the one Henry had taken earlier that day. 'It's a good statement.'

Henry tilted his head. 'And that from a subordinate.'

'Thing is, something struck me,' Rik went on, ignoring Henry. 'About a fortnight ago there was a similar drugs-related death in Poulton-le-Fylde, which, as you know, is in Northern Division. I've been out for a pint with the DS up there, Jack Broughton –'

'Good man.'

'– good man,' Rik agreed. 'He was dealing with it. Young girl. A concoction of drugs wild enough to make any dealer's heart go bump ... not an unusual thing, maybe ... but' – he held up his right index finger – 'the similarity doesn't end there. I mean, I might be adding up and getting five, and maybe the mix in the Carter girl's body will be nothing like, but the similarity is in a name...'

'Jonny Sparks,' Henry guessed quickly.

'Nail on head,' Rik confirmed. 'Ex-boyfriend of the dead girl in Poulton.'

Henry sat back, thoughtfully sipping his brew. Over the years he had spent a lot of years policing Blackpool and he knew a lot of the young buckos who reckoned to rule the streets, if not personally, then by reputation. One he knew personally was Jonny Sparks, a product of an infamous family of lawbreakers. He'd arrested Jonny a few years back when the lad had been only ten for assault and killing a cat by stamping on it. All the warning signs were flashing, even back then, but Henry hadn't had any dealings with him since. Even at ten, he'd been a handful, Henry recalled fondly.

'He's a dealer now.'

'No shock there.'

'And you just wonder if...' Rik began wistfully.

'If he supplied Bethany with the lethal dose?'

'As well as the girl in Poulton.'

'How far has that investigation got?'

'Not very – mainly for one reason: the dead girl's family have been very reluctant to help us because, word is, they're going to sort the matter out themselves.'

'And who might this family be?'

'The daughter is called Jane Grice.'

Henry went cold. He knew the Grice clan well. Big time crims. Violent, nasty people. 'Ronnie Grice's crew.'

'Exactly ... and he's out for blood, so they say.'

'I take it Jonny's been interviewed over the matter?'

Rik nodded. 'Nothing came of it, hard little twat that he is.'

'So, to recap: Beth Carter's and Jane Grice's deaths are similar and Jonny Sparks is connected to both?'

'That's the nutshell.'

The older detective rubbed his temples, his

156

hangover and headache not having quite left him even now. He felt tired and drawn. 'So Jonny needs speaking to, but like you say, he doesn't crack easily ... perhaps we could bring some pressure to bear on him.'

Rik frowned.

'What's the up-to-date intel on him?'

Rik screwed up his face. 'So-so.'

'What about pulling a level two operation against him?' Henry suggested. That meant an undercover operation with test purchasers. 'If he got caught red-handed, maybe that would open other floodgates.'

'Worth a try.' Rik sounded doubtful.

'But in the meantime, I'll fast-track the forensics on Bethany.' Henry sank his coffee and pushed himself up. 'And in the other meantime I need to go back to the Carter household and tell them where we're up to.'

'Oh, the Royal "we".'

'It's always the Royal "we" when I'm about to dump a job in somebody else's lap.'

Which brought Henry full circle to where he was right now – leaving Mark Carter's home, having heard the youngster mutter 'The Crackman' under his breath.

Up to that point, Henry had been pretty indifferent about the case.

Yes, he was very sorry a young girl had died in such tragic circumstances, but he didn't feel particularly involved in it. He'd covered the job more as a favour than anything and done what was expected of him and had been happy to hand the package over for someone else to deal with whilst he scurried off back to headquarters.

But not now.

Mark Carter's utterance had changed things for ever.

And all because Henry wanted some glory that he could shove right up the noses of his ex-bosses who had binned him from FMIT.

The police had been chasing the elusive Crackman for a number of years now without success and Mark's under-the-breath utterance had suddenly gripped Henry and made him think, What if I could catch this guy? What if he was the dealer behind these two deaths? What if Jonny Sparks could be broken? How good would this make me look?

Henry's gut instinct told him that the Crackman was lurking somewhere on the periphery of this investigation and if he could just think of a way of getting to him ... maybe headquarters could actually survive without him for a while longer.

Hell, he thought, what if I could nail the Crackman?

Eleven

Mark sat on the beach underneath Central Pier and ate his ill-gotten goods. He was famished and the food tasted amazing, all the better because of the way in which it had been obtained. The rush had been tremendous and for a while he relived the moments again and again in his mind's eye.

Only when he'd eaten and drunk and lain back on the cold sand did he start to come down and his brain clouded over once more, images of death and the discovery of Bethany's body intruding on his euphoria. He could not shake it, so, realizing he needed to do something to keep busy, he walked back into town and started trawling the streets for Jonny Sparks.

He spent the rest of the morning drifting from arcade to arcade, mooching, killing time, watching, waiting, but unable to track him down. It was like he had gone into hiding, or maybe he was just well camouflaged in the jungle that was Blackpool.

Hunger revisited him about midday. He considered stealing his lunch, but decided not to. He didn't want his luck to run out.

He walked back to Tony's Burger Bar, which had now opened for business. He cadged a hamburger and fries from Ray, the owner, in return for clearing out the rear yard, which he had promised to do with Bradley, but never did. It was obvious from Ray's stilted behaviour that he had heard something about Bethany, so Mark avoided any conversation, did the tidy-up and took the food, which tasted vile today.

Then he was back on the streets.

Jonny Sparks was nowhere to be found. In the end Mark gave up, came back to Tony's – managed to cadge another burger, this time for nothing – and got on his bike and rode home.

It was time to do his evening paper round, but the thought of being bombarded with questions about Beth and why he hadn't turned up that morning, put him off. Stuff 'em, he thought.

He stood outside his house. Didn't have the courage to go inside. The memory of what happened last time was vivid, upfront. He took a deep breath and remounted the BMX and started more aimless cycling around the estate. He didn't avoid anywhere, even the areas which, it was said, were no-go for cops.

Lots of kids lounged round, even though it was still school hours. Some played football, others just hung around, looking dangerous. They watched him, but did nothing to him, as though they could sense he was more dangerous than they were that day.

There was an aura about him, he thought. It was all about attitude with this lot, and by showing he wasn't afraid of them, they let him be, didn't want to mix it. At least that was what Mark believed. There was something festering in him that meant he didn't care; an anger, a rage so deep he would have fought anyone, and it showed in his demeanour.

He turned in to a narrow passageway, high-walled, with a dogleg in it, which cut from the estate out to a pretty dilapidated row of shops on the edge of Shoreside. The passage was called Songthrush Walk, but had been nicknamed locally Psycho Alley, somewhere you walked at your peril. Folk had been mugged here, people beaten up in the dark. Drug addicts injected themselves here; used, bloody needles littered the ground. An awful place. A girl had even been abducted from here once, it was rumoured.

Mark couldn't have cared less.

At that particular moment in his existence, nothing scared him other than the prospect of going home.

He wheeled the BMX around and through the gear-strewn alley, left into the dogleg, then right, where he put his head down and powered out, emerging into the car park behind the shops.

And it was here he saw Jonny Sparks.

He was dealing, that much was obvious. With his pair of henchmen, Eric and Sam, at his shoulder to protect him and keep nicks, he was handing over a tiny package to a lad Mark had never seen before and the lad palmed a return package to Jonny, probably money, which was quickly pocketed. It was over in the twinkling of an eye, but Mark witnessed it all go down.

But that wasn't what bothered him, because at the exact moment he saw Jonny Sparks, his rage instantly boiled up and he found he couldn't stop himself from doing what he did next.

In his mind that morning, he had mulled over the options as to exactly how he would approach Jonny. He'd eventually decided that, if at all possible, he'd talk calmly and rationally to him. Discuss matters.

But as soon as he spotted him, that was all chucked out of the window.

Jonny Sparks was going to die!

A surge of strength and energy ripped through his whole being, like a great beast, the Incredible Hulk, maybe. He forced his right foot down on the pedal and accelerated toward Sparks.

Eric and Sam saw him straightaway.

On their words of warning, Jonny looked up with surprise on his face.

Jonny's customer saw Mark approach too. Without any hesitation, he ran for it, not knowing who Mark was but obviously sensing trouble.

Jonny held his ground, Eric and Sam slightly behind him in their usual defensive positions.

Mark just focused on Jonny. Total concentration was on him, like a racehorse with blinkers, everything else chopped out but the target.

Three metres short of Jonny, Mark yanked on the brakes and slithered to a spectacular, grit-spraying halt. He dropped his BMX in a way he'd never done before, just letting it clatter to the ground, then on foot ran at Jonny, his head low like a rugby player, and drove his shoulder into Jonny's guts before he could work out what was hurtling at him.

He bowled into Jonny with all the force he could command, ramming into him like a runaway express. With Mark's right shoulder in his belly, Jonny bent double and emitted an unworldly gasp as every drop of air inside him whooshed out. Jonny staggered backwards, forced by Mark, arms flailing like a wind turbine, and landed on his backside, smacking down on the concrete, jarring his spine as he hit it hard.

Then Mark laid into him.

Mark had rarely been in fights, but from somewhere inside he found the strength and power to begin pummelling a yelling Jonny Sparks with blows and kicks, rained in with perfect accuracy, like he was a brilliant street-fighter. The reality was he was just a young boy driven by that volatile mix of grief and anger.

He felt like he had smashed Jonny a hundred times.

Jonny rolled into a protective ball, unable to do anything other than cover himself as much as possible from a surprise onslaught virtually impossible to defend against.

And though it seemed like the beating went on for ages, it was only seconds ... long enough for Sam and Eric to react.

Suddenly Mark was yanked roughly up, kicked in the side and pushed off Jonny, who, satisfyingly from Mark's perspective, was whimpering like an abused puppy.

Eric had grabbed him. Sam had kicked him.

Mark staggered away, but that animal-like driving force inside him propelled him back toward the whining Sparks, savagely heaving Eric out of the way, pounding a fist into Sam's face and diving between the two, back on to Jonny who, with a face full of terror, was attempting to scramble away.

Arms and fingers outstretched, Mark landed on Jonny, and with the force still raging inside him, tried to drag him to his feet by the collar. Jonny screamed as Mark kicked his arse with as much power as he could muster, sending him sprawling again.

He landed hard, flipped around and like a terrified crab, scuttled backwards on all fours trying to get away from Mark.

'No, no, no!' Jonny yelled. 'Don't hit me, please,' he begged.

'You killed my sister,' Mark roared.

'I never,' Jonny began, his eyes darting this way and that, working out how to escape.

'You ... *argh!*' Mark gasped, his words getting nowhere, because Sam had come in behind him, having picked up a piece of wood as long and heavy and handy as a base-ball bat from a pile of fly-tipping, and whacked Mark across the shoulder blades. It was a good job he hadn't smashed him across the back of the head, because he could have killed him. Even so, the blow was spectacularly effective. A shockwave rippled through Mark's body all the way down to his knees, weakening them to rubber. They gave way and he crashed down, suddenly all his pent-up power deserting him. He dropped on to all fours and his head sagged. Sam de-livered another blow across his back at right angles to Mark's spine, smashing against his kidneys. Mark yowled like a kicked hound.

Jonny Sparks, true to form, recovered instantly. He was up on his feet in a second and delivered an almighty kick into Mark's ribs which flipped him over, leaving him open for Jonny to drop like a ton weight on to his chest, straddle him and pin him to the ground, a cruel expression on his face.

Jonny's knees fastened Mark's arms down and though he struggled he didn't get any-where because Eric dropped on to his legs

165

and held them.

Mark was beaten. He'd had a few moments of vengeful victory and now it was over.

Jonny wiped the snot and spit off his face with the back of his hand and caught his breath. A swelling visibly rose around his right eye.

Mark glared contemptuously at him, now unafraid, knowing he had the ability to beat him up on a one-to-one, without the two goons to protect him.

'I'm gonna get you,' Mark snarled.

Jonny gave a cruel laugh, then lunged at Mark's face and grabbed it in his right hand so that his fingers dug painfully into Mark's cheek, his ragged nails cutting into the soft skin, distorting his face and mouth as he squeezed hard. There was a feral grimace on Jonny's harsh, weasel face.

'I don't know what the fuck you're talking about, boyo, but you're barking up the wrong tree here.'

'Liar,' Mark managed to say through his misshapen mouth. 'You're a dealer, you gave her the stuff.'

'Lad,' Jonny said, 'you're talking shit. I didn't give her owt, got that?' With that he smacked Mark's head down on the ground. Mark braced himself for what was about to come – the biggest battering of his life. His eyes took in Sam and Eric itching to kick the shit out of him. But something incredible happened. 'Now you just sod off and leave me alone, you mad twat,' Jonny said, rising off his chest. 'And consider yourself lucky we're not gonna beat the living crap outta you, cos you well deserve it, Carter.'

Jonny stood up, taking a step back to give the, metaphorical, gobsmacked Mark room to stand.

'We're not gonna kill the twat?' Sam whined in dismay.

'No, we're not,' Jonny said, wiping his face with his sleeve.

'But why...?' Sam continued.

'Because we're not, OK?' Jonny said, infuriated at being questioned by a lesser mortal.

'What?' Sam sneered, not getting this at all. 'Dun't make sense.'

Mark clambered to his feet. Surely this was a wind up. Jonny Sparks letting him go?

'Now piss off,' Jonny spat, 'before I change my mind.' Mark hesitated, was about to ask why, too. 'Just 'effin' go.'

Mark turned to get his bike – but didn't get chance to go anywhere.

Before he knew what was happening, the four lads were surrounded. Four vehicles screamed on to the car park, tyres screeching, engines revving, and screeched to a halt around them. Two were marked police cars, their blue lights flashing, one was a police van and the other was a plain car. Like well-drilled ants, six uniformed cops shot out of the vehicles shouting like mad men (even the

167

woman) and with a blur of speed, the four lads were slammed face down on the ground, hands pulled behind their backs and hand-cuffed painfully. They all demanded to know what was going on.

Mark was pinned face down by a uni-formed cop, his face crushed into the gravel.

Jonny had the same, but was heaved to his feet by a burly cop, whilst Sam and Eric were held down like Mark.

Mark twisted his head and saw two plain-clothed cops getting out of the unmarked car, the uniformed lot obviously having done the dirty work for the detectives. Mark instantly recognized DCI Christie. He took a moment to work out where he'd seen Christie's colleague – then it hit him: it was the lad who'd just bought some smack from Jonny Sparks!

Sparks had been set up. An undercover cop had just bought drugs from him and now he was being locked up for it. A sting.

Mark tried to keep watching the proceed-ings from ground level and only really with one eye as Christie sauntered up to Jonny, who was being manhandled by a cop.

'Hi, Jonny.'

'Mr Christie,' Jonny responded morosely, obviously knowing him.

'Let's have a look-see what you've got on you, shall we?' Christie stepped up to him and patted him down, chatting pleasantly while he searched. 'You look a bit of a mess.

Someone give you the slapping you deserve?'

Jonny's mouth sneered. 'He came off worse – anyway, what the hell's going on? I ain't done nowt. This is an illegal search. You haven't even told me who you are.'

Christie obviously couldn't resist it. 'Your worst nightmare, that's who I am.' He grinned as a hand slid into Jonny's back jeans pocket. 'Ooh, what's this?' The hand came out bearing a tightly packed roll of banknotes. 'Nice amount,' he said appreciatively. 'Where did this come from?'

'It's mine,' Jonny said, then for the first time got a proper look at Christie's companion and recognized him as the person he'd just sold drugs to. Jonny's shoulder's fell as though his lungs had just been taken out. 'Shit.'

Christie smiled at him, a smile of triumph. His hand went into another of Jonny's pockets and emerged with several wraps. Christie blew out his cheeks, tutted and shook his head sadly. 'Jonny, Jonny, Jonny,' he said sadly. 'You're under arrest on sus of supplying controlled drugs – oh, and suspicion of murder, too.'

'What you talking about?'

'We'll chat down the nick, eh?' He cautioned Jonny and told the cop holding him to bung him in the back of the van, then he quickly searched Eric and Sam, found wraps on them both and arrested them, too. They were bundled into the back of a car each.

Christie turned his attention to Mark, still flattened on the ground. 'Let him up.' The cop on top of him heaved him to his feet. 'Running with a bad crowd, eh?'

'I don't run with them.'

'Yeah, right,' the detective said disbelievingly.

'Honest, I don't.'

'As if.' Christie's face showed even more disbelief. He searched Mark and found nothing.

'See,' Mark said, 'and anyway, ask your undercover cop. He knows I wasn't here when Jonny was selling stuff.'

Christie shrugged, indifferently. 'But you did turn up.'

'Yeah – to hammer him.'

'And why would that be?'

'None o' your business.'

'Everything's my business – you're under arrest, too.'

'What for? What for? I haven't done nothing.'

'Drug-dealing and shoplifting. How's about that for starters? I'm sure once I get into your ribs, there'll be more. Much, much more.'

Mark's gut did a classic back flip. He was shoved into the back of the plain police car and all four vehicles then drove off the car park at a sedate pace, past the group of gawping onlookers who'd gathered to watch proceedings. It was a group of people that included Katie Bretherton and Bradley Hamilton.

Mark looked out of the back window of the cop car as it drove past. The expressions on the faces of his friends told Mark all he needed to know. He sunk into the seat and stared dead ahead, wishing he could be sucked into a black hole, never to reappear.

Twelve

The inside of a police cell. Eight feet by six feet, Mark Carter estimated, maybe a tad bigger, but not much. It had a thick steel door with a hatch in it that slid up and down, perhaps a foot square. The door was locked and bolted – slammed shut, actually – and the hatch had been snapped shut. Above the hatch was a spy hole. Nothing high-tech, just a round hole about the size of a two pence piece with a cover on the other side. The cell walls were painted a sickly cream colour and had names and obscenities carved into them, such as 'Kev', 'Rocky', 'Moose ere 12/4' (Mark knew Moose), and four-letter swear words. The toilet was stainless steel, fitted to the wall with hidden screws, designed for use without a normal toilet seat, just two curved raised ridges of wood on either side of the bowl on which your bum rested. Mark hadn't been anywhere near the bog. It stank, hadn't been flushed, was blocked with tissue, looked disgusting. There was a full-length bed, built as part of the cell structure, and high in the wall above it was a window made of thick, translucent, but not see-through, blocks of glass, a kind of green colour. There was a thin plastic mattress on the bed and a folded, thick blanket which looked itchy and flea-ridden.

God, the smell. The whole cell complex hummed, not just this cell. Mark guessed there were about fifty cells altogether and the reek was a combination of urine, sweat, alcohol, vomit and fear: the aroma of caged human beings. It hit Mark as soon as he was marched from the custody office into the cell corridor, an odour that sent a shiver down his spine, made him afraid and disorientated, too. He had been taken into the custody office and booked into the system so quickly and efficiently that he had lost track of everything, his head in a spin. When he'd been put into the cell, he could not work out where he was. Geographically he couldn't fathom out where the cells were in relation to the exterior of the police station, which he'd seen a million times. Mentally, he was zombified.

He sat on the bed, elbows on knees, facing the cell door.

'Don't normally put kids into adult cells,' the less than friendly, harassed gaoler had explained as he'd propelled Mark into the cell, 'but needs must when we're full to brimming. Just be thankful you're not sharing.' That was when he slammed the door shut with a gut-sickening finality.

Mark had also lost track of time. Couldn't work out how long he'd been banged up. Minutes, certainly. An hour, possibly. More ... he wasn't sure.

Being arrested had had a gigantic effect on him, completely blown his mind, having his liberty taken away from him. What a power that was, to take someone's freedom away from them. He knew kids who revelled in being locked up, a big kudos thing, something that built up their status amongst their dumb, like-minded mates. Mark had always thought of them as futureless idiots. Kids who would never get jobs, who would spend most of their young adult lives in and out of nick, living a hand-to-mouth existence with no end in sight; growing up to be drunks, wife-beaters and drug-takers. Mark couldn't work out when he'd actually seen through the futility of this kind of life and decided against going down that path. He had seen it for what it was, what it did to people, and he wanted far more from life.

Yet here he was in a police cell.

Mark Carter, prisoner.

He dropped his head into his hands and started to sob.

By the time the gaoler came for him, Mark had curled up on the hard mattress and cried himself to sleep. When the key went in the cell door he awoke groggily, as if he'd been out for hours, and stood up in his socked feet – because when he'd been booked in his trainers had been taken from him.

'Time to be interviewed,' the gaoler announced.

Mark rubbed his eyes. 'Right.'

'You can put your footwear on.' The gaoler pointed to the trainers outside the cell door in the corridor.

Mark slid his cold feet into them and walked ahead of the gaoler, who directed him back to the custody office. Which was heaving with prisoners, all lined up at the reception desk accompanied by their arresting officers, or chucked into the holding cage. Mark recognized one or two faces. The gaoler steered him to another desk on which DCI Christie leaned, a pack of tapes in his hand, some papers, too.

Mark was almost pleased to see him. A familiar face.

Christie grinned amiably, but Mark sneered at him because that's what was expected when you were locked up. Mark didn't actually want to let on he was glad to see him. His sneer, though, seemed to make Christie grin even wider.

'How you doing?'

'A'right,' Mark replied in a surly way.

'I'm glad.'

The two eyed each other cautiously, then Christie signed something on the custody record and said, 'Follow me,' turned and walked down another corridor to an interview room, opened the door and pointed. 'In there.' Mark edged past into the room, which was pretty bare: table, chairs, tape recorder, TV and DVD/video player and a guy sitting at the table with a pen and pad. Mark didn't know who he was. He looked young and eager, if a little frayed at the edges. 'Sit down.' Christie motioned to a chair next to the stranger, whilst he himself sat down on a chair at the opposite side of the table. 'This is Mr Gregson, Social Services.'

'Hello Mark...' Gregson extended a hand. Mark recoiled as though the hand was a cobra.

'What do I want Social Services for?' he squeaked worriedly.

'Because I've been unable to contact either your mother or brother,' Christie said. 'Mr Gregson will just be here for the interview.'

'I'm not going into care,' Mark blurted, panic-stricken, but with fire and defiance in his voice.

'Nobody says you are,' Mr Gregson said softly. 'I'm here just to ensure you are looked after properly and are treated in accordance with the law. Nothing else.'

It calmed Mark only slightly. He was feeling distrustful and extremely nervous, all those horror stories he'd heard about the cops and Social Services colluding and getting kids sent to care homes, stories he'd hardly even listened to in the past, were becoming a reality for him. His stomach felt as though it had been scraped empty, but yet he felt a desperate need to empty his bowels all of a sudden.

Christie inserted the tapes into the machine and gave Mark a forced smile. 'Let's have a chat,' he said and pressed the recording button. He checked his watch and the wall clock. Mark followed his eyes and it was then he realized he'd been in custody for three hours.

Time passes so quickly when you're having a good time, he thought grimly.

Mark guessed that Christie had probably interviewed hundreds of people, but there was no way in which he was going to divulge anything to him, other than the truth, no matter what the pressure. He knew the cops twisted your words and set you up for things you hadn't done and there was no way he was falling for any of the detective's little ruses. Mark decided to keep it straight down the line and tell it as it was. Ultimately the truth couldn't hurt and for a while it seemed a good option.

They had talked for a while about the Jonny Sparks' scenario. Christie seemed to accept and be very interested in Mark's version of events, leading up to and including the fight, but he wouldn't tell Christie why they were fighting. As far as Mark was concerned, that was none of his business. It was

177

personal.

'OK, I'll have that,' Christie said finally, wrapping up that part of the interview. 'Now, do you want to tell me about the shoplifting?'

Mark's mouth clammed shut.

'Cat got your tongue?'

'Don't know what you mean,' he said, fidgeting.

Christie snickered. 'A lad fitting your description went into Boots this morning and nicked sandwiches and a drink.'

That statement relieved Mark. 'A lad fitting my description! That's a bit thin, isn't it? There's a thousand lads fitting my description in this town. Anyway, I was at school,' he bluffed. 'Check.'

Christie gave him the tight smile. 'I did – and you weren't.' He picked up a TV remote control and pointed it at the TV fixed to the wall. It suddenly came to grainy life. Mark's heart nearly stopped. 'What's that ad on TV?' Christie asked rhetorically. 'You're captured 300 times a day on camera?'

And Mark had been well and truly captured by Big Brother. From going into the shop – cut – to picking up the food and drink – cut – to waiting at the till with the woman buying perfume – cut – to legging it out of the door, goods in hand, nicked.

'Not exactly crime of the century, is it?' Mark said belligerently.

'Not, it's not, Mark,' Christie agreed, turning off the TV, 'but it's a start, isn't it?' His thin, tight smile now looked unpleasant and dangerous.

Mark felt Christie's hooks digging into him.

They were going to give him police bail, meaning he would have to come back to the station in three weeks' time and present himself to the custody officer. By then, Christie told him, a decision would have been made on what to do with him.

After the interview, Mark was bunged back in the cell for what seemed an age whilst the paperwork was sorted. He was then escorted back to the custody desk where a bleary-eyed, seen-it-all, bored-looking sergeant got him to sign the bail forms. Mr Gregory, the Social Services guy, was the co-signatory. Mark's property was handed back to him and the sergeant gave him a wave.

As he turned away from the desk, Christie was there waiting for him.

'I'll give you a lift home.'

'You're all right, I'll walk,' Mark said.

'No, let me say it again: I'll give you a lift home.'

Mark ground his teeth and regarded Christie.

'You're a juvenile,' Christie explained. 'We, the police, have a duty of care, so I'll be taking you home.'

'Where's my bike?'

'Safe – it'll be dropped off at the same time as you. Follow me.' He turned and Mark, shoulders hunched, a big, pissed-off sigh coming from him, traipsed after Christie up a narrow corridor and into the secure garage area on the ground floor of the cop shop. A Ford Focus bleeped and flashed its lights as Christie walked toward it. 'Get in the front,' he said as he slotted in behind the wheel. He waited for Mark to settle in and strap up before he said, 'We need to talk.'

The automatic roller door started to rattle open as Christie started the car and then crept to the exit.

Mark sank low in his seat, very uncomfortable in more ways than one.

Christie swung the car out left, then at the next junction did another right toward the prom, then at the sea front headed south.

'Fancy an ice cream?'

Mark stared blankly at the detective. 'You a perv or summat?'

Christie chuckled, then shrugged his shoulders. 'I thought we could talk and eat. Maybe you'd like a KFC instead?' He looked at Mark and raised a knowing eyebrow.

'Neither,' Mark snarled. He sat back, folded his arms and stared dead ahead, both defiant and scared at the same time, like a trapped rat. He made one or two surreptitious glances at Christie, trying to weigh the man up. Mark had been lucky enough never to have been in the company of cops for any length of time and he just didn't know the truth. Did they beat you up? Did they fit you up, or 'verbal you', as his mates called it? Could they be trusted, or what? And the bigger, burning question for Mark was – what the hell did this particular cop want?

'I live on Shoreside, not down here,' Mark said as they drove straight past the junction with Squires Gate Lane which would have taken them in the direction of the estate.

'I know. As I said, I want to chat.'

'This is child abduction!'

Christie gave him a sidelong squint. 'Shut the hell up, sit the hell back and chill,' he instructed.

With his nostrils flaring angrily, Mark did the first two.

Thirteen

Christie drove down to St Anne's, the more genteel resort just to the south of Blackpool, on to the sea front and stopped at the white café on the beach, set amidst the sand dunes.

'Probably safe enough to talk here,' the detective murmured. 'Come on.' He led the unwilling Mark inside and bought him a Coke and ice cream, which tasted wonderful. Christie had a bottle of water which he sipped. They sat at a corner table with Christie taking the seat tucked into the angle so he could see all the comings and goings. 'So, how you doing?'

'What d'you mean?' Mark eyed him suspiciously.

'Coping, you know? Since Bethany died. I know it's only early days.'

Mark shrugged manfully. 'Doin' OK.'

Christie scratched his head, opened his mouth to say something, hesitated, closed his mouth and started again. 'You're a good lad, aren't you?'

'So-so.'

'Keep your nose clean, don't you?'

'Up to a point.'

'Do you do drugs?'

'No way.' Mark was horrified at the question.

'Know lads and lasses who do?'

'I know one who died,' Mark responded, a sudden lump in his throat.

'Yeah, true. Must be really, really hard.'

'Yeah, in a way you don't know,' the youngster snapped, but because of the strange dark shadow that crossed Christie's face, Mark gulped and wished he hadn't said it.

'Whatever,' Christie said, with a tinge of sadness, then his expression became businesslike again.

Mark licked his ice cream, looked out across the sand dunes to the Irish Sea.

'I got the results back from the forensic lab.'

'What results?'

'I told you I'd be fast-tracking the samples taken from Bethany's body, remember? I was wrong about the heroin being dirty.' Mark waited. 'But she took a concoction of drugs that were simply too much for her – a mix of heroin, amphetamines, ecstasy and crack...'

'Hell.' Something moved inside Mark, suddenly making him nauseous. Mark scanned the sand dunes again. His whole body was quaking, giving way.

'She died one horrible death.' Christie had leaned forward on to his elbows and whispered these words hoarsely to Mark.

'Why are you telling me this?' Mark demanded, very close to the edge, tears welling in his eyes.

'So you know everything.'

'Why, though? Why do I need to know?'

Christie sat back, regarding Mark critically, but saying nothing.

Mark visualized Bethany's body lying grotesquely on the kitchen floor. He began to try and conceive of what hell she must have been through. From injecting something she thought was going to give her pleasure and taking all that other stuff, too, and possibly then realizing she had actually taken something that would kill her, like letting a venomous snake bite you. What agony had she endured? A pain unknown to anyone other than the person foolish enough to take the damned drugs. Did she scream? Did she call for help? Or did she just writhe and squirm and accept her fate?

'It's unlikely she would have taken that mix of drugs willingly,' Christie said. 'It's more than likely she was fed them until she died.'

'So she was murdered?'

'Looks very much that way,' the detective confirmed.

Mark shot to his feet, knocking the table. His coke tipped over. Christie held on to his bottle of water.

'Need the bog,' Mark uttered and staggered like a drunk between the tables, bouncing off them, drawing curious glances from other customers. The thought that she was killed whilst he, Mark, was asleep upstairs in the same house hit him like a body blow.

'Who's this "Crackman" you're on about?'

Mark had returned from the toilet, pale, drained, ill-looking. Christie had mopped up the coke and bought a new one, which Mark used to wash away the taste of his vomit.

'Don't know what you mean.'

'You mentioned him, not me.'

'I don't know,' he said sourly.

'Who is he?' Christie persisted.

'No idea,' Mark said.

'Where does Jonny Sparks fit in?'

Mark jerked his shoulders noncommittally.

Christie shuffled with growing irritation, Mark saw with satisfaction.

'Did you love your sister?' Christie said brutally, out of the blue.

'What sort of question is that?'

'Did you?'

Mark looked down at his hands, his fingers intertwining nervously. He nodded.

'Do you want to find out who supplied her with these drugs – and who therefore murdered her?'

'You know I do.'

'Hurray, well that's a start ... So do I, Mark, and not just because she was your sister, but because whoever did this has also killed at least one other person and if we don't stop him, or her, more people will die. Do you see that?'

185

'Yeah ... and?' he asked helplessly.

'You think Jonny Sparks did it, don't you?'

'Stands to reason. He's a dealer, he was going out with Beth, she was a druggie ... y'know ... two plus two and all that.'

'I think he did it, too,' Christie declared.

'What? Well, he's locked up, isn't he? Has he been charged?'

Christie shook his head and glanced at his watch, frowning. 'He'll be getting out just about now, I guess. He'll be back on the streets soon, after having admitted nothing in interview.'

'Why?' Mark demanded, as though Christie was stupid.

'Because there's a difference between suspecting something and knowing it and proving it. There's no evidence against him as regards Beth.'

'What about dealing on the streets?'

'He's caught bang-to-rights, there, but because we have to have the powder found on him analyzed, which takes time, and because he's a juvenile, he gets released. He'll get reported and be at court sometime in the future, who knows when?'

'So he just carries on like before?' Mark said, aghast. 'Then he goes to court and gets a slap on the wrist?'

'Something like that,' Christie agreed blandly. He was watching Mark intently, weighing him up, judging him. 'Unless...' he added mysteriously.

'Unless what?' Mark asked uncomfortably.

Christie rotated his jaw, squinted thoughtfully, then asked, 'Who's the Crackman?'

'Like I said, I don't know. Look, you're talking in riddles – what the fuck do you want with me?' he hissed.

Christie ignored him. 'If you don't actually know who this Crackman is, who do you suspect he is?'

Mark sighed. His body deflated and, as though he was reciting something boring for a teacher, said, 'I don't know who the Crackman is, OK? All I know is that it's some mysterious guy, some big-time drugs dealer who controls all the drugs sold on Shoreside, and maybe other places, dunno. He's got a network of people who sell for him and as far as I know, none of them even know who he is. That's it, OK?'

'But no name?'

Mark shook his head. 'Could be Troy Costain, possibly,' he ruminated. Costain was one of Shoreside's biggest criminals, one Christie knew well. 'He's a dealer – and everything else, thief, handler...'

Christie nodded sagely. 'And you think Jonny Sparks is one of this Crackman's dealers, whoever he might turn out to be?'

'Pretty sure. Look, come clean with me, eh? I basically know nothing. I don't do drugs, don't go anywhere near them, I don't mix with people who do. I don't steal – well, with the exception of sandwiches – and I go

187

to school every day. Eventually I want to get out of this town, get a decent job somewhere, maybe like Jack ... and that's me. Beth got involved with the wrong crowd and paid the price. It happens. I hardly ever see Mum, who sleeps with just about every guy who gives her a wink, and I'm me. I try to be good. I try my best.'

'Yeah, I really think you do.'

Mark slurped his Coke, stunned he had revealed so much about himself so quickly to a complete stranger – and a cop at that! Must be going soft in the head, he chided himself, although it actually felt quite good to get that off his chest.

'All right, Mark, you've been open with me, so it's time for me to tell you where I'm coming from.'

'This should be fun.'

'Shut it, smart arse,' Christie said with a grin. 'The Crackman exists,' he began after a breath. 'I don't know who he is or where he operates from, though I have some suspicions. It could be Costain, but then again it might not be. Whoever it is, we've been after him for about two years now. He plays his cards very close to his chest, is very careful. He never meets his dealers face to face. As far as I know he operates by dropping off and picking up drugs and cash through various secret locations, like spies used to do with hard copy information and payments in the old days.'

'Dead letterboxes, you mean?'

'Exactly – how do you know about them?'

'I've read John Le Carré.'

'I'm impressed.'

'Don't be – carry on.'

'One dealer who tried to unmask him came a cropper ... six months down the line he's still recovering, but says he doesn't know who the Crackman is – or won't tell. You want to deal with the Crackman, you do it on his terms and don't step out of line – apparently.'

'So nobody knows who he is?'

'Some people do, obviously. And there's some talk of a turf war bubbling. You know what a turf war is?'

'Oh, please!'

'Some dealers are stepping on each other's toes, and the Crackman is involved – but our intel isn't good.' Christie took a sip of the coffee he'd acquired while Mark was in the bathroom and grimaced. 'I know Sparks, had a few run-ins with the little runt, and I'm pretty sure he is one of the Crackman's dealers, too.'

'And?' Mark waited.

'Ultimately the Crackman is the person who is responsible for Beth's death.'

'Even I worked that one out,' Mark said stonily.

'And I've worked out that you want to find out who killed her, hence the little fisticuffs with Sparks. Am I right?' Mark said nothing, but kept his eyes firmly on Christie. 'Not the ideal way of getting a result, if you ask me.'

'No one is.'

'You,' Christie said with a sharp jab of the finger, 'are the closest I've come to nailing the Crackman, which must tell you something.'

'That you're crap at your job?'

Christie scowled, but did not rise to the jibe. 'No, what it says is that he is very difficult to nail.'

'But I don't know him.'

'True.'

'So what are you getting at?' Mark demanded angrily. 'Stop piss-balling me about and tell me.' He had pretty much reached the end of his tether with the cops, and this one in particular. It was about time he came to the point of this conversation, at which moment Mark would tell him where to get off and stick it where the sun don't shine.

Christie clasped his hands on the table in front of him.

'We both want the same thing. You for personal reasons; me for professional. You want justice for Bethany; I want justice to hammer down on the Crackman. The two desires are closely interlinked.' He raised his clasped hands, fingers intertwined with each other. 'Like this.'

'You're wrong, actually. I don't want justice, I want revenge.' Mark glowered coldly at the DCI.

* * *

'Here'll do.'

Christie stopped the car on the road that circled Shoreside. Mark had no wish to be seen being dropped off by the police outside his house, even if it was a plain car. Everybody knew cop cars on the estate, marked or unmarked. He opened the passenger door and swung out his legs. Christie clamped a hand on his shoulder. Mark looked back.

'Think about it. I'll get your bike dropped off,' he said.

Mark gave a quick nod. Christie removed his hand and the young man climbed out and began walking away, no backward glance at the copper, nothing to show he was remotely interested in the proposal which had just been made to him. He just knew that Christie's hard-edged eyes were burning two holes in his shoulder blades.

With a fixed expression, Mark strode home in five minutes.

Home: the empty house. The rooms echoed.

He entered the kitchen. It was back to normal now, after he and Jack had cleaned it up. He gulped, cleared his mind, crossed the floor where Beth's body had lain and, realizing he was now famished beyond belief, heated up a big can of spag bol and put four slices of slightly stale bread through the toaster. With a glass of Vimto, he retreated with his feast up to his room and scoffed until he felt he was bursting. Then, belly full like a lazy lion, he lay on his bed and thought about Henry Christie and their conversation...

'I can't talk in great detail until I know you're up for it and can be trusted,' Christie had explained.

'Up for what?' Mark said guardedly.

'Playing a part ... setting a scene ... pulling a scam, sort of...'

'I don't follow.'

'OK ... I think you've been deeply affected by your sister's death—'

'Yeah, so what?' Mark snapped irritably. 'I think we've covered that, don't you?'

They were on the beach, walking side by side, out of earshot of anyone.

'Hear me out ... you are so devastated that you start going downhill. The clean-livin', good citizen Mark Carter goes right off the rails, which you might already have started to do' – Mark opened his mouth to protest. Christie held up a silencing hand – 'Shush ... you've stolen from a shop, you've publicly assaulted someone, you've been arrested, you're on bail ... and these are things that I think should continue. You need to get arrested a couple more times to secure your street credentials, you need to alienate your mates – for a while, anyway – you need to become someone who has lost it, y'know. Become vulnerable and ready to be manipulated ... and then you need to gain the confidence of somebody you hate; you need to worm your way into them and use them to discover the true identity of the person who killed Bethany.'

Mark soaked it in. 'You mean go under cover and set up Jonny?'

'I mean exactly that. Play it right with him and he'll lead you to the Crackman ... not directly, because we know Jonny doesn't actually know who he is ... but he has ways of contacting him, as we've discussed, and that leaves a trail. Contact is always a weakness.'

'What about his mobile phone?' Mark asked. 'Didn't he have that on him when he got arrested? That would've had the Crackman's number on it, wouldn't it? That would have been a start for you.'

'Good thinking – except Jonny didn't have a phone on him,' Christie told him. 'He's pretty savvy like that. He doesn't deal with a phone on him – and neither did Sam or Eric.'

Mark sneered. 'So are you asking me to be an undercover cop?'

'Sort of.'

'And a grass?'

'Depends on your perspective. Are you a grass or someone out for revenge?'

Laid out on his bed, Mark ran it all through his head repeatedly. It was scary on one hand, exciting on the other. If Mark had two more hands he would have said it repelled him on the third hand and lured him on the fourth.

The thought of helping the police did nothing for him. He had avoided them all of his life and though he didn't dislike them like other kids did, he always knew they were trouble.

But the thought, the possibility, of bringing down Jonny Sparks and the Crackman ... well, how challenging was that?

But so very horrendously dangerous.

'Yeah, it is dangerous territory,' Christie had admitted when Mark put that to him.

'If Jonny Sparks ever found out I was grassing on him, he'd kill me,' Mark said simply, but with a terrifying casual reality. 'That's if I ever even got as far as getting him to trust me. One slip, I'd be dead meat.'

'Always a possibility, which is why you'd have to do things very carefully.'

'And then the Crackman! Jeez! Even if I got past Jonny, then I slipped up, I'd be sold as burger meat down on the prom.'

'I'd protect you all the way,' Christie promised. 'I can't go into detail as to how, but you'd always be covered and this operation wouldn't go on for ever. It'd be time-bound. A few weeks at most. I couldn't ask you to do any longer ... less, if possible.'

★　★　★

Very bloody dangerous, Mark thought, lying on his bed, his mind twisting and turning like a rollercoaster on Blackpool's Pleasure Beach. One foot wrong and he'd be hammered at best, or at worse, dead meat, as he'd said, sold between two halves of a sesame seed bap.

'Thing is,' Christie had said as they headed off the beach towards his car, reading Mark's mind, 'you cannot tell anyone you've had this conversation, because this conversation hasn't happened. If you want to think about what I've said, the only person you can run it past is yourself. You can't have a chat about it to your brother or your mum or mates, because if you do the whole thing will crumble and I'll just deny it. Even if you decide to help, you still can't tell anyone. You have to understand that.'

Mark thought carefully. 'How legal is this?'

'Which bit?'

'Any of it.'

'We use kids as test purchasers, buying alcohol and fags from off-licences who sell to minors.'

'With consent from parents, presumably?'

'Yep.'

'But you want me to do this with no consent at all?'

'Er, yep.'

'Bit of a step up from buying alcopops to nailing a violent drug dealer, isn't it?'

Christie shrugged unsurely. 'Yep.'

195

'Have you got permission to do this?' Mark asked incisively, seeing that the detective was starting to squirm a little. 'Y'know, like, from your bosses?'

Christie pulled at his collar. 'Yeah,' he said unconvincingly.

Mark snorted with disbelief.

'Look, Mark' – Christie stopped and spun to face him – 'whilst this is going on, every normal way of trying to ID and arrest the Crackman will also be going on. This is just in addition to everything else, something extra that might or might not work. You'll be protected every inch of the way and because I'm good at doing this sort of thing, there's no way you'll end up in court giving evidence or even having them suspect you were involved in their downfall. If we do it right, that is. Trust me.'

Mark nearly belly-laughed at that. Trust a cop. Think not.

Back on his bed he laughed again, then got up to go to the toilet. On the landing his laughter faded as the emptiness of the house hit him once again. He peed quickly, brushed his teeth and quickly scooted back to his room, slotting the bolt to lock himself in. He stripped, pulled on his night shorts and slid under the duvet, switching off all but the bedside lamp.

'I wonder if I can do it?' he pondered out loud. 'I wonder.'

Could he endure living a lie? Was he good enough at lying to pull it off in the first place? Did he have the bottle to wear a wiretap? Christie had mentioned this might be necessary. Then did he have the ability to steer conversations in particular directions without the other person realizing he was doing it? Could he put up with having no friends, making them believe he'd gone bad, even if it was only for a short period of time?

He didn't have the answer to those questions, but what he did know was that he would be doing Blackpool a hell of a big favour by bringing down Jonny Sparks and the Crackman.

Fourteen

Other than through an occasional day of sickness, and because of recent events connected with Bethany's death, Mark Carter had never had a day of unauthorised absence from school in his life. Something he was proud of. School was a good place as far as Mark was concerned. A safe place – usually – somewhere he felt he belonged, somewhere to enjoy, make friends, be appreciated and work hard for the future he had mapped out in his head. He intended to stay in education for as long as possible, because the thought of stepping out of its comfort zone worried him a little.

But for the past four days he had not been at school.

It was very strange, playing truant, playing hooky, knobbing off.

At first he rattled around the house, messing about up in his room, watching daytime TV – which he squinted at with a great deal of puzzlement, wondering who on earth actually sat down and seriously viewed it; he kicked a ball round on the street outside, practising keepy-uppies, but he was an enthusiastic but crap footballer and the best he could manage was six before the ball went flying into someone's garden. By midday on the first day, he was bored out of his skull.

It was time to get going and do something constructive.

He wheeled out his bike and set off towards the prom. Once he reached the front he weaved up the pavement between holiday-makers and swerved into the alley behind Tony's Burger Bar, dismounted and fastened the bike to a downspout. He was about to walk off without even talking to Ray when, grease-laden, he appeared from the shop heaving a bin bag full of rubbish into the yard.

'Oi!' he called. Mark stopped in his tracks. 'You did a crap job clearin' up this,' he said, heaving the bag into a huge, lidded skip. Job done, he wiped his dirty hands down his greasy apron, and waved his hands at the tip that was his back yard.

'So?' Mark said.

'No more freebies until you come back and sort it.'

Mark shrugged. 'Yeah, yeah – whatever.'

'Effin' kids,' Ray muttered, turning back towards the business which ensured him a healthy winter suntan every year. Then he stopped and turned back to Mark. 'Should you not be at school?'

'Yeah – maybe ... but when your sister's been murdered, it kinda puts you off that sorta shit, y'know.'

Ray's jaw dropped.

Mark turned, giving him an angry, dismissive gesture by chopping the air with the edge of his hand and walked away.

Ray's face screwed up. He shook his head sadly and thought, Another one bites the dust. Seen bloody thousands.

Mark made a point of not looking back. He had a pocketful of change and he was going to go and either lose it all, or make a killing.

Amusement arcades were fine – in short doses. But spending more than ten minutes in them was driving Mark scatty. They were so utterly boring. What was the attraction in losing your money, just giving it away? His mind was being well and truly numbed by the experience, but he kept at it, moving from arcade to arcade. He saw a few other kids he knew, the ones who were always missing from school, and had passing conversations with some, making sure it was known he, too, was out and about when he should've been at school. He did not link up with any of them, even though the offer was made. Some were going on shoplifting sprees, some going to hang around in flats with some older kids – 'to chill, have a spliff, watch DVDs, maybe get wanked off', one lad confided, scaring Mark a little. He said a quick goodbye to that one. The prospect of going to some perv's flat left Mark feeling cold.

As he drifted, though, he realized quickly how easy it would be to get sucked into this feckless lifestyle and whilst it had no attraction for him, it was apparent that lots of other kids were already in it and may never ever leave it.

Mark shuddered at the thought.

He found himself in one of the biggest slot machine arcades on the sea front, feeding the bandits with ten pence pieces, when he heard a shout. He spun around, but couldn't get out of the way as four lads he didn't know, all about his age, ran towards him, mad, crazy expressions on their faces, throwing themselves down the aisles, like a pack of wild dogs, whooping, yelling, screaming. Two were carrying plastic shopping bags. Mark stepped back tight to the machine he was playing, but even so, two of the lads barged into him, sending him spinning on to all fours. One tripped over him, shrieked an obscenity and dropped the bag he was carrying before getting back up to his feet and legging it behind his mates, leaving the bag behind.

Mark got quickly up, looking around, and there they were – two uniformed cops on foot and in pursuit of the gang. Without hesitation, Mark kicked the plastic bag slyly down the side of the fruit machine, turned back to face it and, as calmly as he could with shaky hands, dropped a coin into the slot and pressed the play button.

Out of the corner of his eye he saw the cops getting closer. They were out of breath. They looked as though they'd been chasing the tearaways for a fair distance, not easy when piled up with all that equipment around their torsos.

'You seen four lads run through here?' one of the cops gasped at Mark.

'Nah.' He dropped another 10p in.

'You sure, lad?' Both cops sidled right up to him, trying a bit of intimidation as, clearly, they didn't believe him. Mark could smell their sweat.

'I'm sure.'

'Why you not at school?'

'On holiday with my family,' he lied glibly.

'Oh – and where are they?'

'There.' Mark pointed to an oldish couple seated in the café adjoining the arcade. 'Me nan and granddad.'

'C'mon.' One cop tugged the sleeve of the other. 'Let's get after the twats.'

The cop who'd asked the questions glared fleetingly at Mark, obviously not a hundred per cent happy, but they were in pursuit and Mark wasn't their prey.

Mark pressed the play button on the machine.

The cylinders rolled then stopped, one by one: click-click-click-click.

Jackpot!

A bucket load of ten pence pieces spewed out of the jaws of the fruit machine.

He played the machine a few minutes longer to make sure that neither the gang of lads, nor especially the cops, returned, and to ensure that no one else had seen him kick the plastic bag down the side of the machine. Then he checked to see if anyone was watching him. Nobody seemed interested. The old couple – his newly adopted grandparents – had gone from the café, which was now empty, and only a few other people were in the arcade. He held his breath, reached down the side of the fruit machine and tried to get the bag. He didn't get it first time and had to stretch – a period of time which could have drawn unwelcome attention to himself – but his fingers got it and, trying to act as naturally as possible, he strolled nonchalantly out on to the prom. A break in the traffic allowed him to cross the road and tram tracks and head to the sea wall, where he leaned on the railings and pretended to gaze out to sea.

He opened the bag.

Inside there was a mixture of stuff: Xbox games, DVDs and CDs – about twenty in total.

All stolen.

In retail price terms there was about £500 worth of goods, all still in their wrappers.

Mark smiled. He wondered how much he

would get for this little lot at Tonno's, the shop where everyone who had anything to fence went.

Mark looked at some of the titles. He would have liked each item for himself, but that was not to be.

By waiting for the right moment behind Tony's Burger Bar, Mark avoided a sticky meeting with Ray, reclaimed his bike and pedalled back through town up to Central Drive on which there were many tacky and sleazy shops of all varieties, including sex shops, shops selling everything for 99p, a selection of iffy takeaways, off-licences and tattoo parlours, and Tonno's – 'Second Hand Goods Bought and Sold'.

Tonno's – the shop that had a reputation for buying and selling anything and everything, no questions asked. It was always being visited by the cops, but somehow managed to stay open and keep trading.

It was a double-fronted premises, with lots of space. Sofas and chairs were stacked in the window display and on the pavement outside was a selection of battered-looking dining room chairs together with an old reclining chair on which Tonno himself usually basked like a fat shark. And there he reclined today. A large, rotund man, strips of wispy hair combed and gel-flattened across his flaking, dandruffy scalp, thick old-man's glasses, and a body dressed in a stained tee-shirt and jeans which always showed his grubby arse-crack when he stood up or bent over. He was drinking from a dirty mug and squinted up at Mark with piggy-podgy eyes.

It was rumoured he was worth a fortune. In reality he lived pretty much hand to mouth, but always had a wad of cash close to hand and contacts to sell anything on.

Mark had heard about him, had only ever ridden past the shop, but never been in or talked to Tonno.

'What?' Tonno demanded, taking a hearty slurp of tea, then wiping his lips with the back of his liver-spotted hand and sniffing up a noseful of phlegm.

'You Tonno?' Mark asked, even though he knew.

'Aye.'

'D'you buy stuff?'

He shrugged a gesture with his hands to indicate the shop front. 'That's what it says – but only clean stuff.'

Mark had the plastic bag hanging from his handlebars. 'I want to sell this lot. It's all my own,' he said defensively. He removed the bag.

Tonno regarded him with contempt. 'I don't know you, do I?'

'So?'

'How do I know it's your stuff? It could be stolen. I don't deal in stolen goods.'

Mark sniggered. 'Crap.'

'Fuck off, then,' Tonno said. He rolled in-elegantly out of the recliner, stood up and tugged his jeans up over his fat arse.

'Hey – you want to buy, or not? Yeah, you don't know me, but it's not like I'm a cop or anything, is it?' He bounced the carrier up and down temptingly.

'Why would you say that?' Tonno asked suspiciously.

'Say what?'

'About being a cop.'

'Dunno, just said it. I'll find someone else if you're not interested.' He started to thread the carrier handle on to the handlebars again.

'Oi! Un-uh,' Tonno waved a finger. 'Let's have a look. Come on in.'

'I want to bring the bike inside. Don't want it getting nicked out here.'

Tonno's big, fatty shoulders rose and fell. 'Whatever.'

Mark pushed the bike in through the shop doorway, propping it against the back of a settee. He scanned the place. It was like entering the Tardis. It was immense, filled with everything imaginable from furniture to bikes, medals to kitchen equipment, DVD players to old style VCRs. There was a counter at the far end of the shop to which Mark trailed behind Tonno, the big man squeezing in behind it and facing Mark.

'What you got?'

Mark placed the bag on the counter. 'Games, DVDs, CDs.'

Tonno peered in and picked out a selec-

206

tion. He chuckled and raised his watery eyes to Mark. He picked up a piece of paper from the countertop and waved it in Mark's face. 'Cops been round ten minutes ago, gave me this list of recently stolen gear. From what I've seen in here, seems to match exactly. Spooky, eh? And they're all yours, hm?'

Impatiently Mark said, 'Buying or not?' He had the urge to grab the gear and leg it, but he knew he had to see this through.

'Cops said I should call them if the stuff turns up.' He sniffed superciliously. 'Seems to have turned up.'

Mark eyed him cynically, said nothing.

There was silence between them as each weighed up the other.

'OK, how much do you want?'

'There's over five hundred quid's worth in here.'

Tonno guffawed. 'New to this game, aren't you?'

Mark felt himself redden. 'And?' he snarled.

'Let me tell you how this works,' Tonno said patronizingly. He lifted all the goods out of the carrier and stacked them into neat piles – games, DVDs and CDs. 'Come off the back of a lorry,' Tonno ruminated whilst casting his greedy eyes over them. He sniffed. 'It works like this ... think of it this way, say: the drugs trade ... heroin, say ... starts with the growers in Afghanistan, then gets passed through the middlemen until it ends up on the streets, yeah? The growers get sod all, but the middlemen and the sellers add on their percentages until the buyers cough up. You, laddie, are a grower. You might be a vital link in the chain, but there's other growers, if you get my drift? Am I making sense?' He raised his bushy, out of control eyebrows and looked meaningfully at Mark.

'In other words, I get what you offer me and be thankful?'

Tonno gave a short nod. 'Something like that.'

'Which would be?'

'Thirty quid, the lot.'

'What?' Mark said, astounded.

'Take it or leave it. As I said, there's other people just like you out there. Stuff like this is easy to get hold of. Bread and butter to me.'

'No chance.'

'Well, go sell it round your schoolmates, then, and see who blabs on you, I don't care. It's hassle-free money for you.'

Mark shook his head. 'One-fifty.'

'You're in a dream world, sonny.'

Mark snatched the bag and began piling the discs back into it.

'Thirty-five,' Tonno upped his offer. 'I know the market ... I'll be lucky to get fifty for this lot myself.'

Mark continued to shove the discs into the bag. 'One-twenty,' he bargained.

'Thirty-seven, final offer.'

'See ya.' Mark grabbed the handles and spun away from the counter. He stalked down the shop to his bike.

'Hey, lad,' Tonno called. 'There is something I'll give you fifty quid for.'

Mark stopped in his tracks, turned slowly, a shiver of dubious anticipation shimmying through him. 'What would that be?'

Tonno's eyes caught his. 'I think you know ... ten minutes at most ... fifty dabs ... what about it?' He made a circle with his thumb and forefinger and jerked it up and down.

'Fuck off you, fat perv,' Mark snarled, grabbing his bike and pushing it hurriedly though the shop door.

He heard Tonno call from behind, 'You'll be back, you little slut. Lads like you need me.'

'Not this one,' Mark muttered. His face was a mask of disgust and he couldn't get his bike to go fast enough to put distance between him and Tonno.

Fifteen

He pedalled furiously until he practically fell off his bike outside KFC on the Prom at South Shore. There was no queue, so he went in and bought a two-piece meal and a Tango orange with his fruit machine winnings. He crossed the road and sat on a bench looking out towards the sea whilst eating the food, settling his nerves as he digested the mini-feast. It had been bad enough trying to sell stolen property, but then to get sexually propositioned by someone who looked like that! And a bloke.

He blew out his cheeks and chomped on his chicken and chips. When he'd scoffed them, he wandered to a public phone box just down the prom and dialled a number he'd memorized. The call was answered immediately and after a short, clipped conversation, he hung up.

The next thing was a matter of timing.

It was a pleasant enough day weather-wise to doss around on the bike and whilst he would have preferred to go down to the quarry with the BMX to do some stunts, there wasn't the opportunity. Instead, after dumping the bag

210

of stolen games and other gear at home, Mark mooched on two wheels round Shoreside and its environs, checking the place out, seeing who was hanging around.

He almost ran slap-bang into Jonny Sparks and his two oppos on one of the estate roads, but they were walking away from him and didn't turn or clock him. He ditched the bike behind a wall, hoping no one would notice and nick it, and played a bit of cat and mouse with them. Eventually they came to rest in the place where Mark had accidentally bumped into them a few days before when Jonny had tried to sell Mark drugs, then decided he wanted the BMX, then got the front wheel rammed up into his goolies. Mark remembered that well. It seemed such a long time ago. Smacking the front wheel into Jonny's nuts had been a sweet sensation.

Mark ducked out of sight and kept surreptitious nicks on Jonny and Co. for a few minutes. It looked like they were settled there for the duration. Mark knew it was a location they liked to hang out in because it was a bit of a crossroads on the estate and plenty of people passed by.

Then, confident they weren't on the move, Mark legged it back to his bike and tried to recall where the nearest phone box was. He could have done with a mobile. It would have made things much easier ... but then again, a mobile could be checked, whereas a public call box could not.

211

The nearest he could think of was outside Aziz's newsagent's and though he didn't particularly want to show his face there, he would have to.

He propped his bike against the phone box and made the call. When he stepped out, Mr Aziz was waiting for him, a glowering look on his face.

Mark's heart sank. 'What?' he asked meanly.

'Where've you been?'

'None o' your business,' Mark replied, feeling dreadful. Aziz had been good to him and behaving like this towards him made Mark feel shitty.

'I know you've got problems, but you should keep me informed. I've a business to run and I've had to do your deliveries myself.'

Mark shrugged, keeping up appearances. 'Tough.' He mounted his bike.

'Mark,' Aziz said plaintively, 'this is not like you.'

I know, Mark thought. I know it's not like me, because it isn't really me.

'I can only keep your job open so long, then someone else gets it. There's plenty of other kids, you know.'

'Do what you have to do.' Mark rose and powered away.

'Don't become like the others,' he heard Aziz shout as he put some distance between them and gulped back a tear.

★　★　★

Mark swore to himself. This was getting a bit too much now – running into people he would rather have avoided – as, out of nowhere, a stony-faced Katie Bretherton stepped into his path and defiantly stood her ground, causing him to brake and swerve at the same time, almost propelling him over the handlebars.

'You nearly bloody—!' he began angrily.

'Nearly what?' she demanded.

'Nuthin'.'

'What's going on, Mark?'

'Dunno what you mean.'

'You got arrested with Jonny Sparks. I saw you get carted away.'

Mark hesitated, said, 'And?'

'What're you doing, hanging around with him?' Katie pleaded. 'I thought you hated him.'

'Nothing to do with you.'

Katie was glaring at him, a mixture of incomprehension, annoyance and frustration. Her hands were shaking. She tried to maintain eye contact with him, but he kept dropping his gaze sheepishly, unable to give her a direct look.

'Yes it is ... and what about us?'

Mark quickly looked her up and down, his young heart fluttering, his breath shallow. She looked really good, stunning, slim, long-legged, boobs and all, skin soft as silk, on the verge of turning into a gorgeous young lady.

A quick memory of her touch made his lower guts stir. God, he just wanted to get hold of her and kiss her and pick up from where they'd left off.

Instead, a sort of disconnected voice came from his mouth. 'What about us?'

Her eyes rolled heavenwards. 'Have you cut me out of your life? You been avoiding me? I thought we were friends ... more than friends.' Her bottom lip quivered. 'Mark, can we at least talk? I know Beth's death has hit you hard, but don't push me out of the way, don't go off the rails.'

Mark forced a horrid sneer on to his face. 'You don't know anything ... I–I can't tell you anything ... Look, just sod off out of the way, eh?'

'Don't do this, Mark,' she said desperately.

'You have no idea what I'm doing,' he said, rising on his right pedal and forcing it down. Katie reached for him. He ducked, avoided her, and sped away, not even glancing back when he heard her call his name.

He held his head up in the wind. He knew if he weakened, he would not be able to do what he had to do. Only when he had done it, would people start to understand and, he hoped, forgive him. He also hoped that Bradley, his best friend, wouldn't suddenly appear from nowhere. He was surprised he hadn't turned up yet as it was.

Jonny was still there, sitting on a low wall

outside the dilapidated Spar shop, Sam and Eric crowded round him, hanging on to his words, laughing uproariously at some crap joke he'd told.

When Mark caught sight of him, he knew Katie had been right.

He hated Jonny.

It was an emotion with which he was uncomfortable. He did not want to hate anyone ... but for what he believed Jonny had done to his sister, he hated him. But he hated the Crackman even more.

His instinct was to turn and fly in the opposite direction. He fought that battle and hoped for the best, taking a deep breath and setting off slowly in Jonny's direction.

He was spotted immediately. Jonny said something out of the corner of his mouth and rose to his feet. All three of them angled toward him, saying nothing, but even from a hundred metres Mark saw the expressions on their faces. It was as if all their dreams had come true and payback time had arrived. Mark was cycling right into their arms and there was nothing to say that Jonny would show any mercy *this* time. Mark was convinced that last time was just a blip.

Each time the pedal went round, Mark intoned the word 'Shit' to himself, repeating it with every beat of his cycling.

He was getting closer and closer.

Fear was starting to grip him now. Icy fear,

215

clawing his innards.

Time seemed to slow right down.

From behind he heard the approach of a vehicle.

'Please, God,' he said.

He was twenty metres from Jonny and the Hyenas and closing. Eighteen metres ... fifteen metres ... Jonny raised the level of his eyes to look beyond Mark, and took a cautious step back ... twelve metres ... still a vehicle coming up from behind ... ten metres now ... please, God ... then the vehicle was alongside Mark, then in front, then it had stopped.

A police van.

Two cops jumped out – the same two Mark had encountered in the amusement arcade, chasing the gang of lads.

Mark yanked his brakes on and screeched to a stop, eyed the cops, then tried to haul his bike away, but the two officers moved on him in a pincer movement.

'We want a word with you, sunshine,' one called.

Out of the corner of his eye, Mark saw Jonny relax, sit back on the wall to watch. He pulled his two buddies back, a restraining hand on each of their arms as one cop came up behind Mark, the other in front.

'Stop right there,' cop number one said. Mark saw that the number on his hi-viz jacket epaulettes was 810 and a name badge on his breast pocket declared he was called

Dave Briggs. He was a squat, muscular and powerful-looking guy, with no hair, a round, cheerful face, but with watchful eyes that intimated years of cynical experience.

'What's up?' Mark asked. He looked nervously around like a trapped dog looking for a means of escape.

'I think you know,' Briggs retorted.

'Nah.' Mark shook his head.

'A lad fitting your description's been into Tonno's trying to get rid of nicked CDs, DVDs and games.'

'Ain't me,' he said cockily.

'And you were the one in the arcade when those lads we were chasing ran through, weren't you?'

'So what?' Mark could see Jonny straining to hear the conversation.

'They dumped their stash with you, didn't they, laddie?'

'Don't know what you're on about.'

Briggs eyed Mark. 'And not only that, the bike's nicked, isn't it?' He nodded down at the BMX between Mark's legs.

Mark was outraged. 'This is my bike and it's not stolen.'

'Yeah, well we checked the frame number on our computer system when you were locked up the other day. This bike was nicked over a year ago from outside a house in Bispham – so you're either the thief, or you've bought stolen property ... whichever, you're coming with us.'

'No way.'

'And we're going to your house to have a look round that on the way to the nick, where I'm sure we'll find those stolen discs.' Briggs leaned into Mark's face. 'Won't we, mate?'

Mark's upper lip reared into a snarl. 'You're so wrong,' he protested.

'And you're so nicked,' Briggs said loudly. 'Suspicion of theft of this bike and handling stolen property – namely those discs that came your way. Now get off the bike and get into the back of the van.'

The other cop, who had been hovering behind Mark, took a firm grip of his left bicep. Mark dismounted, apparently acquiescing to the officers, but without warning, he wrenched free of the grip, ducked low, did a back kick which sent his bike clattering against the police van – and started to run for it.

He'd managed to get maybe three metres when the full weight of the law, literally, crushed him to the ground. Briggs moved a whole lot faster than his bulk suggested he would have been able to do. He dragged Mark down on to his knees, then slammed him face down on to the pavement, knocking all the wind out of him.

'If that's the way you want it to be, sonny – no problems.' His big hands wrestled Mark's arms behind his back as Mark struggled and cursed underneath him.

'Hey, cop! Watch it!' Jonny Sparks shouted. He and his little gang were on their feet, bouncing on their toes, approaching the scene of the arrest, ready to intervene and have a dig at the cops.

Mark twisted his head round, his cheek misshapen as it was crushed against the concrete.

Briggs, the big cop, who had a friendly face, suddenly turned aggressive. 'Don't even think about mixin' it, Sparks,' he warned. He cuffed Mark and dragged him painfully to his feet, one big hand gripping the solid bar of the rigid handcuffs, the other on Mark's shoulder, his fat fingers digging into the flesh. He spun his prisoner round and frogmarched him to the van, whilst the other cop warily eyed the Hyenas with a warning hand wrapped round the handle of his still holstered baton. A clear gesture that, if necessary, it would come out and be used.

The rear door of the van was pulled open, the internal cage door opened, and Mark was shoved in roughly. He staggered to the front, bent double, turned and glared at Briggs, who said, 'Siddown.' Mark complied and perched on the bench seat.

The two cops heaved Mark's bike into the cage as well, slammed both doors shut with a metallic finality and jumped back into the cab, driving quickly away from the scene.

Breathing heavily, wrists restrained, knees sore from being dragged to the ground,

Mark peered out of the rear window of the police van through the steel mesh cage and saw Jonny Sparks by the kerbside, watching with great interest.

Once out of sight and off the estate, Mark leaned back against the side of the van, his head tilted on the metal panel. 'What the hell have I done?' he said stutteringly. 'What the hell have I got myself into?'

Sixteen

'You complete arsehole!'

'Don't, OK?'

'You told me that bike was kosher.'

'I thought it was, OK?'

'But it was nicked.'

Mark shrugged. 'Whatever.'

'And what's the story behind the games and DVD's? How the friggin' hell did you happen to get them in your possession?'

'I found them, OK? By accident.'

Jack Carter, Mark's older, respectable brother, had been going on at him, browbeating him, strutting up and down the carpet, gesticulating angrily, for what seemed an eternity. Mark had pretty much had enough.

'You, my lad, are going down the shitter faster than a greasy rat.' He towered over Mark, hands on hips, head shaking in dismay. Mark looked directly into his eyes once, then looked away. Jack exhaled a long, pissed-off breath, then his body wilted and he sat slowly down next to Mark on the settee. He leaned forwards, elbows on knees, fingers intertwined, his body angled in Mark's direction. 'Look, I know this is a tough time for us all, but you've got to keep yourself together for Bethany's sake. You're better than this, Mark. You're not a thief. I know that.'

'It's all right for you – you're out of this shit hole. I'm stuck in it here by myself. Beth's gone ... Mum's ... *Mum*.' He frowned. 'I'm by myself. Where's big bro when I need him to keep me on the straight and narrow? Eh? Swanning about, doing business with clients.' His head fell into his hands and he stifled a deep sob. Jack's arm slid around his shoulders.

'Yeah, sorry, kiddo. Been all tied up with business, I guess. It's been my escape, in a way. Kept my mind off what's happening and I've obviously forgotten about you in the process. Not good,' he admonished himself bitterly. 'Look, tell you what' – he gave Mark a reassuring, gentle shake – 'after the funeral, then, when you've been sorted by the cops – I mean, they're only going to caution you, aren't they? I can't see you going to court. First offence and all that – so after you've answered your bail and been dealt with, we'll go away, eh? Just me and you. Let's bog off to the Costa del Sol for a week, just us guys. How does that sound, mate?'

Mark raised his head. 'Sounds bloody fantastic, actually.'

'Something to look forward to, eh, when all this bad stuff's over. I've been thinking about buying a place out there, anyway.' He ruffled Mark's hair, bringing a begrudging smile to the young man's face.

'I'd really love that, Jack.'

'Me too. But in the meantime' – Jack tapped his nose with his forefinger – 'nose clean, OK? No more stunts.'

'Yeah, sure.'

Jack's mobile phone rang. He fished it out of his pocket and looked at the caller display. 'Need to get this.' He stood up and left the room.

Mark answered the door.

Bradley stood on the front step. He said, 'Long time, no see.'

Mark muttered something, then looked past Bradley and saw Katie hovering at the garden gate, her arms folded haughtily.

'Well?' Bradley insisted.

'Well what?' Mark's eyes half closed.

'Well let me tell you this, matey' – Bradley poked him in the chest. Mark staggered back a step, knocked off balance at the unexpected assault – 'I don't like thieves and I don't like people who get into fights ... I know you're going through a tough time and you want to have a go at the world, but it doesn't give you the right to diss me and Katie. I thought we were friends – and you turn to friends when the going gets tough, or so I thought. But you've obviously lost your mind ... so don't come crawling to us when you get your sense back, because we're not interested.'

Mark saw tears forming in Brad's eyes. He desperately wanted to say something to his best mate, his best pal. But he knew he couldn't. He had to ride out this storm alone. A casual, thoughtless word would bring it all crashing down and Mark did not want that to happen. He just had to trust that, despite Bradley's rant, these guys were truly his friends and that at the end of it all, they would still be there, whatever was said.

He slammed the door in Bradley's face.

The police had confiscated the bike, making Mark feel like he'd had some vital organ removed. He was lost without it and the only alternative he had was Shanks's pony – walking. A very strange experience, on foot on the estate. He killed time mooching along the roads and footpaths, rediscovering long forgotten short cuts. It was pretty quiet, no one about, and he found himself back at home without having achieved anything.

After filling the kettle, he sat back, waited for it to boil. He liked tea with three sugars and was looking forward to a nice brew in his big, cracked mug.

Before the kettle boiled there was a knock at the door.

Fearing a rematch with Bradley and Katie, Mark dragged his feet sullenly down the hallway and opened the door.

His senses tingled when he saw who was standing there.

Jonny Sparks.

Mark's first instinct was to slam the thing, but Jonny, obviously experienced on the doorsteps of people who didn't want him there, jammed his foot and shoulder in, preventing closure.

'Wait!' Jonny said. Mark thought quick and hard about smacking the door against Jonny, but relented. 'I'm alone, if that's what's worrying you,' Jonny said with a sweeping gesture, proving to Mark that his two stooges, The Kong and Rat-head, were nowhere to be seen. Mark surveyed the area suspiciously. 'I come in peace,' Jonny said earnestly. 'Word of honour, cross my heart and all that shit.'

'Why?'

'Just want to chat, eh? No violence, no fisticuffs.'

'I don't know if I want to talk to you,' Mark said. 'What are we going to talk about? We have nothing in common.'

Jonny gave him a knowing look. 'That's where you're well wrong,' he said, and almost winked. 'We've got loads in common, you and me. We just don't know it.' Jonny looked down the hallway to the steaming kettle in the kitchen. 'You brewing?'

'Aye.' It was said reluctantly. Deep in his chest, Mark's heart was pounding. He imagined this whole thing was like trolling for a fish. Suddenly, when it nibbled the bait and you could feel it on the line, you would have to resist the urge to just yank it in otherwise the fish would be lost. It needed to be allowed to swallow the bait, chew on it – and then! Heave back on the rod and drive the barbed hook into its upper lip so that it could never escape, no matter how much it writhed and twisted.

Trouble was, Mark had never been fishing in his life.

'Four sugars – sweet tooth.'

Mark piled them into Jonny's mug, wishing he could have added a measure of arsenic, stirred, handed it across.

'You need to know something right now, Mark,' Jonny said earnestly.

'What would that be?'

'I didn't give any heroin or nowt to Beth. I'll hold my hand up' – he held up his free hand, palm forward – 'I did give her a bit of weed once, but never anything stronger. I swear.'

Mark regarded him, sipping his tea as he did. 'Why should I believe you? You're a dealer, you were going out with her, she was on drugs ... stands to reason it came from you, don't it?'

'Nah ... not me. Honest.'

'OK, say I believe you – is that why you've come here, to plead innocent?'

'Partly.'

'What's the other bit?'

'I want us to mate around together.'

Mark spluttered his tea and almost dropped his mug. 'You what?'

'I actually like you, respect you.'

Mark's face screwed up in disbelief at the admission.

'No, it's true. You're not frightened of me and there's not many who aren't. The wheel in the balls, for example. You attacking me. Not many would have a go at what you did. I respect that. You're not like them sucky-up gits who trail around after me. I want us to be friends. We're not so different.'

'I wouldn't be sure of that.'

'Nah – you reckon you're all goody-goody, but you fight dirty and you steal. Qualities like I have. And ... I could use someone like you.'

'How?'

'I lost a lot of my market when I got booted out of school. You could pick it up for me ... Mr Clean, the guy no one would suspect. Fucking ideal, if you ask me! And I'm getting hassle from up above.' Jonny jerked his thumb up to the ceiling. 'The boss, y'know? You're in a great position ... and you'd get a percentage ... soon buy another bike with what I'd pay you, from a proper bike shop, even.'

Mark snorted. 'Me and you?'

'Think about it.' He slurped his tea. 'And not only that, I can get top whack for anything you need to sell ... like stolen property, if you know what I mean? And I can lay my hands on virtually anything you might want.'

'How about an iPod?'

'Easy – on the house.'

'How do you know you can trust me?'

'Put it this way – if you ever do the dirty on me, you're dead.' Jonny held out a bony hand. 'Deal or no deal?'

Reluctantly, Mark placed his mug down on a work surface. He did not want to appear too eager just in case Jonny sniffed something he didn't like the reek of. With a slight tremble in his fingers, he took Jonny's hand. Jonny held on longer than he should have done, his eyes beaming a sort of contemptuous victory which made Mark's skin crawl. He wanted to pull his hand away and chuck Jonny out of the house because he was certain that if this went wrong, he'd be in Jonny's debt, and there was nothing more certain ... Jonny would come collecting.

'Don't look so bloody worried,' Jonny said in a way that did not reassure Mark. 'I don't bite.'

Mark eased his fingers out of Jonny's grip and considered the irony of the situation: both thought they had the other one hooked.

Jonny hung around for another hour. They talked about the cops, and Mark's bike, with Jonny loving it that the bike Mark had so jealously guarded, said was straight, was – apparently – stolen. A belief that Mark did nothing to dispel.

'You'll never see that again,' Jonny declared confidently.

'I'll have to start saving – unless I nick another,' Mark said glumly.

'What is the dosh situation?'

'I've got bugger all,' Mark admitted. 'That is why I was trying to sell those games and stuff.'

'Police got 'em?'

Mark shook his head and grinned. 'No, they missed them when they searched the house. Still got 'em.'

'Let me see.'

Mark climbed on to the kitchen sink and reached up on top of a cupboard, his fingers stretching until they found the carrier bag. He jumped down and handed it to Jonny, who appraised the contents. 'Good stuff here. What did Tonno offer you?'

'Forty,' Mark exaggerated slightly.

Jonny winced, then thoughtfully raised his eyes as he calculated things. 'I'll get fifty-five out of him,' he guessed. 'If I give you thirty now, then another fifteen when I sell 'em ... a tenner for me. How does that sound?'

Mark pretended to consider the offer.

'Take it or leave it,' Jonny pushed, 'but I'll throw in an MP3 player, not an iPod.'

'All right,' Mark said slowly.

Jonny reached into his back jeans pocket and eased out a wad of folded bank notes. Lots of them. Mark's eyes widened. He peeled off three tens and handed them across wedged between his first and middle finger. Mark eased the money off him.

Jonny beamed. 'I think we're in business.'

Mark was relieved beyond belief when Jonny eventually left his house and almost collapsed behind the front door after he'd locked it. He felt as though he had just got into bed with Satan.

Seventeen

Mark and Jonny were seen out and about together on several occasions over the next few days and it was disconcerting for Mark suddenly to become Jonny's biggest mate. Only a matter of days before they had been trying to rip out each other's throats.

They didn't get up to much and Mark wondered what Sparks did with all the spare time he had on his hands. Mostly, it seemed, very little. Didn't get up till late then dossed around; Mark was even invited around to Jonny's house where there was no sign of any parents; here they watched DVDs (mostly ultra-violent ones which made Mark squirm), played games on a brand new Xbox 360, ate rubbish, then in the afternoon wandered down to town. Here, with Sam and Eric in tow, they meandered around the arcades, striking poses, looking tough and mixing with the other kids doing much the same thing: bunking off school and living an aimless life with one eye over the shoulder for cops or Education Authority officials.

Mark hated it, but stuck at it. He missed his old life desperately. School. His bike, of course. His mates ... Katie; he was really pining for her and could not rid his mind of the point they'd reached together. Mark wondered if he'd blown it completely with her, or whether he'd be able to pull it back when this was all over.

Yes, he hated it, but he did a damned good job of convincing Jonny that he was born for this life.

Bethany's funeral, which loomed ominously over Mark like a storm cloud for days, put a bit of a dent into this new lifestyle, at least for a day.

On the morning of the event, Jack turned up in the Porsche Cayenne, suited and booted and bearing a suit, shirt, tie and black shoes for Mark, and a sombre new dress for mum. Mark dressed in his new clothes, pulling them on as though he was a death row prisoner getting ready for the trip to the electric chair. They fitted him well. Then, with the others, he waited for the arrival of the hearse and funeral car.

It was the second worst day of Mark's life: sat in the back of a long, black limo with his Mum and Jack, following the hearse to the crematorium.

Shite, he kept telling himself.

Tears began to roll. He could not contain them. He turned to his mother for a hug, but she sat there cold and brittle, staring dead ahead, making no move to take Mark under her arm and hold him tight.

Mark blubbered when he realized that there would be nothing there. He sat bolt upright between his mum and a sombre-looking Jack, trapped his hands between his knees and attempted to get a grip of himself.

He couldn't remember the rest of the morning.

When it was over and they were back home, he retreated to his room and lay on his bed, hands clasped behind his head, staring un-blinkingly at the ceiling, trying to come to terms with the fact that his sister was now just a pile of ashes. Which made him even more determined to finish off what he'd started.

He was out on the streets with Jonny that same evening, knowing that the events of the day had had a bad effect on him. He was on the lookout for trouble and if trouble found him, it had better bloody well watch out.

Jonny picked up on Mark's dark mood with an amused pleasure and went with it because he could sense Mark's wildness and knew something would come of it.

Mark, Jonny, Sam and Eric barged their way around the arcades in the town centre, an air of violence emanating from the way in which they entered a premises and stalked through it. Like hungry hyenas. Smirks of superiority on their faces. Pushing for a fight. Hoping someone would stand in their way, or give them a dirty look.

No one did.

Everyone shied respectfully out of their way. No challenges, no disrespect tonight.

Underneath the façade, though, Mark was unhappy. Yes, this was his true mood. He was angry and frustrated and at that moment in time he hated the world and wanted to lash out, but the truth was that everything inside him was really directed at Jonny, although he did not allow that to show. He had to keep that in check, but a big part of him wanted them all to get into a fight which they couldn't win, one in which Sparks would get the hammering he deserved without Mark blowing his cover.

But it was unlikely to happen.

Jonny breezed through everybody. His fearsome reputation made them step aside and cower. No one would be taking them on tonight.

They'd gravitated to a cheapo greasy-spoon café near the Winter Gardens. Over Cokes, they had been laughing at the patheticness of every wimp in town, and wondering what to do later that evening, when Jonny got the call on his phone. The ringtone, as ever, 'Boulevard of Broken Dreams' by Green Day. Mark's favourite. He cringed.

Jonny suddenly became businesslike – just like on the day he'd got the call when he and Mark had faced each other over the BMX.

Mark sat back, tried to act natural and pretend he wasn't interested.

It was obviously an important call. Business.

'Need to get this,' Jonny said. He stood up and left the other three sitting at the cracked, Formica-topped table. Jonny walked out of the caff and took the call on the street. Mark watched him discreetly whilst at the same time trying to give the impression he was interested in the dumb-arse ramblings of Sam and Eric who, in truth, struggled to sling two coherent sentences together. They really needed schooling, Mark thought sadly. He'd learned neither could really read or write and their futures looked bleak. He'd also learned that Jonny *could* read and write, which put him one step up the evolutionary ladder from his mates. Perhaps made him a chimp. That said, Mark believed that Jonny was canny enough underneath his toughness to have a better future than the one already mapped out for him, if only he could see it.

Mark slyly eyed Jonny on the phone. It was a phone call during which Jonny did most of the listening. A few nods, some monosyllabic responses.

'Bet it's the Crackman,' Eric said suddenly.

'Eh?' Mark turned to him – too quickly – then tried to disguise his interest by taking a swig of his Coke. He needn't have worried. Neither goon saw his body language.

'On t'phone.' Eric put his thumb to his ear,

235

little finger to his mouth in the well-known gesture to imitate a phone.

'Who's the Crackman?' Mark asked dumbly.

'Don't effin' ask me. I dunno,' Eric said.

'And that's the Crackman on the phone, is it?'

'Er … probably, that's his ringtone I think,' Eric said dumbly, losing interest in the conversation. He had started cracking his knuckles one by one, loudly, by bending his fingers right back. Mark winced and felt queasy.

Then Sam joined in, making a stereo, knuckle-cracking symphony which was weirdly in tune, giving Mark the perfect excuse to get up and walk away with an 'Ugh!' on his lips.

Jonny's phone call ended. He was about to return inside as Mark shouldered his way out of the door and met him.

'Those two are going to have arthritis big style when they get older,' Mark said disgustedly.

'Knuckle-cracking?' Jonny said knowingly.

'Yep.'

Jonny raised his right fist and, using the palm of his left, spectacularly cracked his knuckles, one by one, like dry twigs snapping. Then he laughed.

'Whatever.' Mark raised his hands in submission. 'Was that business?' he asked innocently.

236

Jonny ran his eyes over Mark. 'What's it to do wi' you?'

'Sorry, mate – just asking. Those guys said it was the Crackman.'

'Pricks!' Jonny uttered. 'Big-mouthed pricks.'

'Hey, hey, no need to get riled.' Mark used his hands in a calming gesture. 'No big deal. I don't know owt, OK? I'm not prying.'

Jonny's eyes blazed, then the fire went out of them and the expression he gave Mark was one of serious consideration. 'Maybe it's about time you started earning your keep.'

'What d'you mean?' Mark kept the excitement out of his voice as best he could.

'OK,' Jonny relented, 'that was the Crackman.' He held up his phone. 'You know about the Crackman, don't you?'

'Only by reputation. Don't know who he is.'

'Nor do I.'

'Yeah, right. You deal for him, don't you? You distribute for him, don't you?'

'Don't push it. I don't know who he is and I don't want to know. I got recommended by a friend of a friend, got a call, then took it from there. The rest is history.'

'But you don't know who he is?'

'Nah.'

'He must know who you are.' Mark desperately wanted to ask about the phone, but couldn't think how to phrase a question so that it seemed innocent ... but then Jonny

237

seemed to sense what was going on in Mark's head and was suddenly suspicious.

'Hey – why all the questions? You an undercover cop or summat?'

'Don't be thick,' Mark responded. He knew it was a question that might come at some time and had rehearsed his reaction to it. Was it a good enough reaction, though? Or did his body language leak the truth? 'You're the one who wanted to mate about with me, remember?'

'In fact, thinking about it, I need to check,' Jonny said warily.

'How do you mean?'

'Better safe than sorry. Maybe I've already said too much.'

'What?' Mark's face was screwed up in puzzlement.

'You wearin' a wire?'

'A what?'

'A wire, y'know? Like summat that records what we say, what I say.'

'Am I fuck!' Mark said, uttering a word he detested, but which Jonny used with abandon. All part of the game plan.

'Well let's check it out, then,' Jonny said. He pushed Mark in the chest, back inside the greasy-spoon, gesturing to the Hyenas that he needed some help here.

Jonny manhandled him into the gents' toilets, Mark's face red, angry, his breath coming hard. Eric and Sam followed, eagerly wondering what the hell was going on, but gladly along for the ride.

'Eric – door,' Jonny barked.

'Eh?'

'Guard the door. Don't let anyone in,' Jonny shouted at him whilst pinning Mark against the wall next to the washbasins. Sam checked all the stalls, found them empty. Not that anyone in their right mind would have willingly sat on any of the cracked, reeking toilets.

'This is stupid,' Mark said, nostrils flaring.

'It's only stupid if I don't find a wire,' Jonny came back at him. 'So if I don't, you can call me stupid, OK?'

Sam completed his bog search, came and hovered by Jonny's shoulder. 'All crappers empty,' he reported back.

Mark looked at Jonny and saw in him the true feral monster he really was. Not the big mate he'd been pretending to be. This guy, even though he was only fourteen, was a truly hardened criminal, in a league of his own. His personality changed on a whim, and Mark guessed this is what they meant when they talked about psychopaths. Charming one minute, breaking your friggin' head the next and laughing while they did it – and maybe killing people by plying them with drugs.

To put it bluntly, Mark, slammed hard against a graffiti-covered wall in a toilet in the back of a shit-hole café, was terrified, even though he knew Jonny would find nothing.

'Take your jacket off and give it to Sam.'

With his lips snarling, Mark did as he was told, peeling off his denim jacket and handing it across to Sam, who went through the pockets and inspected the stitching. He found some cash, nothing else.

'Now the shirt.'

Mark removed his short-sleeved tee-shirt with a breast pocket in which was clipped the MP3 player Jonny had given him in a moment of generosity. Sam searched it, found nothing incriminating.

'Just this,' Sam said, holding out the MP3 player, which Jonny took. He turned it over in his fingers and held it up to his mouth.

'Hey – can you hear me, pig bastards?' he screamed at it, making Mark jerk. He handed it back to Sam. 'This is the one I gave him, it's OK.'

'Turn around and face the wall. I want to see your back.'

Mark did as instructed, his nose inches from a felt-tip scrawled, *'All coppers are bastards'*. At that moment, he could not have agreed more with the sentiment.

'OK, turn back and drop your keks.'

'No chance,' he said, defiantly facing Jonny, teeth gritted.

Jonny looked eye to eye with him. Mark noted the line of wispy bum fluff growing over Jonny's top lip. And his blackheads. And his zits, their creamy heads ripe for popping.

'Do it, or I'll cut you.' Suddenly there was a click and in his hand was a flick knife, which he held up to Mark's left eye.

A beat.

The point of the knife was only a centimetre from Mark's eyeball.

Mark unbuttoned his jeans, pushed them down and stood there with them around his ankles, just his boxers on.

Jonny's eyes dropped to Mark's hairless body.

'See,' Mark growled. 'Nothing.'

At which point Jonny burst into laughter and Eric bundled the clothes back into Mark's arms.

'No hard feelings, mate?' Jonny had easily reverted back to the big-hearted friend again, laughing off the intrusion he'd made into Mark's privacy.

Inside, Mark still shook, his guts churned and his lungs dithered as they expanded and contracted. Outwardly, he hoped he exuded confidence and a bit of street savvy. He wasn't completely sure how to deal with the situation and he hoped his reaction was the right one.

The four of them were walking down the prom. Jonny had wrapped his bony arm around Mark's shoulders. Mark shrugged him off and turned angrily to him, so they were face to face.

'Just what the fuck were you hoping to find?'

'Can't be too careful in this business.'

Mark sneered. 'You think I'm a grass?'

'Like I said,' Jonny responded playfully, 'call me stupid.'

Mark's mouth snapped shut as he held back the urge to do that, only because he knew if he did call Jonny names, he'd just get angry again. Even when Jonny invited you to call him stupid, you would have to be a fool to take up the offer.

'Look – it's a good lesson for you. Trust no bugger.' Jonny raised his eyebrows. 'Anyway, what's done is done. We got over it and now we're out the other side. You want to start earnin' some dosh? Need a new bike, don't you?'

'Yeah, yeah I do.'

They were in McDonald's opposite central pier. Generous Jonny bought them all more Cokes, then he and Mark slid into one of the booths by the window whilst Sam and Eric went to another table, keeping nicks, as Jonny and Mark talked.

It was obvious the two big lads were nothing more than hard men and gofers. Jonny seemed to keep them well out of the loop of his business dealings. They were his muscle, his enforcers, nothing else.

They faced each other across the table.

'Before I got excluded, I ran the whole of

the drugs trade in that school,' Jonny opened up. 'One or two others were dabbling, but I took care of them.'

'How?'

Jonny gave him a withering look. 'Remember Paul Eaves?'

Vividly, Mark thought. Paul Eaves, tough nut troublemaker. He had ended up being beaten up in odd circumstances, with no witnesses. It had been a brutal attack and he'd ended up with a broken arm amongst other serious injuries. The story was that his attackers had beaten him up at the side of the road, then laid his arm on the edge of the kerb and stamped on it, breaking it in five or six places. He'd been repaired with lots of bits of steel and nuts and bolts, but would never have full use of his arm again. Jonny saw these recollections whizzing through Mark's brain.

'I did the arm,' Jonny said simply. 'Stamped on it like a twig.'

Suddenly Mark's throat went dry. He sucked on his straw and knew then, if he hadn't known before, that he was out of his depth. This guy, this fourteen-year-old sitting opposite, coolly sipping a fizzy drink, maimed people for life if they got in his way.

'Tony Wright?' Jonny said.

'Shit,' Mark gurgled. Another one who'd come to serious grief. He'd been flattened by a stolen car, had only just survived and never been seen at school since.

'Both muscling in. Had to get rid. On the Crackman's instructions, of course.' More Coke disappeared up Jonny's straw. 'You got to understand there's a lot at stake, here ... I mean, how many kids go to our school?'

Our school? Mark thought. That's a bit rich coming from you. He didn't say it. 'About thirteen hundred.'

'See! Big market, big money. On a bad week, say five hundred quid.'

'Jesus!' Mark's eyes opened, literally and metaphorically. He simply had no idea of the extent of the drugs trade that went on. He knew it happened, but had no conception of its size.

'And then I have the estate and I control a couple of the arcades, too. My patch,' he said proudly. 'You work it out.'

'Bloody hell.'

'Money for old rope. I mean, don't get me wrong. I get a percentage and the rest goes upwards to the big guy. From my percentage I got to pay my runners, like those two idiots, Bill 'n' Ben, the Flowerpot Men.' He thumbed at Sam and Eric, both hysterically knuckle-cracking again and not keeping nicks like they should have been. 'But I need someone with a bit of nous to get back into the school because the bastards won't let me in again. I can only do so much from the gates. You'd be ideal, mate. A goody-goody who'd never be suspected in a million years. Piece of piss.'

'I'm up for it,' Mark said seriously, hoping he hadn't jumped too quickly.

'Glad to hear it ... but first' – he sucked on his straw and made a noise like a drain – 'you need to do some errands for me, just to show willing, like.'

Eighteen

He didn't look back. Just turned out of McDonald's and went for it, needing to get away, needing to get his head together, wondering – not for the first time – just what the hell he'd got himself into. He knew it wouldn't be the last time he wondered that either.

Two hundred metres south of the restaurant, he stopped and looked into the window of a shop selling rock and other teeth-rotting sweets. He pretended to look, anyway. In reality he was checking to see whether or not he'd been followed. It would not have surprised him to see one of Jonny's Flowerpot Men ducking and diving behind him. After all, this was his first assignment, and whatever Jonny might say, he would remain highly suspicious of Mark until the job was done without any hitches.

No one seemed to be there.

Mark walked on quickly and turned left into Yorkshire Street, then increased his pace even more – almost, but not quite, legging it, wishing like hell he had a mobile phone. Was he the only kid in the world without one? He had never really seen the point of them until now – because he needed to make an urgent call and standing in a bloody telephone box in broad daylight was asking to get spotted.

He dinked quickly through the streets, weaving his way on to Lytham Road, which ran more or less parallel with the prom. Here he found a phone box which worked and quickly tabbed in the number he had memorized.

It was answered on the second ring.

'I need to talk,' Mark uttered. 'Now.'

The car was there within five minutes. Mark, who had been hovering like a burglar casing up a joint, was glad to throw himself through the back door, which had been opened for him, to prostrate himself across the back seat.

'Keep your head down,' said the man at the wheel as he accelerated away.

Mark didn't need telling twice. He lay face down in the leather upholstery and covered his head with his hands, wishing the world would open up wide and swallow him whole.

'I don't have much time,' Mark ranted. 'This is insane. I'm not sure I can do this. In fact I know I can't do this. These are dangerous people. They are wary people. If I let anything slip, I'm dead. I swear it, I'm dead – or worse, a bleedin' cripple for the rest of my life.'

DCI Christie, the man responsible for getting Mark into this mess, let the boy have his say without interruption.

'And as for this!' Mark ripped the MP3 player out of his pocket and dangled it in front of Christie's face. 'You can keep it. You know what they did? Eh?'

'No.'

'Made me strip to see if I was wearing a wire. The only place they didn't search was my arsehole.'

He shook the MP3 player under the detective's nose. 'And the thing is – I was wired! With this, wasn't I?'

Christie looked at the MP3 player, the one Jonny Sparks had given to Mark and which the police Technical Support Unit had opened up, then replaced its innards with some new gubbins which turned it into a voice-sensitive recorder with the capacity to hold over three hours worth of conversation at the touch of the 'on' button.

'I'd've looked well good if he'd wanted to listen to Green Day, wouldn't I? I'd've been stuffed – probably into a mincing machine. Jonny Sparks makes the Godfather look like Santa.'

'But they didn't find it, did they?' Christie shrugged. 'Didn't even suspect it.'

'That is not the point.' Mark shook his hands angrily as though he wanted to wring Christie's neck with them.

'Can I just say something, Mark? I've been

there. I know what it's like and it's nerve-shattering ... but the thing is this – you came through it unscathed. With shining colours. You held your nerve, and that's brilliant. OK, it's only right to let off steam, only natural, but just think what you've achieved in such a short space of time.'

After having picked Mark up, Christie had driven them to Fairhaven boating lake on the sea front at Lytham and they were walking around it, stepping carefully over duck and goose shit.

'It's going well,' Christie cooed soothingly. 'You've got results already. He trusts you and now he's given you a job to do.'

'Which I'm not happy about.' Mark was so charged up he was almost dancing on the spot.

Christie stopped, turned to him and laid two hands on his shoulders. 'Calm down. This'll all be over soon – and then you can walk away from it.'

'Pardon me for being cynical.'

Christie chuckled. 'Trust me.'

'You mean like in, trust me I'm a cop?'

'So you're going to carry on?'

Mark took a breath and got a grip. 'Suppose so.'

'Good lad ... once you've identified the Crackman, we'll work out some sort of exit strategy for you so that you can bow out without anyone suspecting you of anything – promise.'

'And that strategy would be?'

'Er ... not quite sure yet. Depends on how the whole thing pans out.'

'That's reassuring – not!'

'Don't worry.'

Mark eyed Christie and shook his head. 'I'm only doing this for Beth.'

'I know you are.'

'So drop me off somewhere and I'll go and collect this package. Knowing my bloody luck, there'll probably be a gun in it.'

He was sweating heavily as he turned in to Ashburton Road in North Shore and found the address he'd memorized – one of many similar houses on the street, converted into a rat-run of seedy flats. There was a panel of doorbells by the front door, each with a name sticker on; at least, they'd all had name stickers on at some time and they were all now either scratched away to obscurity or had been ripped off. He knew he wanted flat number three, but didn't know which button referred to it.

Instead he tried the big, paint-peeling front door. With a push, it creaked open and he stepped into the ground-floor hallway.

The place reeked. Mark instinctively covered his nose. Urine, vomit, shit – a nice combination of odours. Not a million miles away from the way the cells had stunk at Blackpool nick.

Underfoot, the soles of his trainers stuck to

the bare carpet.

Flats one and two were at this level. He went upstairs and found number three on the first-floor landing. There was no one around, but he could hear sounds of habitation through the doors. Music. Shouting. A kid skriking. He hesitated, then knocked timidly and waited. No one came. The baby, somewhere else in the building, cried even louder. Standing in the dingy, dank landing made Mark feel vulnerable. He knocked again, harder, wanting to get this over and done with. This time he heard movement from inside. Footsteps approaching. Mark braced himself as he heard someone on the other side of the door. A key turned, a bolt slid back with a metallic crack. The handle twisted and the door opened a fraction, a thick security chain hanging in view and an eye inspecting him.

'I've come for the package,' Mark whispered the words he'd been told to say.

'What?'

'The package – I've come for the package,' he said more audibly.

The door slammed shut, making Mark jump. Then nothing. Mark considered doing a runner, but hovered uncertainly by the door. After a good two minutes, the door opened again and this time the chain was slid off. A hand bearing a big, padded envelope, A4 size, shot out. Mark took it, the door closed.

He headed back down the stairs immediately.

The envelope was thick, heavy, bulky and fastened securely with masses of parcel tape wound round and round it.

Now, Mark knew, he was on a timer.

'Once it's in your hand, you've got exactly fifteen minutes to deliver,' Jonny had told him. 'As soon as you've got hold of it, a phone call is made and the person you're supposed to deliver it to will be counting. One minute over – mission aborted. You're dead on the street. But don't worry, fifteen minutes is plenty time.'

Mark ran, and then, as instructed by Jonny, went to a nearby phone box and placed a call to a number Jonny had made him memorize, not being allowed to write it down under pain of death. 'C'mon, fuck!' he breathed. The phone was answered and an undistinguishable male voice gave him an address that he had to repeat. He hung up and started running. Twelve minutes to make it – and that included another stop on the way – into Henry Christie's waiting car on Dickson Road.

He jumped in, kept his head down and recited the address to Christie who was at the wheel – then almost jumped out of his skin when a voice from the back seat said, 'Give me the parcel, lad.'

'Jeez!' Mark almost laughed. He handed the envelope over and saw some sort of cool hi-tech contraption on the seat next to the guy in the back. It looked like a portable grill. There was also a laptop computer hitched to it.

'That's John, my technical support guy,' Christie explained, jerking his head.

'And this, in case you're wondering, is a portable X-ray machine,' the officer called John said proudly. 'And as you can't obviously open the package and reseal it without giving the game away, we'll have a clandestine look instead.'

He placed the envelope inside the mouth of the machine, the bit that looked like the grill, and pressed a few keys on the laptop.

'Don't we need some protection or something?' Mark said worriedly. He'd once had an X-ray on a bust wrist and remembered everyone else getting behind lead screens and loads of warning signs about radiation and stuff.

'I have,' John, the tech-man said, tapping something on his chest like a bullet-proof vest, then pulling a ski mask down over his face. 'You don't need anything, though. The rays are pretty weak.'

He tapped the 'enter' key. There was a bright flash of light from inside the machine, then an A4 size sheet of plastic spewed out of the top of it, which he held up to the light. Mark immediately saw what was in the envelope.

'It's a pistol and two spare magazines and

a lot more spare bullets in a bag,' John said to Christie.

Up to that point Christie'd been concentrating on his driving, but the news caused him to swerve and swear simultaneously.

'This is what is known as an ethical dilemma in the trade,' Christie said. 'Do we let you deliver this gun and ammunition, thereby taking the chance that someone could get killed? Or do we seize it now and put you in danger? Hm?' Christie touched his chin contemplatively. 'Which is the lesser of the two evils, and does the bigger picture count more than the little one?'

'You're going to have to make up your mind real soon,' Mark said quickly, 'otherwise I'm dead anyway. I've got six minutes to get it delivered!'

'I know,' Christie said tetchily, his mind obviously racing.

'Shit – come on, man,' Mark urged him.

Christie blew out his cheeks, decision made: 'Deliver it.'

The address was just off Talbot Road near the town centre, another building with a rat-run of flats. This time he was after number six, top floor. He knocked hard this time and as soon as the door opened, he thrust the parcel through and legged it as fast as his legs could manage.

Next thing he had to go and meet Jonny

Sparks again outside the entrance to North Pier. He had half an hour before this and spent this time walking quickly through the town, trying to pull himself down from the heights of panic.

He had just delivered a gun and bullets to someone, though he wasn't supposed to know that.

But he did know.

And he knew the muck he was in was creeping inexorably upwards. Soon it would be filling his wellies. Next stop it would be lapping around his chin, just before he sank and drowned in it.

'Good job,' a beaming Jonny Sparks remarked, handing Mark a screwed up £10 note, the fee for the delivery. Mark took it. It was the least he deserved. 'No hitches?'

'Nah.'

'Sure?'

'Yep – sure.'

'You didn't peek?'

'No, I didn't, OK?'

'Fine, fine.'

'I need to get home,' Mark said – but didn't add it was in order to lock himself in his bedroom, where he planned to curl up in a ball and stick his thumb in his mouth and cover his head with a pillow.

'Why, what's there for you?'

'Just need to get home.'

'I never hardly go home.'

'Well, that's up to you, but I'm going.' He turned. 'See ya.'

Jonny grabbed his arm. 'No you're not.'

Mark spun back and shook Jonny's grip off his bicep. 'Why?'

'We have things to do, you and me.' His eyes were challenging. 'You work for me now, Mark Carter. I tell you where and when you can go and right now, you're staying with me.'

Mark's bottom lip drooped open as his eyes surveyed Jonny. He closed his mouth, which became a tight line of anger, and realized the power Sparks possessed, the fear he engendered, and how, just by delivering something for him, he had come under Jonny's control.

Mark swallowed dryly. He set himself firm, then nodded. 'OK,' he said quietly, bringing a wide smile of triumph to Jonny's cruel, mean, rat-like face.

'Let's go chill.'

Nineteen

They were in town, the four of them. Big mates, big pals, cruising, brushing people out of the way, Mark playing the part of the tough guy as well as the other three. Intimidating. Scaring.

In one of the arcades, Mark spotted Bradley and Katie playing the machines. His heart seemed to stop, yet there was a pounding in his head at the sight of his best friend and his girlfriend having a good time together. They were standing side by side at one of the bandits and Katie was leaning casually on Bradley, her hand resting on his shoulder in a curiously intimate gesture, laughing along with him in a way which had Mark's nostrils flaring angrily. Deep inside, something moved. Jealousy.

Jonny's quick eyes caught what Mark was seeing. He laid a hand on Mark and pulled him to one side.

'You shagged her yet?'

'Eh? No,' Mark said, affronted.

'She's your girlfriend, though.'

'Uh, yeah, suppose so ... was.'

'And he was your best mate?'

257

'Yeah.' Mark shot a snarling look at them, playing oh-so-nice and friendly, Kate's hand still on Brad's shoulder. At that moment, Mark considered walking away from all this. Telling Christie to shove it. Telling Jonny Sparks to eff off, and taking the flak from them both. He just wanted to walk up to Brad and Katie and explain everything, make it all OK again. And get Katie in his arms.

Then the feeling passed.

He was in this predicament for Bethany – and if it meant losing a friend or girlfriend, then so be it. When it really was all over and they knew what it had all been about, then if they were truly his friends, they would understand and it would all be OK. If they didn't want to understand, then they weren't real mates in the first place. He'd find others...

What was it Christie said ... something about the bigger picture?

'Yeah,' Mark snorted, back in role, 'was.'

'Look at me,' Jonny ordered and Mark looked into his eyes. 'I'll personally break his arm for you, if you want.' It was said in such a matter-of-fact manner that Mark almost reeled away in shock. Jonny meant every word. 'Drag him to the kerb and stamp on it, like I did Paul Eaves. Breaks like celery.'

'No, he isn't worth it.'

'Did she ever wank you off?' leered Jonny.

'No, she didn't.'

'I think I might have a crack at her if you're not interested,' Jonny declared, and looked across at Katie. 'Nice girl, getting nice tits.'

It was all Mark could do not to launch himself at this sick, violent bastard and pound him to a pulp. What stopped him, as much as anything, was the knowledge that Katie would probably do the same if Jonny made any advances toward her.

Jonny eyed Mark shrewdly.

Mark could see this was another loyalty test and if he reacted badly, it would be the end of him and Jonny. 'Whatever.' Mark shrugged. 'Can we just get out of here for now, eh?'

As the gang quit the arcade, Mark didn't notice Katie looking over in his direction. He did not see the sadness in her eyes, nor the sigh she took; nor did he pick up the desperate telepathic messages she was trying to send to him. Mark neither saw nor felt any of these things as he and the three others tumbled back on to the streets that evening.

Nor did he notice that someone was following the gang.

The 'things to do, you and me' as promised by Jonny Sparks turned out to be nothing more than simply bumming around. Mark was getting more and more frustrated as the evening dragged on ... but just after eight, Jonny got a call on his mobile.

It was the Crackman, Jonny's mysterious

boss. Mark could tell by the ringtone and he wished Jonny would use another ringtone to announce an incoming call from the devil himself. He hated that his favourite tune was being used for such a thing.

Jonny held up a hand to keep the others quiet, then stuck the hand over his ear and bent to listen whilst edging away so no one else could hear.

Mark and the Flowerpot Men, as he had now permanently named them, watched Jonny with anticipation.

They were on Church Street in Blackpool, opposite the Winter Gardens complex. It was busy, lots of traffic, lots of people. Mark glanced across the road and the billboard announced that the Counterfeit Stones were appearing in the theatre that night. That meant nothing to him.

Jonny was still in deep conversation. Even though the words could not be heard, Mark sensed something was not quite right.

Eventually Jonny came off the phone, approached them wiggling his fingers to indicate he wanted them to gather round. He suddenly looked haggard and worried.

'Wor is it, J?' Sam grunted.

'Bad news, guys.'

Mark tensed up.

'Very bad news ... one of his dealers' – and by 'his', Jonny meant the Crackman – 'has been attacked up in Bispham. Been flattened by a car – and it doesn't look good.'

'Shoulda watched where he were going,' Eric ventured.

'Tit!' Jonny sneered. 'It were deliberate. Somebody run him over, tried to kill him.'

'Oh.'

'That's not all.' He paused for effect, having got their undivided attention. 'Another's been shot at in Fleetwood ... missed, like ... a drive-by ... looks like there's a turf war starting and we need to get off the streets. We could be targets, too.'

'And what's the great Crackman doing about it?' Mark asked cynically.

'Sortin' it, OK? But we need to move. We could be next,' he said dramatically and a little scarily.

They hurried across town and up to Shoreside on foot. Mark's mind whirred, wondering what the hell it all meant. Turf war? He knew what such things were and not long ago, although it seemed a distant memory now, he'd witnessed a drive-by shooting. His thoughts stopped abruptly and his eyes narrowed, but he still kept up with Jonny and Co. Surely not, he thought.

'Come on, nearly home,' Jonny urged. He had obviously been rattled by the news from the Crackman and was desperate to get holed up. Even though Mark was also a bit scared by the warning, he secretly revelled in seeing how it affected Jonny. He was shit-scared by it and the way in which he'd set off across town with the others at his heels doing their best to keep abreast of him, was almost comical.

Mark jogged up and came alongside him.

'Did he say anything else?'

'No, just that he was sorting it.'

'What's that mean?'

'He's got lieutenants, I think. Guys who do the real rough stuff for him. They'll be workin' hard tonight. Reckon there'll be bloodshed.'

'Shit,' Mark gasped, not happy that he was now linked to the Crackman. Not happy at all.

It took twenty pretty hard minutes to get up to Shoreside and all four of them were knackered by the time they reached the row of shops on the edge of the estate, the row behind which was the car park where Mark had attacked Jonny, where Jonny had been arrested for pedalling drugs.

'Made it,' Jonny said happily.

Two good words, making all four of them feel better and safer. The town centre might well have been their stomping ground, but Shoreside was their home and even Mark felt secure here, as much as he disliked the place. The town was an ambiguous place; Shoreside, on the other hand, had its boundaries. The town could throw up nasty surprises; Shoreside was under their control.

There was a chippy in the row of shops.

Jonny's bravado had returned now and he

said, 'Bag o' chips each, I'll buy,' magnani-
mously.

'Great,' enthused Eric.

'I'll have that,' said Sam.

'Cheers,' said Mark, still desperate to get
home.

'We can crash at Eric's place,' Jonny said.
'It'll be empty, won't it?' – Eric nooded in
agreement – 'We can watch *Tokyo Drift* on
DVD.'

'Yeah,' Sam said, well up for it.

Jonny turned to Mark. 'You?'

'Yeah, OK.'

'Good man.' Jonny whacked him on the
back. 'Chips all round.'

They had them in a tray each, covered in
viscous, but fabulous curry sauce, and ate
them with two-pronged wooden forks – and
gusto. They tasted fantastic, especially after
the tiring haul across town. A few minutes
were spent standing in the light from the
chippy window before they set off walking,
going to the end of the shops and across the
unlit, litter-strewn car park towards Songthrush Walk to cut on to the estate proper.

Suddenly the darkness of the night seemed
to envelop them.

Suddenly it seemed a long way from the
back of the shops to the alley.

Suddenly they all instinctively put on a
spurt.

The shadows were dark, very, very black.

As they approached the mouth of Psycho

Alley, the shadows were no longer still. They moved. Three black shadows came towards them and Mark knew they were in big trouble. This was an ambush.

It happened quickly, faster than anything he had ever experienced. It also happened quietly.

It was over in seconds, yet Mark's brain recorded everything in minute detail because as soon as he knew it was an ambush, his senses heightened and suddenly he could see everything more clearly in the darkness, hear everything with amazing clarity and feel his own terror coursing through his veins.

Three of them. Emerging from the shadows. Like Ninja warriors. All in black. Ski masks with eye-holes. Black wind-jammers, black jeans, black trainers.

Mark's head jerked and he looked from Jonny, to Eric, to Sam. They were still engrossed in stuffing their faces with chips and curry. Not even a flicker that anything was amiss. They were on home territory, so they thought they were safe and sound.

The black shapes burst silently out of the shadows where they had been hiding.

Mark tossed his banquet away, opened his mouth to give a warning. No sound came, nothing.

The shapes were only metres away.

Still no reaction from Jonny and the boys, other than to give Mark a puzzled look.

Their relief at arriving on home ground had dulled their senses.

'Why've you chucked your—?' Jonny started to say.

Mark wanted to scream a warning.

Then he saw the glint of a blade in the black-gloved hand of the dark figure in the lead.

It shimmered, just caught the available light.

A thin blade, maybe five inches long.

Jonny was just ahead of Mark, who stood slightly to his right, maybe a step behind. Eric and Sam were behind Mark.

The rushing sound of footsteps, padded trainers.

And then they were face to face.

No words were spoken.

The figure with the knife was directly in front of Jonny.

There was a moment of stillness, before Jonny tried to utter a warning.

Then he sagged to his knees, dropped his chips and both his hands clutched his body.

The knife had been plunged into him at an upwards angle, under his ribcage, piercing his heart. One hard thrust. That's all it needed.

Nothing said.

Mark stood transfixed, knowing he would be next.

Sam and Eric – Bill and Ben – hadn't even reacted.

Then the shapes were gone as quickly as they had appeared, surged past, sprinting towards the shops, having carried out their allotted task.

Mark span, watched them go, too terrified to give chase. A car screamed on to the car park and they hurled themselves into it. Even in the darkness, Mark knew where he had seen the car before – KFC. The drive-by shooting. The Subaru Impreza. The one he and Jack had witnessed. Doors slammed, the engine revved and it screeched away, lights out.

Mark turned back to Jonny, who was still on his knees, doubled over, holding himself, a horrible gurgling, gagging sound coming from him.

'He's been stabbed,' Mark yelled. He looked desperately round at the two others, who simply hadn't got a clue what had happened, their mush-filled brains not computing any of it.

'What do you mean?' Eric demanded, looking quizzically at Mark and Jonny.

Mark twisted down to Jonny, still balancing on his knees. His hands were cupped under his chest and he was staring down at them, dumbfounded, unable to comprehend anything other than a dreadful numbing sensation in his chest. He looked back at Mark. 'Help me,' he said pitifully.

'Guys, come on,' Mark said, 'we've got to get him back to the shops and get help.' He didn't know what else to do. He put his hand under Jonny's elbow. 'Come on, get up.'

Somehow Jonny rose to his feet, assisted by Mark and giving the latter the hope that maybe this wasn't so bad. Neither of the other two reacted, watching stupidly. 'He's been fuckin' stabbed, you idiots, help me, help him.'

The Kong and Rat-head exchanged a glance with each other as though they were feeding off one another's brainwaves, if they had any to share.

'Looks bad,' Mark said, holding on to Jonny as he staggered on rubbery legs.

Only then did the big guys react. Both tossed away their chips and ran for it, leaving Mark open-mouthed and astounded and with a seriously wounded Jonny who could hardly stay upright.

'Bastards.'

'Yeah, bastards,' Jonny agreed. His legs crumpled under him and Mark could not hold him, but managed to prevent him hitting the ground too hard. Jonny folded down and lay on his back. Mark knelt next to him.

'I'm gonna call an ambulance, OK?'

Jonny's mouth opened and closed like a carpeted goldfish as words tried to leave his lips. Mark leaned closer, his ear next to Jonny's face.

'Mobile phone,' Jonny managed to utter, 'call him ... warn him ... tell him they got me...'

'Tell who?'

'Crack—'

Jonny convulsed and coughed. Mark felt the splat of warm, thick liquid across the side of his face causing him to rear back and wipe it off disgustedly, knowing he had been sprayed with Jonny's blood.

Suddenly Jonny creased up in agony. 'Jesus!' Then he relaxed.

And died.

Mark knew it, but somehow, something in him forced him to pat down Jonny's pockets and find his precious mobile phone which he then stuffed into his own pocket. He took one last look at Jonny's face. In the poor light he could see a faint reflection in the still-open eyes.

Then he ran back to the shops, fast, as though he was being chased by evil spirits.

The only shop open was the chippy. He ran to the door and screamed, 'Call an ambulance – there's a lad been knifed out back.'

Then, before the evil caught him, he spun on his heels and ran for his life.

Twenty

The sight in the mirror in the hallway terrified him.

Mark Carter: fourteen years old; sister dead from drugs overdose, possibly murdered; basically living alone in a house because his mother is either out working or shagging; a boy who knows right from wrong; a boy who thought – wrongly – that he had the ability to work undercover for the cops, who now knows the game in which he is involved is way too tough, too dirty, too horrendous for him to handle; a boy in way over his head; a boy who has witnessed a cold-blooded, brutal murder.

Mark Carter, fourteen, schoolboy.

Mark Carter, idiot.

Mark Carter – blood splattered all over his face, hands and clothes.

Maybe the devil *had* caught him.

His eyes looked drawn and he had a hunted, panicky expression on his face. His lips curled back into a snarl of contempt as he dragged off his bloodstained denim jacket and threw it furiously down on to the hall floor.

269

He took one last look at himself, despised what he saw, and ran upstairs, tearing his clothes off as he went so that by the time he reached the bathroom, he was in his underpants.

It took for ever for the shower to warm up, but he didn't care. He stood under the needles of cold jets and shivered, rubbing Jonny's blood off his hands. Then as the water heated up, he soaped himself thoroughly from head to toe whilst wondering what the hell he should do next.

He knew he had to call the cops, but some niggle inside told him to wait with that one.

Also, he now had Jonny's phone and the precious number of the Crackman on it – unless of course the Crackman had already changed it because of the troubles.

But he couldn't know about Jonny, not yet, could he?

Jonny Sparks, dead on a car park, heart skewered like a kebab.

The image of the murder in the shadows stayed with Mark as he towelled himself off and then wrapped another bath towel around his middle whilst he picked up his discarded clothing and dropped the blood-stained items into an ASDA carrier bag. The cops would need them. Forensics, he thought.

Next he changed into a clean set of clothes and made himself of mug of tea which, with a packet of biscuits, he carried up to his room.

As he sipped the hot, sweet, brown tea, his hand quivered. But it tasted good. Something special, something soothing, about tea.

It settled him. Slightly. Stopped him from dithering like he had the flu. Allowed him to get his mind ticking over again.

Maybe Jonny wasn't dead, he thought. Maybe it was just a bad wound. Maybe an ambulance had come and he had been saved.

'Yeah, sure,' he said with a sniff, knowing he was dead all right. And as for those two useless goons, Sam and Eric ... already, part of Mark's mind was contemplating some poetic retribution for those two cowards ... he picked up Jonny's mobile and inspected it.

Though Mark had never owned one, he knew his way around them; Bradley had one, as did Katie ... his two friends – his ex-friends, to be exact.

Jonny's keypad was locked. Mark pressed the required combination of buttons and the wallpaper display came up, an animated, naked woman, with huge breasts wobbling obscenely. Mark winced, but wasn't surprised. Jonny had been a disgusting git. He thumbed the keypad and displayed the list of the last ten numbers Jonny had dialled from the phone.

Only there weren't ten numbers, there was just the one.

Mark looked at it carefully. There was no name with the number to identify who it belonged to. Just the number. It had to be that of the Crackman.

Mark's thumb hovered hesitantly over the keypad, over the redial button.

If he dialled, the Crackman would think it was Jonny calling him, but as soon as Mark said anything, he would know different. Because the Crackman was so careful, Mark doubted if he would get chance to say much. What he blurted out would have to be pretty quick and to the point and worded in such a way that the Crackman wouldn't hang up, would listen and respond to Mark.

Mark's heart beat solidly. Visions of the knife disappearing up to the hilt into Jonny's body were still vivid in his mind.

Surely he had to be dead. Certainly the Crackman would want to know and if Mark could just say the right words and hook him – maybe by claiming he knew or could ID the killers – then perhaps he could arrange to meet the Crackman face to face.

A sneer spread over Mark's face.

But then again, maybe not. The Crackman would be far too canny to even listen to a stranger's voice. He would hang up immediately and that would be the end of it. The Crackman would ditch his phone and everything would be back to square one, or even further back than that because of Jonny's murder.

Mark's thumb clicked the exit button on the keypad and the screen returned to the wobbly-chested woman. Put simply, Mark did not know what to do for the best.

His decision, when it came, was simple: phone the cops and speak to Henry Christie. He was the puppet master, he would know what to do. Let that manipulative bastard make the decision.

He tabbed in Christie's number and was about to press call when the phone rang in his hand, vibrating and pumping out Green Day's number, now so ironic: 'Boulevard of Broken Dreams'.

Mark almost dropped the phone in surprise. Eyes popping out of his skull, he stared at the screen aghast. A withheld number. Must be the Crackman.

Panic struck him like an electric shock, but instead of throwing him across the room, he froze.

Then the ringing stopped and the screen came up, 'Missed call'.

'Shit.'

He lowered himself to the floor and looked at the phone and for no reason, other than he did not know what to do, he began thumb tabbing through the menu whilst he considered his position.

'Why don't I know what to do?' he whined plaintively.

Under the heading of 'Gallery' he pressed 'Select', then, again, for no particular rea-

273

son, he chose 'Video Clips'.

There were about six clips stored in files, each with a name.

One that stood out was 'Bethdeth'.

Cold dread coursed through his mind as he pressed 'Open'.

At first he hardly heard the pounding on the front door. His mind was in a far distant place, shocked beyond anything he'd ever known. Then the desperate knocking permeated and he dashed to the window, expecting to see the cops at his door. But looking down, he saw Jack, holding his shoulder, kicking at the door. For a moment Mark wondered why Jack didn't just let himself in. He had a key, after all. Then he remembered locking the door from the inside when he'd returned home, blood-soaked.

Jack looked up and saw Mark at the window. 'Let me in,' he screamed.

Relief flooded through Mark at the sight of Jack at the door. Now he could spill the beans to his elder brother, seek guidance from him. He would know exactly what to do.

Pushing the phone into his pocket, Mark ran downstairs, trying to work out where the Cayenne was, Jack's car. It wasn't parked out front.

He leapt down the stairs in one bound, using the banister, and dropped into the hallway.

Jack hammered on the door, not letting up.

'I'm coming,' Mark muttered impatiently.

As he got to the door, one of the four-inch square windows in the frame shattered and there was a terrifying whooshing sound just to the side of Mark's head, making him spin and duck.

He knew a bullet when he heard one.

'Open the fuck up!' Jack yelled.

Another window smashed as another bullet crashed through, narrowly missing Mark's forehead and imbedding itself with a thud into the kitchen door jamb.

Mark dropped to his hands and knees and crawled to the front door and reached up to the Yale lock, which he thumbed open and unlocked.

As the door opened, Jack crashed through, tripping over Mark, then turning and slamming the door closed behind him.

Mark stared up at him, petrified.

There was a gun in Jack's hand and blood pouring from a wound in his left shoulder.

Twenty-One

Another bullet slammed into the front door, making a sound like a cricket ball striking a bat for six.

'Get down, keep down,' Jack said. 'Come on.'

He started crawling down the hallway towards the kitchen, but his left arm couldn't hold his weight. It folded weakly under him and he hissed in agony.

'What's going on?' Mark asked fearfully, totally mystified and terrified by the events of the last minute.

Jack managed to ease himself painfully into a sitting position, propping himself against the wall, smearing blood on the wallpaper.

'Put the light out, Mark, otherwise they'll pick us off.'

'What?' Mark asked incredulously. 'Who ... eh?' He was dismayed and disorientated.

'Just do it!' Jack ordered him, then winced.

Mark complied, but not before he had seen the mess that was Jack's left shoulder. Jack had started to peel the leather jacket off to get a look at the wound. Under the jacket he was wearing a white tee-shirt which was now soaked in crimson blood.

'Oh God,' Mark gasped. 'What the hell's happening, Jack?'

'Is the back door locked?' Jack asked as though he hadn't heard Mark's question.

'Yeah – think so.'

'Good. I don't think they'll try to get in, least I hope not.'

They were close to each other. Mark was on his haunches, Jack leaning against the wall. In the half-light coming through from the streetlights, they could see each other clearly.

Jack coughed. Spittle flecked across Mark's face.

'Sorry, pal,' Jack apologized, wiping his mouth with the back of his right hand – the one in which he held the gun.

'Jack, I'm scared ... what's going on?'

'Don't be, don't be ... it's me they want ... I...' His words of explanation were cut short as two more bullets slammed into the door. What was really scary was that there was no sound of a gunshot to accompany them as whoever was shooting had a silenced gun. Mark ducked instinctively at the sound of the thuds.

'We need to call the police,' Mark declared.

'*No!*' It was almost a scream from Jack, who pointed the gun into Mark's face, creating a terrible queasy feeling inside the youngster. 'No ... no cops, OK?' he said more gently.

Jack glanced at his damaged shoulder and Mark's eyes turned to it also. Blood was constantly oozing out of it.

'You need a hospital.'

'No,' Jack said again, waving the gun dangerously. 'Get me upstairs to the bath-room. Need to clean it, then I'm gone. Come on, help me, pal.' He gasped painfully as he moved, his eyes searching Mark's face desperately.

Mark was speechless, torn between a plethora of conflicting emotions, but the one which overrode all was the love for his brother. In spite of not understanding anything and once again feeling he was in the vortex of something he had no control over, his gut instinct took over.

'Tear it off, tear it off.'

Hesitantly, Mark took hold of the blood-soaked piece of clothing and, using all his strength, ripped Jack's tee-shirt apart to expose the ugly, gaping wound, making him feel woozy at the sight. It was horrible, like some bloody black hole, just in the fleshy part of Jack's shoulder, near to the breast-bone.

Jack twisted his head and peered at it. His mouth contorted with the immense pain he must have been experiencing.

'Looks bad,' he admitted. 'I think it's gone down into my chest. Ahh!'

'Is it a bullet wound?' Mark asked ridiculously.

Jack managed to give him a withering look. 'No, I caught it on a thorn bush.'

'Sorry.'

They were in the bathroom, having made it up the stairs, no more bullets having been fired. Jack had used up a lot of energy and was weak from loss of blood. Uncovering the wound and seeing it clearly had confirmed their fears.

'Ambulance,' Mark said.

'No,' Jack insisted.

'Look, Jack, I don't know what's happening here. I'm not sure I want to, but you're my brother an' I don't want you to die. I've already lost a sister, OK? If nothing else, an ambulance turning up'll see them away, whoever they are.'

'No, no ambulance, no cops.' Jack picked up his gun. It was a pistol, one with a magazine of bullets up the handle. Looked very similar to the X-ray picture Mark had seen of the gun he'd delivered for Jonny. Jack thumbed a lever and the magazine slid out and clattered on the tiled floor of the bathroom. 'Back jeans pocket.' He sat forward with a groan. 'There's another mag in there. Get it out for me, will ya?' He lifted one cheek of his arse as Mark, once more, did as he was told, and fumbled in the pocket to bring out a fully-loaded magazine. Jack handed the gun to Mark. 'Just slide it in and slam it into place.'

279

Mark took the pistol, his hand dithering. He slid the magazine into the butt and rammed it into place.

'Now you need to put one into the chamber.'

'How the hell do I do that?'

'Get hold of the top of the gun between your thumb and forefinger, then slide the breech back, then let go.'

Mark complied.

'Good lad. Armed and dangerous.' Jack took the weapon back. 'Now, get a towel and wrap it around the wound, then get me some painkillers, then I'll call in some reinforcements and we'll keep low and wait for the cavalry.' Jack smiled crookedly, then winced and gasped and his face went the colour of puce.

Jack positioned himself on the floor just below the window in Mark's bedroom. He was still losing blood and now sweating profusely and shaking uncontrollably. The towel was already soaked in blood. Mark wondered if this was Jack going into shock.

'I need a drink,' he said. 'Throat dry.'

He pulled himself up on to his knees and, from the darkened room, took a quick peek into the street outside. He could see nothing, but he dropped quickly back down when a bullet shattered the window just above his head and embedded itself in the wall above Mark's bed head. The streetlight outside the house was then shot out, pitching that portion of the street into blackness.

'Still there,' Jack said unnecessarily.

'Why doesn't anyone call the cops?' Mark whined.

'Because this is Shoreside,' Jack said cynically. He placed the pistol down by his side and fumbled for his mobile phone in his jeans pocket. He began to thumb through it, glancing up at Mark as he did so. Perspiration teemed down Jack's face and his breathing was harsh and rattly. He raised his eyebrows. 'Drink?' he repeated. 'Good lad.'

'Yeah, yeah, sorry.' Mark scuttled out of the room on all fours and slithered down the stairs head first on his belly, crawling like a reptile. He kept low in the hall and crept into the kitchen.

Upstairs he could hear Jack's muffled voice on the mobile. Probably calling those reinforcements he'd been talking about.

Mark froze. A dark shape moved across the kitchen window, then a hooded figure pressed his face up to the glass, covering his eyes with a hand, trying to peer into the kitchen. Mark lay on the floor, too terrified to move, certain he was going to be spotted. The man – Mark assumed it was a man – had his hands against the glass and in his right was the ugly black shape of a gun. He moved away and tried the handle on the back door. Mark held his breath, suddenly unsure whether he had locked it or not. A gunman at the door tends to give you those sorts of doubt. It was locked and the man put his shoulder to it and tried to force it, but it held. Then he took a step back and flat-footed it. Mark cringed every time the foot connected. But again, it didn't budge. Mark knew the man would have problems forcing it open in such a way. It had been tried before when one of his mum's boy-friends who she'd fallen out with had tried to batter his way in. He'd been one hell of a big guy, pissed up and enraged, but the door had held firm from his onslaught. So unless the guy outside shot the lock off, like they did in films – which Mark always suspected was an iffy way of opening a door – he was going to struggle.

The man cursed. Then he was gone ... but Mark knew he would be back.

He released his breath then waited a few seconds before crawling across to the fridge and getting out a bottle of pop.

Upstairs, Jack was still on the phone.

Mark took his chance at that point and did something he hoped he would not regret ... then, that done, he edged his way back upstairs into his bedroom and handed the pop to Jack, who drank from it like a man in a desert.

'Cheers, mate.' He put the bottle on the carpet beside him and picked up his phone again. 'Not long now and we'll be out of here ... one more call to make.'

He pressed a button on his phone.

There was a short delay.

Then Mark felt the vibration from the mobile phone in his jeans pocket, then heard his favourite Green Day tune which was its ringtone: 'Boulevard of Broken Dreams'. Jonny Sparks's phone was ringing.

At first neither of them could work it out, one of those surreal moments.

Mark fished the phone out of his pocket and looked at the display.

Jack took his own phone away from his ear. His look of pain evaporated, replaced by one of shock. He thumbed the end call button.

'Jonny Sparks is dead,' Mark said simply. 'This is his phone.'

'Did you kill him?'

Mark shook his head. 'I was there when he died. Somebody stabbed him, one of your enemies, I'll bet.' His voice was calm and controlled. 'Before he died, he asked me to phone the Crackman and tell him what had happened. I guess I don't have to do that now, do I, Jack?'

'Don't know what you mean.' His voice sounded frail. 'I must've misdialled.'

'Did you know I was working for Jonny?'

'I don't know what you're on about,' Jack said faintly. He picked up the pop and gulped down a few mouthfuls.

Mark snorted a gush of derision. 'Liar,' he said bluntly. Without warning he grabbed

283

Jack's phone and wrenched it out of his weak grasp. 'Let's see, eh?' Jack tried to snatch it back, but Mark twisted away, now very much in charge. He held up the phones side by side. They were the exact same models.

'Mark,' Jack said pathetically, reaching out, twiddling his fingers.

'There's only one number in Jonny's phone, because this is the phone he used when he was out dealing drugs. He used it exclusively to contact the man he worked for – the Crackman – and this was the only phone the Crackman ever contacted him on. Let's see, eh?' Mark pressed the appropriate button on Jonny's phone.

Mark and Jack eyed each other. The gunmen outside were forgotten in those moments.

Nothing happened for a few seconds, then Jack's phone rang out with a crazy voice which declared, *'Here's Jonny!'*

'Was it a misdial?' Mark asked cynically. 'I don't think so.' A feeling of rage began to burn fiercely inside him, coupled with one of betrayal. 'You're the man, aren't you, Jack?'

His big brother looked away.

Mark desperately wanted him to deny it, but the words never came.

'Jesus, you are, aren't you?' Mark blurted, still not wanting to believe, all churned up inside. He threw down Jack's phone in disgust.

'Mark, look,' Jack said reasonably, 'we've

got to get out of here. Help'll be here soon. Let's get out and then we can talk, OK?'

'This ... this' – Mark gestured towards Jack's shoulder, then the window – 'this is a turf war, isn't it?'

'Mark, you don't know what you're saying.'

Suddenly he saw Jack in an altogether different light. Now, as far as he was concerned, he was no longer his brother ... his brother was as dead as his sister. It was all beginning to fall into place.

'That day at KFC! They were after you, weren't they? Not those two lads who I thought were drug dealers. It was you, wasn't it? You were the bloody drug dealer!'

'Mark, not now, eh? More important things to get through.'

'And you supplied the drugs that killed Bethany and that other girl, Jane Grice, didn't you? Those deaths ... Bethany ... that other girl, you supplied the heroin and all the other drugs, didn't you?'

'No, you're wrong, mate ... look, can we just—?'

'Just what?' Mark interrupted. 'Pretend it didn't happen?' Mark's voice rose. 'I looked up to you, respected you. I thought you'd dragged yourself away from this shit. But' – he gestured desperately with his hands – 'but you're one of the people who make it shit living here. You're a drug dealer, Jack.' Tears formed. 'And Beth died because of you, and so have others – even Jonny Sparks. All

285

because of you!'

'No, you're talking rubbish, mate ... this is all a misunderstanding.' Jack would not relent.

'Getting shot is a misunderstanding? And stop calling me "mate", and stop denying it.'

Mark's face was a smear of tears and snot as he started to cry.

'Come on, let's just get out of this and I can explain it all.'

Mark wiped his face. 'No ... the cops are coming. I called them.' He held up Jonny's phone. 'When I was downstairs.'

'You did what?' Jack exploded and moved suddenly, sending pain rocketing through him. 'I said no cops.'

'Tough, they're coming – and whoever's out there can just fuck off.'

'You idiot,' Jack snarled. His hand dropped on to the pistol which was at his side. He picked it up and pointed it at Mark. 'I said no cops,' he growled. 'I can't afford cops.'

'Your problem, not mine.' Mark stood up. 'I'm going to walk out of here and then out of the front door and I'm going to shout that the cops are coming and if they want to wait, then it's up to them, whoever they are ... if they want to shoot me, that's up to them, too, cos at this moment in time I don't feel like I've got very much to live for.'

'Mark!' Jack aimed the gun. Mark could see the 'O' of the muzzle pointed directly at his chest. He would now have bet his life that

286

this was the gun he'd delivered for Jonny. Part of a chain of events that led to Jack now holding it.

'Shoot me then, then you'll have killed your brother and your sister. Good going.'

Jack's aim did not waver. His finger curled on the trigger. Sweat dripped off his forehead, through his eyebrows and on to his eyelids, making him blink. The effort of holding up the weapon was taking its toll. It began to shake.

'Shit,' he gasped, and lowered his gun.

The brothers stared at each other for a timeless moment, then Mark spun out of the room, taking the stairs two at a time, switching the house lights on as he went, and unlocked the front door.

As he opened it, the first police car screamed into the street, blue lights flashing ... many more followed.

Twenty-Two

They were in a sealed and secured visiting room, Mark on one side of a screen, Jack on the other. A thick Perspex window separated them.

Mark looked at his brother through the scratched pane.

Jack had been pretty close to death and the surgeons at Blackpool Victoria Hospital had battled to save his life because the bullet that had skewered down through his shoulder into his chest had nicked a major artery. He was patched up now and, six days later, though weak, was well enough to be in custody at the Blackpool cop shop.

'I didn't think you'd come,' Jack said. He shifted on his plastic seat, gritting his teeth with pain.

'Nor did I,' Mark responded flatly. 'What's happening with you?' He felt distant and unresponsive to anything, recent events continually washing over him like a tidal wave.

'I've been charged with some offences,' he said vaguely. 'I'll be up at court in the morning and then the cops want to talk to me here for another couple of days. After that I'll probably be remanded in custody until my case comes up.'

'When's that?'

'Who knows?'

'Guilty or not guilty?'

Jack didn't answer, just stared at Mark.

'So,' Mark said, taking a breath, 'you are the Crackman.'

Jack gave a barely perceptible nod.

Mark shook his head in disgust. 'How long?'

Jack gave a short laugh. 'Started when I was your age ... it was the only way to survive, specially after Dad left ... it just got bigger and I got further and further away from the streets.'

'And I thought you were a legit business-man,' Mark snorted. 'What a fool I was.'

'I was – am – a businessman,' Jack said defensively.

'Don't kid yourself, you're nothing of the sort. You're a death dealer,' Mark said, keeping a tenuous grip on his anger. 'And you killed Beth, didn't you?'

'No – don't try to lay that one on me. I'm not having that.'

'But Jonny was one of your dealers and he gave out the drugs you supplied, some to Bethany and she died. Do not try to wriggle out of that.' Mark jabbed a finger at Jack's face. He would have liked to punch him hard and repeatedly. He was glad there was a screen between them.

His brother remained silent.

'I have nothing more to say to you,' Mark said, rising from the seat and turning out of the visiting room without looking back.

'My head's a shed,' Mark complained, using the quaint northern term to describe emotional turmoil.

On the table in front of him was a toasted bacon sandwich – filled with really crispy bacon – and a mug of sweet tea courtesy of DCI Christie. The two of them, Mark and Christie, were seated in the canteen on the top floor of Blackpool Police Station.

The food looked and smelled appetising, but whilst Mark may have been famished, he didn't feel like eating.

'You did good,' Christie said. 'You were brave, a bit cunning, and you did the right thing.'

'Why the hell does it feel so bad, though?'

'Because it was a tough call.'

'My head's still a shed,' Mark admitted.

'I'd be surprised – nay, astounded – if it wasn't.' Christie, hunched over the table looking at Mark, had his back to the dining room door. He turned to glance over his shoulder when a noisy group of people barged in and formed a ragged queue at the counter.

Mark's lower jaw dropped and his mouth popped open in astonishment. 'They're the lads who...' he spluttered.

'Yeah, they are,' Christie confirmed with a smirk. 'Christie's little helpers.'

Mark had immediately recognized the four youths who had entered the room, all about his age, all wearing the same sort of ID badges around their necks that he'd had to put on and sign for before being allowed into the inner sanctum of the cop shop. They were the four lads, the 'thieves' who'd hurtled past him whilst he'd been in one of the arcades, chased by the police; the ones who'd dropped their ill-gotten gains in a plastic bag at Mark's feet – the Xbox games, CDs and DVDs – and then legged it, hotly pursued by the two uniformed cops on their tails.

'They work for me occasionally,' Christie said to the gobsmacked Mark Carter, who couldn't keep his eyes off them.

'I knew it was all part of the set-up,' Mark said, 'but it was all so real.'

'It had to be,' Christie said, indicating the lads with a gesture of his thumb. He went on, 'They're all in some sort of care, but they're straight, dead-ahead, honest kids and perform a valuable function. Sometimes we need the help of youngsters like that' – he paused for effect – 'like yourself. Anyway, like I said when you eventually agreed to help, everything you did from that moment on, everything that happened to you and around you, had to be totally realistic, including your response as much as possible – which is why your arrest for stealing the bike worked so well. It was something you weren't expecting and you reacted just right and in a way that drew Jonny Sparks in.' Mark couldn't help but beam a little at that. 'We just had to ensure you were in the right place at the right time ... and what could be more realistic in Blackpool than four little scallies legging it from the police, or someone on Shoreside being locked up for nicking a bike? Happens all the time.'

Mark smiled proudly. 'But what about the stuff in the bag, the games and all that?'

'Provided by a big retail chain which often helps us out when we need it ... and which, incidentally, we need back at some stage.'

Mark reddened slightly. 'I'd forgotten about them.'

The lads at the counter got cakes, biscuits and fizzy drinks then headed for a table in the far corner. One nodded amiably at Mark as he passed and Mark grinned back like a Cheshire cat.

'Thing is, the two officers chasing the lads didn't know it was a set-up. They had to believe the lads were thieves and had to behave exactly like cops do, just in case you were being observed – which you were, actually.'

'Oh? By who?'

'Recall the oldish couple having a brew in the arcade caff?'

292

'My grandparents!' Mark exclaimed, recalling them clearly and how he had pretended to the cops that he was their grandson.

'Two neighbourhood watch coordinators who do a bit of town-centre watching for us. Both retired cops.'

'Bloody hell! You've got people everywhere.'

'Better believe it,' Christie said. 'Anyway, even when you were arrested for stealing your own bike, the two officers didn't know that was a set-up either. They were acting on information supplied by me. The whole thing had to be as real as possible, otherwise Jonny would've seen right through it. What could've been worse than you getting a nod and a wink from a cop who was in on it? Would've given the whole game away. Even now I haven't told the officers the whole truth ... which I must do,' he finished thoughtfully.

Mark's appetite suddenly returned. He picked up the big sandwich and chomped into it, melted butter drooling down his chin. 'How often do they do stuff for you?' he asked about the lads.

'Quite often ... if nothing else they do test purchases, y'know going into off-licences to see if the storekeeper will sell them booze, fags, that sort of thing. Sometimes they get involved in other, more complicated stuff. Why?' Christie eyeballed him. 'Interested?'

'Could be,' Mark said through a mouthful

of bacon and toast. He swallowed. 'Jack's not coming out for a while, is he? Sorry to change the subject, like.'

'No.' The detective shook his head with a pout. 'The more we dig, the more we unearth. He's a very big operator, worth millions – money which is currently being chased by our financial investigators.'

'Hell.'

'Hell, indeed,' Christie agreed. 'But it wasn't a turf war he was involved in, by the way.'

Mark stopped chewing, frowned, washed down his mouthful of food with the tea. 'What was it, then? Why were people after him with guns?'

'Remember me mentioning Jane Grice?'

Mark nodded immediately. 'She died of a drug overdose. She went to our school. It got mentioned at assembly.'

'That's the one. She was actually the daughter of a very iffy businessman from Poulton who's an even bigger villain than Jack, a real gangster.' Mark winced slightly at the words, still finding it hard to imagine Jack as a criminal, let alone a gangster. Christie said, 'He was after Jack in revenge for Jane's death. At least that's what I believe, but proving it is more difficult. He and his family were trying to destroy Jack because they think he supplied her with the drugs she overdosed on.' He let that sink into Mark's brain.

'So you know who shot him, then?'

'No. Jack does, but he won't tell us. We think it was someone from out of town, hired by Jane's family.'

'Hired killers?' Mark gulped.

Christie shrugged. 'Maybe.'

'And the drive-by shooting at the KFC?'

'Their first attempt to kill Jack.'

'And they very nearly killed an innocent person, that girl who works there.'

'Would it surprise you to know that Jane Grice had been going out with Jonny Sparks?' Christie asked.

'I think I vaguely knew that,' Mark said ponderously. He narrowed his eyes and looked at Christie. 'Did he...?'

'Give her the drugs that killed her? Think so. She'd been told by her father to dump Jonny and I think it was his revenge for being jilted. Jilted Jonny, you might say.'

'The bastard,' Mark whispered hoarsely.

'Jonny was a psychopath, a very dangerous and manipulative one,' Christie explained. 'I think he deliberately gave Jane Grice the overdose and did the same to Bethany – although I don't think I'll ever prove either. He loved the power, loved manipulating people – a bit like a Harold Shipman character, you know, the doctor who killed all those old people who were his patients?' Mark nodded. 'Which in a way was why it was relatively easy for you to gain his trust – because he thought he had power over you, had a hold.'

'Y'know, I could never work out why he was always after me. I never did owt to him, yet he was always chasin' me. He was just crazy, I suppose. Wanted to control me.'

'Which doesn't mean to say I don't want to catch his killers. I do, and I won't rest until they're behind bars.'

'No, I get that,' Mark conceded. 'However,' Mark went on bitterly, 'he got what he deserved and he *did* kill Bethany ... and do you know why? Because she dumped him, just like Jane Grice did. I had a real go at her for seeing him, she must have realized she was being an idiot knocking about with him and so she decided to ditch him, which is why he killed her—'

'Whoa – hold on! Impossible to prove now,' Christie said.

'No, it isn't,' Mark said. 'Jonny did it and those two lads who traipsed around after him, Sam and Eric, helped him out and stupid as they are, they're guilty of murder too. I just didn't know these things at first. I do now.'

Christie leaned back with a sigh, folded his arms and looked pityingly at him. 'Mark, Mark, Mark,' he said sadly. 'I know you're upset...'

'Don't patronize me, Henry,' he warned the detective. Mark fished out a mobile phone from his pocket, the one Jonny had given him just before he died. The one Jonny used to contact the Crackman with. He selected the media programme, pressed start on a particular file and handed the phone to Christie.

'Watch this. This was happening while I was asleep upstairs,' he said, swallowing back something in his throat.

Christie did, appalled by what he saw. When the clip ended he said, 'I need to keep this.' Mark nodded. 'Unbelievable, the bastard recorded Bethany dying, bragging about it, laughing ... Jesus ... and his mates helped too, plying her with more and more drugs, coaxing her to swallow them.'

Christie watched the clip again, which concluded with Jonny Sparks leering into the lens and saying, 'So, girls, never dump Jonny, otherwise you'll suffer.'

One of his mates, either Eric or Sam, had been recording the mini-speech and as it finished, the camera moved away from Jonny and was pointed at Bethany down on the kitchen floor, her body convulsing and retching horribly as she approached death.

'He told me he had nothing to do with her death,' Mark said stonily, 'and you know what? I almost believed him. I feel so stupid.'

'Their feet won't touch the ground, I promise,' Christie said earnestly, referring to Sam and Eric.

'Whatever,' Mark shrugged. 'Beth's not coming back, Jack's in jail and me mam's a slapper.' He looked as though he was going to cry.

'And you are one helluva lad,' Christie said, placing a hand on his shoulder.

'Yeah, right, that's me, a helluva lad.'

'What are you going to do?'

'Get back to school. Get my job back at the newsagent's, if they'll have me. Make my friends again.' He raised his eyebrows. 'I have unfinished business with Katie, if you know what I mean? Get my head down and get out of this shit hole – eventually. But, first things first.' He pointed at Christie. 'I want my bike back.'

Epilogue

Once again, Henry Christie was sitting in an excuse for a car on a rainy night, just after the witching hour, parked up in a dimly-lit back street, but the location had changed: this time he was somewhere in Rochdale, a grimy town to the north of Manchester. Again, he was shivering as the heater wasn't working properly and as he reached forward to crank up the temperature – without success – and had to wipe the screen with his hand, he wondered if it was the same bloody car.

He glanced at Rik Dean in the passenger seat. 'OK, mate?'

'Yep.'

'How's the leg?'

'Had a bullet in it, y'know?' He shrugged. 'Still not great.'

'But good enough to be out here tonight?'

'Oh yes,' he said enthusiastically.

Henry smiled and looked forward again, snorting a quiet puff of amazement down his nose. Incredible, he thought, how things could snowball.

Who could possibly have known what

would have happened as a result of him picking up his mobile phone four months ago and reluctantly agreeing, despite his terrible hangover that day, to turn out to what appeared to be a run-of-the-mill drugs OD.

What had started as a routine, though tragic, set of circumstances which had not really interested him all that much initially, had led to the brutal murder of a teenager and a shoot-out on a council estate in which one man was almost fatally injured, that man being Jack Carter, the Crackman.

Who Henry had nicked.

Following Jack's arrest, Henry had pounced on Jonny Sparks's running mates, Eric King (The Kong) and Sam Dale (Rat-head), finding them easy meat. Two dumb-ass no-hopers who'd completely screwed up their lives by associating with Jonny. They had blabbed until the cows came home when confronted with the evidence on Jonny's phone.

Despite their being teenagers, they had been charged with murder, even though he knew it would probably be reduced to manslaughter when, or even before, it came to court. That wasn't his problem. He'd done his bit.

And then they were boxed away. Henry had quickly moved focus.

Like a terrier on a postman's leg, he went for the Grice family.

As much as he was sympathetic to the fact

they had lost their daughter through drugs, he did not like the way in which they had gone about exacting their revenge.

The hiring of professional hit men to kill Jack Carter, to drive a knife into Jonny Sparks's heart and to mow down one of Carter's dealers in Fleetwood, was not something Henry could tolerate.

Not only that, an innocent girl had nearly lost her life in the Kentucky Fried Chicken drive-by shooting that had been the first attempt on Jack's life. She had almost been forgotten in the mess, but Henry had decided – in a high and mighty way – that someone had to seek justice for her.

He had decided *he* would be that seeker and would not rest until he had ground the Grice family into the dust and hunted down the killers they had hired.

Rik Dean looked at him. 'How good is this intel?' he asked impatiently.

'Of the very highest calibre,' Henry assured him.

'Only my leg's getting stiff.'

Henry was aware that this was the first time that Rik had stepped out operationally since the shooting. 'You could've stayed in your shiny-arsed office.'

'Yeah, right.'

Their good-natured bickering ended and silence came down on the pair.

The Grice family had been tough and unapproachable and Henry had got nowhere with them. Not that he had expected anything more. They were all hardened criminals, top professionals, and ran a tight operation, but not as tight as their lips. There was no way they would incriminate themselves, so Henry decided to try and come at them from another angle, but try as he might, that angle eluded him for a long time.

Then, three weeks into it, as he shuffled and reshuffled everything in his mind, something struck him, something that Mark Carter had told him.

Henry had been in Rik Dean's office at the time, filling in some paperwork when the thought hit him. He looked out of the narrow, floor-to-ceiling window and tried to remember if it had rained at all over the last twenty-one days. He was sure it hadn't, not to any great degree anyway.

With an inner whoop, he grabbed his jacket and shot out of the cop shop.

He was at Mark Carter's house within ten minutes.

It was late afternoon as Henry battered at the front door, still bearing the signs of a shoot out. He shouted Mark's name through the letterbox and knew the lad was home because his precious BMX was propped up in the hallway.

Eventually, the door was answered. Mark stood there looking rather flustered, red-faced.

'Mr Christie!'

'Hi, Mark, not an inconvenient moment, I hope?'

'Er, er, no.'

It obviously was, but nevertheless Henry said, 'Can I come in? Need a word.'

'Yeah, yeah, sure.' Mark stepped aside and Henry entered the hallway. His eyes caught sight of a girl at the top of the stairs who ducked quickly into Mark's bedroom when she realized she'd been spotted.

Henry raised his eyebrows and smiled. 'Ms Bretherton, I assume?' He gave Mark a completely salacious, OTT wink.

Mark squirmed, shrugged and gave a lopsided grin.

'Friends again?'

'Er ... we managed to make up ... anyway,' the young man pulled himself together, 'what can I do for you?'

'Kitchen.' Henry pointed down the hall.

Mark followed him, chuckling as Henry caught his shin on the pedal of Mark's BMX, cried out in pain and limped into the kitchen.

'Can't you keep that bloody thing somewhere else?' Henry whined.

'Beth used to say that...' Mark began, but his voice faded into sadness. His mouth twisted with the pain of it.

'You OK?' Henry asked.

Mark screwed up his features and nodded bravely. Henry realized just how much he had come to like Mark at that moment.

'Good lad.' Henry turned and looked around the kitchen. 'When you and Jack were pinned down in the house, you said you sneaked down to the kitchen, didn't you?' Mark nodded. Henry went on, 'And when you were in here, some guy came looking through the window, yeah?'

'And tried to boot the door in. Scared me shitless!'

'Which window did he look through?'

'That one.' Mark pointed to the window behind the sink. 'Why?'

'And he tried to boot the door down?'

'As I said.'

Henry opened the back door, stepped into the back garden, then looked at the panels in the door, which were made of UPVC. His lips pursed when he saw that on the surface there were marks which looked like the sole of a shoe, a trainer by the looks, which had been worn by the bad guy who'd attempted to flat-foot the door open. Some of the marks were better than others. Some were just smudges, some distinct patterns.

'Don't touch the door,' Henry said, then took a step sideways to inspect the window. 'He looked in through this window?' he confirmed with Mark, who nodded.

This time Henry's heart soared.

'Anyone been near this window since?'

'Not that I know of.'

'It's not been cleaned?'

'As if we can afford a window cleaner.'

Henry bent his knees and angled his head to look across the pane of glass so that the light fell on it in such a way he could see any marks on the surface.

And marks were there: the marks left by the edges of two hands, left and right, which had been cupped over the man's eyes as he tried to see inside the kitchen where the terrified Mark Carter had been cowering.

Henry's smile grew and his bum twitched.

He pulled his PR out of his jacket. 'DCI Christie to Blackpool...' When the acknowledgement came, he said, 'As a matter of urgency, please contact a CSI and turn them out to' – he recited Mark's address on Shoreside – 'as soon as possible. I'll be waiting here.'

'Shouldn't you have thought of this before?' Mark asked cheekily, indicating the window and door. 'Would've saved so much time.'

Henry eyed him levelly. 'Fuck off, smartypants.'

The fingerprints came back with an immediate hit – but the shoe impression took a little time. Henry felt like rushing in to make an arrest, but held back while the footwear databases were checked in Lancashire and Greater Manchester.

It was worth the wait. The shoe prints were an exact match for a pair of trainers belong-

305

ing to a young man who'd been arrested only six weeks earlier for a suspected murder in Moss Side, Manchester, a drive-by shooting. He was out on police bail pending further enquiries.

The prints from the window also belonged to the same male, an extremely violent individual who was suspected of many brutal crimes in Manchester and who, intel reports suggested, was a gun for hire and cheap at the price.

And now, in a joint operation with Greater Manchester Police, the home of the suspect was surrounded. A surveillance team had tracked the man to the address in Rochdale earlier in the evening and now it was hoped he was tucked up in bed, ripe for the picking.

Henry shivered – but not from the cold. A strange sense of unease had flitted through him.

'Call me a suspicious old geezer,' Henry said, holding up his hands to prevent Rik from doing just that, 'but this guy has been trailed to this address and seen to walk in through the front door at eight and hasn't moved since ... pretty unusual behaviour for someone like him, wouldn't you say?'

'Having a night in, you mean?'

'Exactly ... people like him are usually out and about, mixing it, aren't they?'

'Even crims stay at home and watch telly occasionally. Maybe *Crimewatch* was on tonight.'

'Mm, maybe,' Henry said doubtfully.

'What time are we going in?'

Henry checked his watch for the umpteenth time: 12.15 a.m. 'Now.'

The suspect's name was Danny Todd. He had been involved in the Manchester crime scene since the age of seven and by the time he'd reached twenty-two, his present age, he had clocked up numerous convictions, been arrested over a hundred times, been in and out of custody, suspected of over fifty things that could not be proved, and made his living with the gun and the baseball bat. He had a fearsome reputation and Henry was itching to get face to face with him.

Only he wasn't home.

Henry waited with growing disbelief as the back-up search team entered Todd's residence after the initial entry by the firearms team and arrest squad, knowing full well that there would be no sign of Todd. He had been seen to enter the house by the surveillance team, but, Henry guessed, he'd gone straight out back and made good his escape along a disused railway line which ran along the back of the house, thereby outsmarting the surveillance bods. Todd was known to be surveillance conscious and Henry suspected this was a ploy he often used to fool the cops, whether he thought he was being followed or not.

There were two people in the house, Todd's seventeen-year-old girlfriend, multi-pierced, tattooed and blessed with a super bad attitude, and smelling of booze, and her sixteen-month-old son, possibly Todd's, who was also pretty cranky.

The girl, Natasha, held on to her offspring defiantly, positioning him on her left hip. Too defiantly, Henry thought as he entered the house following the negative search for Todd, and faced the sneering teenager and bawling baby, both in their night attire.

He looked coldly at her.

Rik stood behind Henry, wondering if she had a knife or a gun, not wishing to find out.

'Where is he?' Henry asked.

'Don't know who you mean.'

Henry's eyes flicked to the kid and back to her. 'Danny – where is he?'

'Shove it right up your arse,' she said, and jerked her middle finger up at Henry, who winced. 'And get the hell out of this house.'

Henry turned his head and looked at the sergeant who had been running the search side of the op. 'Has she been searched?'

Natasha took a defensive step back, clutching the baby.

'No, boss.'

'I'll do it with pleasure.' A well-built female officer stepped up and shouldered her way towards the girl.

'No effin' way are you touching me!' the girl snarled aggressively and suddenly she dipped her hand down the back of the baby's nappy and pulled out a short-bladed kitchen knife which she waved threateningly at the police. 'I'll stab you, I will.'

'Out of my way,' the large female cop growled. She heaved her way past Henry and Rik, surprising both of them with her speed and strength, and in a flash she had grabbed Natasha and twisted her arm back and disarmed her. The knife dropped out of her grip and she was suddenly being held in a well-rehearsed wrist lock, whilst still holding the baby who was staring wide-eyed and stunned at the events unfolding in front of it.

'You friggin' bitch ... Argh!' she gasped as the officer applied some pressure to her wrist, making her jerk in pain. The officer then manoeuvred her down on to the settee, the baby still clinging on.

'Sit there and shut it.' The officer looked at Henry. 'Boss?'

Henry was inclined to keep Natasha pinned down for the moment. 'The choice is yours, girl ... the offences are stacking up on you ... threatening behaviour, offensive weapons, threats to kill, breach of the peace, drunk in charge of a child ... if you get locked up now, Social Services will have a field day with you and I guarantee you won't be cradling your little babbie for a long, long time—'

'You bastard!'

The officer twisted her wrist – just a little bit.

'Where is he? That's all I want to know. If you don't tell me, the baby goes into care and you go on remand ... that's a threat.'

Natasha's face contorted with pain, but she was doing the sums.

'He's gone on a job,' she relented.

'What job?'

'Can't tell you, can I? He'll bleedin' kill me, yeah?'

'What job, Natasha?'

'Tell this bitch to let go and I'll say.'

Henry nodded to the policewoman who slowly eased off the pressure.

Natasha shook her head.

'Well?' Henry asked. 'I keep my threats,' he assured her.

'Look, all I know is, yeah, he'd been paid to do some guy who's at court later today ... that's all I know, yeah? I haven't heard any-thing more than that.'

Henry glanced worriedly at Rik, then back to Natasha. 'I want more – otherwise you're going down, lass.'

'I don't know any more.'

'Well in that case, you just lost babykins here.' Henry looked at the snotty-nosed kid with what looked like a candle dripping out of its nose.

'You complete and utter twat!' Natasha responded in a ladylike manner.

'If the cap fits,' Henry acknowledged. To

the policewoman, he growled, 'Lock her up and turn out the on-call Social Services.'

The largely-built lady's face morphed into one of delight. She turned on Natasha, ready to grab her.

'No, no!' Natasha screamed. She looked desperately at Henry, who shrugged indifferently in an 'it's your choice' gesture. 'You utter, utter bastards,' Natasha wilted, beaten. 'You'd take a kid away from its mum?' Henry remained silent, hard faced. Shaking her head disgustedly, she licked her lips and seemed to struggle for a few moments with her conscience, such as it was. Then her watery eyes rose to meet Henry's. 'He can never know it was me,' she begged.

It was 9.45 a.m., later that same morning. Henry Christie and Rik Dean paced the corridors of Blackpool Magistrates Court, each man wearing a ballistic vest underneath his jacket. The court was teeming with customers and their relatives, uniformed and plain-clothed police and a few members of the public out gawping for the day.

'Think he'll show?' Rik said. They paused outside court number one.

'Who knows?'

They moved to the entrance foyer where a couple of sullen private security guards were searching people as they entered the court building, then making them walk underneath the arch of a metal detector before being allowed in. Such were the modern security requirements of any court these days.

Henry watched the filter of people, a great tiredness welling over him. He had been up over twenty-four hours and was flagging. He checked his watch and nodded for Rik to follow him to court number two, in which the remand hearings were being held that morning.

At that time the court was virtually empty. The clerk was arranging her papers on the desk below the bench and the prosecuting solicitor was doing the same on his table, which faced both the bench and the clerk. A sight Henry had witnessed hundreds of times in his career. The wheels of justice getting ready for the day ahead.

He crossed to the prosecutor and spoke quietly to him, then took a seat next to Rik at the side of the court, which gave him a good view of the whole room.

A few people drifted in. Henry recognized one or two of them, people he'd had dealings with over the years. There was no nod, or how do you do.

Rik was looking at them, too. 'You know you're a cop,' he said reflectively, 'when you think that seventy-five per cent of people are a waste of space.'

'I thought I was the cynic,' Henry said. But he did have to acknowledge that it some-times seemed hard for cops to think well of people. Then he suddenly forgot what he was thinking about and jerked upright when he saw Mark Carter come into the court-room. 'Bugger,' he said. He stood up and approached the boy.

'What're you doing here?' he demanded.

'Bit of moral support for Jack,' he said sheepishly.

'I thought you'd ditched him?'

Mark gave a gesture that encompassed a shrug and a wince, letting Henry know he didn't really have a proper answer. 'He's my brother,' he said simply, 'and he's up at court on remand and I thought it would do him good to see I haven't deserted him – as much as I hate what he did, what he was.' He gave the gesture again.

'I know,' Henry said. 'No need to explain.'

'What time is he due up?'

'First one.'

'Well, at least I won't be hanging around all day.'

Henry left it at that and returned to sit next to Rik.

'What've you told him?'

'Nothing,' Henry said.

The court convened at 10.15 a.m., only fifteen minutes later than it should have done, which wasn't bad, Henry thought im-patiently. The wait had been getting to him, but he sat back and tried to give the impres-sion of not being bothered and chatted amiably with Rik, mainly about women and football, although the latter did not do much for Henry unless he was laid out on a settee with a beer in one hand and a remote control in the other. His eyes and Mark's often caught and Henry wished the lad wasn't here. He didn't want him to get involved in anything that was going to happen that morning.

In his left ear, Henry had a tiny earpiece; in his right lapel he had a miniature microphone. Together they made up a mini personal radio which kept him in constant contact with the team of plain-clothed officers roaming the court in several disguises, from cleaners to court staff, and the firearms team on standby in the police waiting room.

Henry knew that Jack Carter had been safely conveyed to the holding cells below the court from the remand centre this morning and that the only time he would be on public display was when he actually stepped into the dock for the remand hearing, formality that it was. Henry doubted whether Danny Todd had the resources to hold up a prison bus, so he guessed that if Todd was going to do anything, it would be when Jack was in court. A hit and run, he guessed.

'Your Worships, the first case on the list today is the remand hearing of Jack Carter.' The clerk was addressing the three dour magistrates on the bench.

Henry checked the people sitting in the

court.

No one looked remotely like Danny Todd.

He might not even come, Henry hoped. If he'd got wind that his house had been raided and that his delicious girlfriend Natasha had been arrested (Henry had gone back on his word to her, just to keep her from getting in touch with Danny ... all being fair in love and justice), then Danny would definitely abort the job. But if he didn't know, then maybe he would chance his arm ... hence Henry's hastily prepared operation.

Henry had been faced with a dilemma.

He could easily have flooded the court with hi-viz uniforms and done a preventative op, but that would have meant that catching Danny would have been much harder ... and the thought of catching him with a gun in his pocket was a very strong motivator for Henry. Just arresting him because his finger-prints were on Mark Carter's window would not necessarily have been enough to prove that Todd was the shooter hired by the Grice family. He would be able to come up with all sorts of excuses as to why his prints were there – but if he were arrested with a gun, that would put a whole new complexion on the matter. Henry could use that as a negoti-ating tool with Todd to get to the Grices.

A chance Henry did not want to miss.

And, amazingly, with his reassurances that no one would get hurt, that Danny Todd would be lifted as soon as he showed his face at court, his bosses and the court had said give it a go.

The chief magistrate leaned forward on his elbows and said to the prosecutor and defender, 'Are you gentlemen set?'

Both nodded.

'Jack Carter,' the clerk said, raising his voice for the benefit of the court ushers who would pass the name down to the gaolers below.

Then the court room door opened and one final member of the public joined the others in the gallery. A young man, dressed in jeans, trainers and a hoodie (hood down) with short-cropped hair with a swastika zigzag cut into it. His eyes were mean, his face pock-marked and his bloodless lips thin.

Danny Todd.

'Shit!'

The clerk gave Henry a look.

Henry ran his forefinger across his throat, then he was up on his feet, crossing quickly to where Todd had taken a seat, right next to Mark.

'He's in court,' Henry uttered over his PR. 'How's he got this far?'

Todd had seen Henry coming towards him straight away. Sensing something amiss, he rose to his feet, vaulted over the railing and legged it towards the door, his animal instincts not deserting him, his innate sense of self-preservation kicking in as soon as he saw Henry approaching.

'Stop!' Henry yelled as Todd ducked out of the door. Henry was only feet behind him, as the man speeded up in the corridor outside. 'Stop, police!' Henry shouted, and saw the black shape of a gun in Todd's right hand, which he was holding against his outer thigh.

The people hanging about in the corridor whirled around at the noise.

Henry had fished out his warrant card, which was in his left hand; in his right he had his extendable baton, which he wrist-flicked open with a crack that sounded like a gunshot in the confines of the court and its echoey corridors. The noise made Todd jump and spin around, his gun hand coming up and letting Henry see clearly for the first time the revolver he was brandishing. Henry would have put money on it being a replica which had been converted into a real gun so it could shoot real bullets. It wouldn't be as efficient as a properly produced one, but at short range he did not doubt it was just as deadly. The fact he was wearing a ballistic vest didn't make him feel much better.

Henry held out his warrant card.

In the periphery of his vision he was aware that lots of things were happening. People were scurrying away, there were warning shouts, pounding feet approaching him, but he remained blinkered on Todd, in the zone, the one in which he had to stay focused to stay alive.

'Drop the gun, Danny.'

Again, behind him he was aware of more running, more bodies, and instinct let him know this was the firearms team deploying.

Todd looked beyond Henry, a hunted, desperate expression on his face, confirming this. Henry knew that MP5s and Glocks were now out, but he didn't want to look round, needed to remain right on Danny.

'Don't be a fool, lad,' he said to Danny. 'Just drop it.'

Todd's eyes zeroed in on Henry. They were wild eyes, the type Henry had seen on so many disaffected kids over the years, because that's all that Todd was, a kid. Nevertheless, he was a kid with a gun.

Henry saw Todd's forefinger wrap around the trigger.

'That will make this a million times worse,' Henry said.

'I've always wanted to kill a cop,' he sneered. The gun jerked up and Todd aimed it at Henry's head.

Henry felt a chill, then flinched away as Todd pulled the trigger and things happened all at once.

The gun, which later was shown to be a badly converted replica, loaded with badly home-made bullets – backfired in Todd's hand, sending an explosion back down his arm and into his chest. This in itself would have been enough to flatten and seriously injure him, but what did the most damage was the double-tap from the Glock of the firearms officer who'd stepped up to Henry's side. Two commercially produced bullets from a superbly maintained weapon slammed into Todd's upper chest and hurled him backwards against the wall, which he slithered down, a look of complete disbelief on his face.

'Henry, Henry, are you all right?'

Mark Carter was by his side, having ducked and weaved through the melee behind him.

'Yeah, I'm OK...' Henry looked at the ashen-faced firearms officer not three feet away from him, holding his pistol in two hands, pointing it at the floor. He looked at the body of Todd on the floor, partly propped up against the wall, air rushing out of his chest wounds, blood bubbling obscenely as he fought for life.

For a moment, the world stood still.

'Ah, Jeez,' Mark said, as he looked at Todd and the blood.

Henry pulled him away, back through the throng of people surging towards Todd.

Henry closed his eyes, held the tip of his thumb and forefinger on his eyeballs and rubbed. The office door opened and Rik Dean entered.

'He'll live,' the DI said, dropping into his seat at his desk. 'And he'll blab ... already has done a bit.' Rik rubbed his leg, which was feeling very sore.

Henry raised his eyes.

'Said a distant member of the Grice family works at the court, would you believe? Secreted the gun in the bog for him.'

'That's a start, then,' Henry said.

'So we can move on the Grice family.'

'Y'know, we could probably go on for ever with this, spend the whole of our careers investigating this.' Henry scratched his head. 'It's like looking under rocks, always finding something more lurking there.'

'Like dominoes falling,' Rik added, tossing in his own metaphor.

Henry blew out his cheeks and put down his pen. He'd been writing his statement, got bogged down, needed a drink. 'Drugs,' he said disgustedly.

'Yeah ... keeps us in business, though. Fancy a pint?'

Henry tapped his fingers on the desk. 'Alcohol's a drug – did you know that?'

'Aye, but it's legalized and that means I can have as much as I want.'

'Me, too,' Henry said enthusiastically.